Rozlan Mohd Noor served as a police officer in the Royal Malaysia Police for 11 years as a crime investigator and court prosecutor before joining the private sector. He has published several crime/thriller novels. Six of them feature Inspector Mislan as the main protagonist, with *Posthumous Child* being the latest. The Inspector Mislan novels are now published internationally by Arcade CrimeWise, New York, starting with *21 Immortals* in 2020, *DUKE* and *UTube* in 2021, and *Soulless* in 2022. In 2022, UK-based Envision Entertainment optioned the mini-series rights for the Inspector Mislan books.

FIXI NOVO MANIFESTO

1. We believe that omputih/gwailoh-speak is a Malaysian language.

2. We use American spelling. This is because we are more influenced by Hollywood than the House of Windsor.

3. We publish stories about the urban reality of Malaysia. If you want to share your grandmother's World War 2 stories, send 'em elsewhere and you might even win the Booker Prize.

4. We specialize in pulp fiction, because crime, horror, sci-fi and so on turn us on.

5. We will not use italics for non-American/non-English terms. This is because those words are not foreign to a Malaysian audience. So we will not have "They had *nasi lemak* and went back to *kongkek*" but rather "They had nasi lemak and went back to kongkek". Nasi lemak and kongkek are some of the pleasures of Malaysian life that should be celebrated without apology; italics are a form of apology.

6. We publish novels and short-story anthologies. We don't publish poetry; we like making money.

7. The existing Malaysian books that come closest to what we wanna do: *Devil's Place* by Brian Gomez; and the Inspector Mislan crime novels by Rozlan Mohd Noor. Look for them!

8. We publish books with the same print run and the same price as those of our parent company, Buku Fixi. So a book of about 300 pages will sell at RM20. This is because we wanna reach out to the young, the sengkek and the kiam siap.

CALL FOR ENTRIES.

Interested? For novels, send your synopsis and first 2 chapters. For anthologies, send a short story of between 2,000-5,000 words on the theme "KL Noir." Send to info@fixi.com.my anytime.

Posthumous Child:
Inspector Mislan and the Playground Murder

Rozlan Mohd Noor

Published by
Fixi Novo *which is an imprint of:*
Buku Fixi Sdn Bhd (1174441-X)
B-8-2A Opal Damansara, Jalan PJU 3/27
47810 Petaling Jaya, Malaysia
info@fixi.com.my
http://fixi.com.my

Posthumous Child: Inspector Mislan and the Playground Murder

First Print: October 2022

Cover and layout: Teck Hee
Consultants: Amir Muhammad and Matthew Yap

ISBN 978-967-0042-27-5
Catalogue-in-Publication Data available from the National Library of Malaysia.

Printed by:
Vinlin Press Sdn Bhd
2 Jalan Meranti Permai 1, Meranti Permai Industrial Park
Batu 15, Jalan Puchong, 47100 Puchong, Malaysia

All men, however highly educated, retain some superstitious inklings.

– H. G. Wells, *The Invisible Man*

1

It is 11 at night when the Special Investigation (D9) office's phone rings and Detective Sergeant Johan Kamaruddin answers it. The standby detective on duty at the front desk informs him of a homicide along Jalan Ampang in the police district of Dang Wangi.

"Where in Jalan Ampang?" Johan asks.

"Shophouses after the AIA building toward the old Bilal Restaurant," the detective answers. "I think there's a 7-E around there a few shops after the Nepal embassy. Syed and Jeff are on their way there."

"OK."

"And Sarge, the station said the victim's transgender."

"Oh," Johan manages, not liking what he is being told.

Johan terminates the call and informs Inspector Mislan Latif, the duty investigator on twenty-four hours shift. Mislan glances at the wall clock and thinks to himself, *It's starting.* Walking out of the office to the car, Johan briefs the inspector of what little he knows of the homicide.

"The station said the victim's a transgender."

Mislan turns to Johan inquiringly.

"That's what the station said."

"Hate crime?" he asks, the first thing that comes to his mind.

The detective sergeant shrugs.

"If it is, I mean hate crime or gay-bashing, you know what it means right?"

"It'll go viral."

"Nowadays every damn thing goes viral, even if you pee by the roadside. The public outcry, the activists and NGOs will be screaming for blood."

"Never seemed to bother you before. What changed?"

The inspector smiles at Johan without answering.

The Special Investigation officers come in from Jalan Munshi Abdullah passing the Dang Wangi District Police Headquarters on their left, onto Jalan Dang Wangi. They keep right over the shrinking, almost disappearing Klang River. At the end of the road they make a right onto Jalan Ampang, passing the historical landmark American Insurance Associates (AIA) Building. In 1975, the building was the focus of the world when the Japanese Red Army stormed it and held fifty foreigners hostage, among them the American consul and the Swedish *charge d'affaires*. Mislan remembers catching part of it on the History Channel. He remembers it all ended well with no one killed or hurt. Not the hostages or the hostage-takers. Through negotiation, the Japanese Red Army members were flown to a third country of their choice or something like that.

Johan almost misses the crime scene as there was only a small crowd gathered. Which is unusual in a city full of kepochis. *Probably it's close to midnight and the pandemic rules are still in force*, Mislan rationalizes. Johan pulls over to the curb by the exit of Lorong Ampang 1, about 30 meters past the crime scene. The crime scene is the pavement in front of a 7-Eleven, more precisely its front door.

Walking towards the crime scene, Mislan notices a trail of blood on the pavement for four to five meters and all the way to where the victim lies, in front of the 7-Eleven. The victim is sprawled face down in front of the store's glass door, partially blocking its entrance. There is smeared blood on the glass door where the victim probably touched it. Mislan believes the victim must have collapsed on the pavement and crawled to the store's door for help.

The victim is not cross-dressed, or has long girly hair or women's accessories. He is wearing dark slacks, a red T-shirt and light brown loafers. Nothing to indicate he is transgender. He is about 1.65 centimeters tall and slimly built. By his complexion and facial features, Mislan believes the victim is of Indian ethnicity. His body position indicates he came from the direction of the blood trail. His left hand is under his upper body, most likely used to prop himself up, while the other hand is stretched toward the glass door. His head lying in a pool of congealed blood is turned to one side, slightly tilted upward like he is looking into the all-nighter convenience store.

Although the scene is in an open space, the smell of blood is still strong. The all-too-familiar pungent metallic smell of violent death.

Mislan approaches Inspector Kevin from the Kuala Lumpur Contingent Crime Forensic (D10), who is examining the victim.

"Kevin, what do we have here?"

"Oh hi," Kevin acknowledges.

Indicating with his eyes, Mislan asks about the victim.

"Johnathan Kutty, 33, from Klang," Kevin says, reading the victim's identity card.

"Anything taken?"

Kevin shakes his head. "Wallet with RM18 and phone, all here."

Just then, a Dang Wangi district investigating officer appears at the glass door on the inside of the store. He carefully pushes the door which is partially blocked by the victim. He manages to open the door wide enough without banging the victim's head and causing additional injury. Squeezing through the small opening, he steps over the victim's head and hops to the pavement.

"Hi, Mislan D9?" he asks, not proffering his hand. "Daim, I don't think we've met."

Mislan nods and introduces his assistant, Detective Sergeant Johan.

"The cashier saw anything?" Johan asks.

"No, but they were here earlier, the victim and his friend," Daim briefs them. "They came in around 10.05 to buy some beers. According to the cashier the victim paid for the beers, and when he gave the change the victim's friend grabbed it."

"How much?" Mislan asks.

"RM4.50. The cashier said the victim grabbed his friend's shoulder and protested. They were arguing as they left."

"Were they joking or serious?"

"Hard to tell. They were talking in Tamil and the cashier did not understand, but he could still hear them after they left."

"It had to be serious," Johan said.

"Fifteen minutes later the cashier noticed something at the front door. He thought it was a dog or something. When he bent over the counter to take a closer look, he saw a man's head and a bloody hand reaching for the door. He immediately called 999."

"7-E has CCTV, right?" Johan asks.

Daim nods. "We viewed the footage and my men are waiting for a copy to be made."

While they were talking, Kevin turned the body facing upward. They see a single slash injury on his left neck. The front left side of his T-shirt is soaked with blood.

"I think the cut hit the carotid artery," Kevin says. "Not enough to sever it but deep enough to nick it. That's the reason the victim managed to crawl all the way here. If the carotid artery was severed, he would've been dead on the spot."

They look at the trail of blood on the pavement where Kevin's men are searching for the murder weapon. Johan excuses himself and enters the 7-Eleven.

"Murder weapon?" Mislan asks.

"Thin with very sharp blade. The cut is clean. My men are searching the area."

Mislan steps away to look at the smeared blood trail. He spots velocity blood spatter on the shutter of the shop next to the 7-Eleven and figures that was where the victim was slashed. He surveys the pavement leading away from the shutter and sees tiny gravitational blood drops about a meter apart. One of Kevin's men is searching the roadside drain with his flashlight. He walks over to him and the man shakes his head to indicate he has found nothing.

They hear a call for the photographer from one of Kevin's men searching along Lorong Ampang 1. Mislan walks to him and is shown with a flashlight a utility or box cutter in the small side drain. After the photographer takes several shots of the utility cutter in the drain, it is retrieved and placed in a clear evidence bag. The bag is handed to Mislan. It is a thin yellow utility cutter, like those used in the office. There are blood stains on the handle and on the casing sleeve tip. He notices about five millimeters of the blade is protruding from the casing sleeve tip and the lock-catch is on. Handing the evidence bag back to the man, he rejoins Kevin and Daim in front of the store.

Johan emerges from the store to join them.

"The cashier said the victim and friend turned tricks and this is their stretch. They usually worked the area from around 7 pm onward. When they picked a client they'd go to the back lane to perform their tricks. The stalls back there close by 6 pm and there is no street light," Johan briefs the inspectors.

"Convenient," Daim says.

"That's the murder weapon?" Johan asks as the man hands it to Kevin.

"Looks like it," Kevin answers.

"It fits. I know most of them carry a box cutter for protection. It's legal if they're stopped and searched by the police."

"So the vic lost his life over RM4.50," Mislan says to no one in particular.

"Are we taking this?" Johan asks.

Mislan does not reply, instead looks into the 7-Eleven.

"Daim, you got the CCTV recording?" Mislan asks the district investigating officer.

"Yes, clear shot of the victim's friend. The photo had been WhatsApped to all MPVs. My detectives believe the victim and his friend were staying around here. There are a lot of rooms for rent along this stretch of shophouses."

"It's almost midnight, everything will close soon. I don't think he's going anywhere tonight. He's probably holed up in his room or at a friend's room," Mislan suggests.

"I'll get the crime prevention unit boys to knock on doors. If he's still around we'll get him," Daim says.

"Looks like you have it all under control."

2

It is 6 in the morning and somehow it had been a quiet night. Mislan pushes his chair away from the desk and stands to stretch his stiff limbs and numbed butt. Get the blood circulation going. Lately, he feels uncomfortable taking cat naps between call-outs by resting his head on the desk with his arms as a pillow. He is getting old and his body is not as flexible and accommodating, Johan points out whenever he grumbles about it. He used to be able to nap soundly in such a position during a twenty-four hours shift and continue working after that. Not anymore.

Walking to the pantry, he sees his assistant engrossed with his mobile phone. Mislan has never been hooked on social media and wonders how much time Johan spends daily looking at it. *Probably most of his waking time.*

"What're you watching?" he asks as he walks past Johan's desk.

"A dead girl," Johan says, his eyes fixed on the phone screen. "Just went viral."

"Where?"

"It says a playground at Jalan Tempinis, Bangsar."

"Wasn't there a case in Bangsar where a body was dumped on the road?"

"That was an old case, a man's body was dumped on the road. This is new. Just posted a few minutes ago."

Mislan makes himself a mug of black coffee and walks to Johan's desk.

"Take a look," Johan says, handing the inspector his mobile phone.

The video is shaky with poor lighting. It is as if the person shooting it was walking toward what looks like a lump on the patch at the foot of a kiddy slide. A man's voice speaking in Malay says, "There's somebody sleeping here, probably drunk or stoned." As the image gets closer, it can be seen that the supposedly sleeping person is in a woman's dress. She is lying in a fetal position at the foot of the slide, facing away from it. As the video focuses on the woman the same voice calls out, "Hello, are you alright?" A man wearing a green work vest with yellow reflector stripes kneeling beside the woman comes into view. The man says, "I don't think she's breathing. Better call the police." The 23-second video ends abruptly.

Mislan hands the phone back to Johan saying, "Could be a D11 case." He is referring to the Sexual, Domestic Violence and Child Abuse Investigation Department (D11).

Johan shrugs. The office phone rings and Mislan swears under his breath, placing his freshly made coffee on his desk.

Leaving the office, Johan tells the inspector that he knows how to get to Bangsar but is not sure where exactly Jalan Tempinis is. Passing the old Istana Negara, Johan makes a left to Sentral taking the long curve out back to Jalan Damansara. They pass Muzium Negara on their right until they reach the traffic light at the junction to Jalan Maarof. Stopping at the red light, Mislan takes out his mobile phone and Wazes for directions to Jalan Tempinis.

"It's on the left after the petrol station," Mislan tells Johan. Enlarging the map on the phone screen he says, "There's a playground there. Make a left after the petrol station, from there you can get on to Tempinis 5, Lucky Garden, where the playground is located."

It is said that Bangsar has more professionals, retired senior police officers and top civil servants per square meter than anywhere else in the country. Property prices have long passed the million-ringgit threshold. Properties here are beyond what middle-class Malaysians, those labeled by the government as M40, can afford. Bangsar is also known as the hotbed for liberal activist groups.

Johan makes a left onto Jalan Tempinis 5 where they spot several police cars parked next to the playground. The playground is shaped like a half-moon with Jalan Tempinis 1 as the circumference and Jalan Tempinis 5 as the diameter. A few sleepy-looking but curious residents are gathered on both roads watching the police, snapping shots or recording videos with their mobile phones. Most likely to uploaded to social media. *The beauty of social media, where news is shared at the press of a button,* Mislan sneers under his breath.

Stepping out of the car, Mislan notices the wet road surface and asks Johan if it was raining earlier.

"Not at the office, maybe just here."

The area around the kiddy slide is cordoned off with police tape and a uniformed policeman is standing guard. Johan introduces themselves to the uniformed policeman.

"Who's the IO?" Mislan asks the policeman.

"Inspector Rachael, she's over there," the policeman answers, pointing to a woman in uniform within the group standing by the slide.

"You know her?" Johan asks the inspector.

Mislan shakes his head. Stepping on the grass, he notices it is wet and the ground mushy, the air clean and fresh with the smell of grass. *What is the smell called,* he tries to recall … *is it petrichor?* Feeling the wet ground under his feet, he reflects, *It must have rained heavy, maybe one of those freak rainstorms. It pours suddenly then stops, something to do with global warming.*

He surveys the surroundings to orientate himself. The playground is divided into two sections. On the side they came from, the area is open with no trees or kiddy play equipment. In its center is an open-air badminton court and around it several concrete benches. Normally, open-air badminton courts are used for dual games, badminton and sepak takraw. But not in this case – the court's line is only for badminton. He supposes, rich Bangsar people don't play poor villagers' games.

A paved footpath bisecting the middle of the playground acts as a boundary between the two sections: the adult and the kiddy.

On the kiddy side, there are several spring-rides in the shape of a horse, an elephant and so on. There are two colorful kiddy slides, one open and one tubed. Two large shady trees with overhanging branches partially obscure the view of the slides from the row of houses. With no playground lighting and only the streetlights, this section is poorly lit. Undeniably, a better section to dump a dead body. *Could the killer be familiar with the playground layout? Perhaps, someone who lives around here or frequents it?*

As the Special Investigation officers approach, Mislan sees Inspector Kevin from the Kuala Lumpur Contingent Crime

Forensic speaking to a woman in an inspector uniform. Kevin turns to greet them. They are both wearing facemasks as mandated by the pandemic rules but are not observing the one and half meter apart social distancing.

"Mislan, Jo, this's Inspector Rachael May from Brickfields," Kevin introduces.

The officers nod their acknowledgement but neither offers their hand for a handshake. The new norm in meeting people.

"Hi," Rachael greets.

Inspector Rachael May is in her late twenties or early thirties. Average height, slender with short straight hair just covering her ears. With her facemask on, Mislan cannot make out her facial features except she has dark clear eyes. She looks smart and elegant. *The type of person that is built to wear uniform, any uniform,* he thinks to himself.

Mislan disengages his thoughts on Rachael and addresses Kevin.

"What's the story?" he asks, stepping closer to the body.

"The garbage collectors spotted something by the slides while emptying bins along Jalan Tempinis 5," Rachael explains, pointing to the road. "They thought stray dogs must have raided the bins and dragged a garbage bag here. When they came to retrieve it, they saw it was a woman. Initially they thought she must be drunk or stoned. They tried calling for her to wake up but when she did not respond, they called 999," she says, pointing to a man in a green workman vest standing by a patrol car along Jalan Tempinis 1.

"You said they, where are the others?" Mislan asks.

"The rest of the gang had gone to collect garbage. They need to complete their round before the residents are up. They don't want any complaints. Don't worry, I got their names and contact numbers."

"Jo, can you tell Syed and Jeff to canvass the area? See if any resident saw or heard anything," Mislan tells Johan.

"I don't think they're up yet," Johan says, looking at his wristwatch.

"You might be surprised. Unlike us poor people, rich people are light sleepers. Constantly worried about their wealth being plundered. They wake up to the slightest of sound and peek out their windows," Mislan jokes. "See if there're any CCTV aimed at the road or here."

"That's a good one … about rich people being light sleepers," Kevin laughs.

X

The victim is in a fetal sleeping position with one arm chicken-winged under her head as a pillow, the other hand holding her knees which are jackknifed toward her chin. Her body is arched inward, and in that position, it is hard to tell her height but she does look petite. Mislan is guessing not more than 1.5 meters tall, slim or more towards skinny, light brown skin, shoulder length wavy hair. Although her hair is wet and clinging together, it was carefully arranged, like she cared how she looked to others. *Am I imagining it or was the hair arranged to give an impression that she was sleeping?* He has not seen a woman sleep for a long time, perhaps he is imagining it.

The deceased is wearing a black flare dress with a back zipper; it looks expensive. The bottom seam of her dress is neatly pulled and arranged to cover her thighs and part of her lower legs. Mislan squats and looks at her face. She is not wearing makeup. She has sharply defined features and looks like she is of mixed Malay-Indian blood. Her long hair and dress are soaked and sticking to her face, neck and body. She has no jewelry or shoes. Examining her fingers and toes, Mislan notices that they are well-manicured and pedicured.

He purses his lips, deducing the victim must have been placed here before or during the freak rainstorm.

As if Kevin read the inspector's mind, he says, "The rain washed away whatever traces left by whoever dumped her here."

"Your men searched the area?"

"Mine and Rachael's."

"COD?"

"No sign of physical injury but I notice light abrasion markings around her neck. I'm guessing asphyxiation. It's best if you get the pathologist to confirm it."

"Suicide by hanging," Rachael prompts.

"Could be."

"The boyfriend found her hanging, panicked, cut her down and dumped her here," she theorizes. "If that's the case, she must be from here or close by."

"Could be."

Mislan does a cursory examination of the victim's face for blood spots and fingernails for blue-ing, looking for signs of oxygen deprivation.

"If it's suicide, why place her body here?" Mislan asks.

"Maybe whoever found her panicked and decided to get rid of her," Rachael suggests.

"Why? I mean why panic? Why not just call it in?"

"Maybe she's somebody's wife and she hanged herself in her lover's place. The lover panicked."

"Or he's married and the victim hanged herself in his house," Kevin speculates.

"And he had to get rid of her before the wife came back," Rachael adds. "Makes sense."

Mislan smiles at the officers' imaginative theories. "TOD?" he asks.

"The rigor mortis has just set in, had to be more than four hours, the forensic pathologist can provide you with a more accurate timing," Kevin answers.

"ID?"

Kevin and Rachael shake their heads.

"Did anyone cover her?" Mislan asks.

The two inspectors look at him questioningly.

"I mean her dress is pulled over her legs, decent like. Did any one of us do it?"

"No, that was how we found her," Rachael replies.

"A caring touch," Mislan says.

"You're thinking someone who knew her?" Kevin asks.

"What I'm saying is, I don't think she was just dropped there by someone who then hurriedly left. Not the way she is. I believe she was carefully placed and staged."

"By someone who cared for her, like I said a boyfriend or lover," Rachael stresses.

Mislan smiles and shrugs.

Johan joins them from canvasing the surrounding area.

"There are CCTVs at houses number 79 and 87 facing the road on Jalan Tempinis 1. From the angle and distance I doubt if they cover the playground."

"I'll get my men to pay them a visit and ask if they can view them later," Rachael states.

"If we're done here, I suggest we get her to the morgue before the crowd gets bigger," Mislan says. "You know the people here are all powerful and connected. You don't want them accusing us of being insensitive and dragging our feet."

"Will D9 be leading this case?" Rachael asks, her voice pleading.

Mislan looks at her inquiringly.

"Kevin thinks it's suicide, shouldn't you pass it on to the OCS?" Mislan suggests. OCS stands for Officer in Charge of a Station. Normally, the OCS or his assistant (AOCS) handles Sudden Death Reports including suicide.

"I know, but the body was dumped, sorry, placed here and you know the type of people who live here."

Mislan knows it only too well. He knows the two things that all rich people have: rich friends and powerful friends.

"I'll brief my boss and see what the postmortem says."

"Thanks."

3

Leaving the crime scene, Mislan asks his assistant to make a detour to a lane behind Maybank just before they hit the main road to the city. When Johan looks at him inquiringly, Mislan tells him there is a roadside stall he used to frequent that sells delicious nasi lemak.

"Do we have time for breakfast, morning-prayer starting in twenty minutes," Johan reminds the inspector, gesturing to the dashboard clock showing 8.05 am.

"Tapau. You want anything?"

"What do they have?"

"The usual stuff, mi goreng and all the side dishes."

"Mihoon, telur mata and sambal," Johan says.

"You want drinks?"

"No thanks. Which stall?" Johan asks as he slowly drives next to a row of stalls.

"That … the second last," Mislan says, pointing it to him.

Johan pulls over by the stall's side and stays in the car with the engine running. As Mislan steps out, his mobile phone rings.

"Yes Kevin."

"Mislan, where are you?"

"Behind Maybank, why?"

"When my guys were moving the body, they noticed, or rather they brushed against something hard on the deceased's stomach. I inspected it and it's a bandage."

"Bandage?"

"Not like medical bandage but masking tape used as bandage."

"Did you examine it?"

"No. Since she's already in the body-bag, it's better for the pathologist to examine it. At the same time, the crowd here is growing fast. A few big guns stopped by asking questions. Don't want any of them taking a peek if I did it here. And Mislan, I need you to bag the bandage for us to check for print and trace evidence."

"But we may not lead the case. Rachael knows about it?"

"Yes, I informed her too."

"She left?"

"Right after you."

"Where're you sending her?"

"GH, or you want her somewhere else?"

"GH is fine with me."

Reaching the police contingent HQ, Mislan heads straight for the meeting room where the meeting/briefing monikered the morning-prayer will be held, while Johan carries the packed breakfasts to the office. Turning left into the hallway leading to the meeting room, he bumps into Superintendent Samsiah Hassan, the Head of Special Investigation (D9).

"Morning, Puan," Mislan greets, falling in step with her.

"Morning. I heard you caught a late one."

"Yes, how did you know? I just got back, haven't filed the report yet."

"Just got a call from Brickfield's OCPD." The OCPD mentioned by her refers to the Officer in Charge of Police District.

Mislan looks at her inquiringly.

"He was asking if we could lead the investigation."

"Any particular reason?"

"Apart from Bangsar being the residential favorite of the rich and powerful, he said D10 noticed a bandage on the victim's abdomen."

"Hmmm, Rachael must have gone crying to him."

It is Superintendent Samsiah's turn to look at the inspector inquiringly.

"The IO," Mislan explains. "She was pleading for us to lead the investigation, saying you know how the people living there are."

"Meaning?"

"Politically influential, rich, connected and a pain in the where-the-sun – don't-shine," he answers with a snort.

"That aside, what do you make of the case?" she asks.

As they are already at the doorway of the meeting room, she stops him from answering. "Let's start the meeting and if there's a need to discuss the case further, we'll do after."

The morning-prayer is a brief gathering of the unit's investigating officers chaired by the unit head. The outgoing investigating officer will brief the others on his or her twenty-four hours shift call-out. They would share experiences of similar cases they had worked on, if any. The meeting is also used by the unit head to disseminate directives and new developments. The meeting is usually short and sweet. As Mislan is the outgoing investigating officer, he kicks off the meeting by briefing the rest on his two call-outs.

Mislan starts with the transgender homicide. Superintendent Samsiah asks about the possibility that it was a hate crime.

"The 7-E cashier knew the vic and the suspected killer. The cashier had seen them many times before. The pavement along that stretch was where they conducted their business."

"Business, what business?" Samsiah asks.

"Soliciting for clients."

"Oh."

"According to the cashier, just before the incident they came in together to buy beer. The vic paid for it, and when the cashier returned the change, the suspect grabbed it. They left the store arguing and a few minutes later the vic was slumped outside the 7-E front door."

"How much was the change?" Inspector Reeziana asks.

"RM4.50."

"That's all a life is worth now?" she mocks.

"Times are bad," Inspector Tee comments.

"Especially those in their trade," Mislan quips. "According to Dang Wangi detectives, there're a lot of rooms for rent in the rows of shop-houses. They believe the vic and suspect were probably staying in one of those rooms. Their crime prevention unit will conduct a door-to-door search. With everything closed at midnight, I believe the suspect is holed up in there until the city wakes up in the morning, then he'll make a run for it."

"He could've run sooner, there's no curfew imposed on movement," Tee points out.

"He could but I doubt it. He'd stand out like a sore thumb walking alone in a dead city after midnight with no public transport around," Mislan refutes. "The MPVs were notified and photos taken from 7-E CCTV distributed."

"I'm sure Dang Wangi's got it under control," Samsiah interjects, stopping the debate. "The second call-out, what are your thoughts on it?"

"The deceased, a woman probably in her early thirties, was laid at the foot of a kiddy slide. Except for abrasion marks on her neck, no other visible injuries. No ID, no jewelry, accessories or shoes."

"Jane Doe?" Reeziana asks.

"For the moment. She was wearing a black flare dress that looked expensive to me."

"Did you check the brand?" Again, it is Reeziana.

"No, why?"

"The brand will tell you if it's expensive or not, it could be a knock-off."

"What I found interesting was that her nails were manicured and pedicured, clean and shiny. The other thing was the way she was laid down. She was in a fetal sleeping position, her left arm was chicken-wing for a pillow and her right arm placed on her knee. The bottom of her dress was neatly arranged to cover her thighs, and her hair too was arranged on her neck and back like she was sleeping."

"Whoever put her there cared how she looked," Samsiah says.

"My thoughts too. Someone who knew and cared for her."

"Boyfriend or lover?" Reeziana suggests.

"Could be, but what bugged me is: Why place her at the playground and of all places in Bangsar? If she committed suicide, why not call the police?"

"Not wanting to be involved, or perhaps there're other insinuating circumstances, like personal issues," Samsiah offers.

"Like a wife or a husband in the equation," Reeziana suggests.

"OK, but disposing of a body is a criminal offence," Mislan comments.

"If we can trace back to whoever did it," Tee reminds him.

"Anyway, Kevin said his men noticed a bandage on the stomach when they moved her to the body-bag. It was not a medical bandage but masking tape used as a bandage."

Before anyone can ask more, Mislan's mobile phone rings. It is Kevin from forensic. He signals to Superintendent Samsiah that he needs to take the call.

"Yes, Kevin."

"Mislan, the deceased is on record. Name, Norita Mokhtar, age 32, permanent address Kampung Lubok Jaya, Kuala Selangor. Last known address 08-03, Flat Taman Pantai Dalam."

"What was she on record for?"

"She was charged under Section 15 DDA, three years back. Fined five hundred with no jail time. The offence was committed when she was working as a GRO at D'Voice KTV in Jalan Putra, Kuala Lumpur."

Section 15 DDA refers to the self-administering of scheduled drugs under the Dangerous Drug Act 1952 (Revised 1980). A GRO (Guest Relations Officer) is a hostess at a bar or nightclub.

"Kevin, can you email me the record?"

"Will do that now."

"Thanks."

Mislan informs the others of the information received.

"The bandage, what was it for?" Reeziana brings them back to their earlier discussion.

"No idea. Kevin did not examine it because he said the crowd was growing and he spotted some big shots asking questions. So he felt it was better to let the pathologist do it in the morgue operating room."

"Could it be that the victim was murdered, the killer bandaged the wound and then strangled her to make it look like a suicide by hanging?" Reeziana probes.

"Could be, but there was no blood at the scene."

"You said it rained heavily, perhaps the blood was washed away."

"If it was the primary crime scene, we should still find traces of blood there. But I don't think it was the primary scene, and I'll check with Kevin if he did the Luminol spray around the area – but I doubt they did."

"Maybe it's more sinister than just a murder," Tee suggests.

All eyes turn to him.

"She could be a drug mule. She swallowed the drugs but then decided not to pass it on to the traffickers. They strangled her and then cut her stomach to retrieve the drugs."

"Now that's imaginative," Reeziana says. "I see that Jo's wild imagination is having its effect on you."

"No point in speculating. I suggest you attend the postmortem and we'll decide once we know more," Samsiah says to Mislan.

"I'll check with Rachael when it is scheduled."

"If I've nothing on, can I come along?" Reeziana asks.

"Why not, the more the merrier."

4

Earlier, before he left the office, Inspector Rachael had called to inform him that the autopsy is scheduled for 3 pm. Arriving home, Mislan manages to get a few hours' sleep before leaving his apartment at 2.30 pm. Despite driving a full circle around the hospital complex, he fails to get a parking spot. He remembers Johan's solution to their parking predicament the last time they visited the morgue. Driving back to the police station next to the Trauma and Emergency Center, he parks in the bay reserved for police vehicles. Entering the station, he introduces himself and informs the personnel of his car parked there. The policeman nods but gives him a disapproving look.

Finding his way through the maze of footpaths and drain lines behind and beside buildings, he realizes he is lost. He stops to ask several hospital staff in the maze, and at long last makes it to the medical forensic department. After scanning the MySejahtera QR code, he surveys the waiting area looking for Inspector Rachael. As all the people in the waiting room are wearing facemasks, he fails to spot her. Mislan walks to the reception counter to inquire on his deceased's autopsy schedule. Approaching the counter, he hears his name being called. Turning around, he sees Rachael waving at him. Walking back to meet her halfway, his mobile phone rings. It is Reeziana.

"Where're you?"

"At the morgue lobby."

"Give me a few minutes, just got a parking spot."

"We'll wait for you here," Mislan says, terminating the call. "Hi, you just arrived?" he asks Rachael.

"I was here earlier, seated over there," she answers, gesturing to indicate where.

"Oh, didn't recognize you with the facemask. Can you lower it for a moment and let me see what you look like?"

Rachael pulls her facemask to her chin and smiles. She has an oval-shaped face with a warm smile.

"Thanks, now I know what you look like," Mislan says, returning her smile. "By the way, one of my colleagues, Reeziana, is joining us."

Rachael rises her eyebrows inquiringly.

"I don't know why, maybe she's just curious or bored at the office. Ask her," Mislan says in response.

They hear a woman saying, "Sorry, just couldn't get bloody parking," as she comes in through the main entrance. "Hi, you must be Rachael, I'm Reeziana," she introduces herself.

Rachael nods, saying "Pleased to meet you," without proffering her hand. "Let's go, we're in room 3."

Autopsy Room 3 is at the farthest end of the brightly lit, quiet, dull gray hallway. Mislan presumes there is nothing to say or consult with the dead, therefore the silence. The bright lights are to ensure there are no ghosts or spirits of the evil dead lurking around.

Reaching Autopsy Room 3, Rachael knocks lightly on the thick wooden door. Mislan pushes the heavy door slightly and peeks inside. Two pairs of eyes stare at him.

"Police," he says.

The man who is examining the deceased says, "Come in, I'm just starting."

Stepping in, Rachael introduces the police party.

"I'm Inspector Rachael from Brickfields, and this is Inspector Mislan and Inspector Reeziana from D9."

"D9, that's Special Investigation?"

The officers nod.

"What's D9's interest in this case?"

"Yet to be determine," Mislan answers. "Sorry, you are?"

"Dr. Matthew."

Mislan remembers working with a Dr. Matthew on one of his cases. He remembers the doctor was meticulous and took the trouble to explain whatever was required of him. Mislan however could not recognize him with the double facemask, face-shield and the plastic surgical overalls commonly used by medical employees since the pandemic.

"I'm guessing D9 is curious to know about the bandage on the abdomen," the doctor says.

"Yes, and the COD," Mislan adds. "And Doc before I forget, I need you to bag the bandaging for forensic examination."

Dr. Matthew nods.

"From external visual examination of the deceased's eyes, lips and neck I would say the COD was most likely strangulation. There're visible signs of petechiae." Dr. Matthew turns to look at the officers and smiles behind his facemask when he sees their blank expressions. "The red spots under the skin. There's also the blood-red eyes. The swollen lips are an indicator of asphyxiation, deprivation of oxygen. Apart from those there's the ligature marks on the neck. That's before we examine what is under the bandage on her abdomen."

"Death by hanging," Rachael suggests.

"Strangulation, but certainly not by hanging."

"The ligature mark, why is it not distinctive?" Mislan asks.

"I'm guessing the strangler used a piece of cloth like a folded handkerchief or bandana, which is of softer texture and would make the choke area wider than if a rope was used. The deceased's complexion is also a factor."

Mislan nods.

"Why do you rule out suicide by hanging?" Rachael asks.

"Come closer," the doctor invites the officers. "Look at the ligature marks, they are lateral, around the neck, horizontal to the shoulders if she is standing. If she had died by hanging, the front ligature marks would be above the larynx closer to the chin," he continues, indicating the neck. "And the marks on the sides of her neck would be running upwards, which would be consistent with someone hanging by the neck."

"Could the strangulation marks be made after she was dead?" Reeziana asks.

"They could, but it would not have caused the petechiae, red spots in her eyes and swollen lips. Postmortem injury can easily be distinguished by its coloration. In the case of postmortem injury there is the absence of hemorrhaging and clotting as the heart has stopped and is not pumping blood."

"TOD?" Mislan asks.

"By the rigor motis and liver temperature, I say between midnight and 1 am."

"Doc, I'm guessing this is going to be a long autopsy, with all that you have explained. Is it possible for you to examine what the bandage is about?" Mislan asks.

"Yes, I'm as curious as you are," he admits, shifting his attention to the abdomen.

The bandage that Kevin mentioned was made using masking tape. From the overlapping edges of the tape, it is obvious several layers were used. The light brown tape is about five centimeters wide and twenty centimeters long. Using some sort of a bent plastic clipper, the doctor carefully clips one end of the tape and peels it off the deceased. It comes off rather easily.

They stare at what the tape concealed: a 12-centimeter laceration at the lower abdomen around the panty line. The cut looks deep and gaping. They can see the layers of stomach wall. Surprisingly there is very little trace of blood.

"Hmmm," Dr. Matthew murmurs.

"What is it?" Mislan asks.

Dr. Matthew examines the inside of the cut and asks the attendant for a pair of forceps. He probes into the gaping cut with the tool. After a moment he puts the tool aside and dips his hand into the wound. When he withdraws his hand, it is full of a dark, grayish, mushy substance. Mislan does not know what it is but it looks and smells awful. The doctor places it in a stainless-steel receptacle and digs in again. His hand comes out with another handful of the stuff. This time around, a cord or intestine is attached to something. He asks for surgical scissors and cuts the cord or intestine.

"What're those?" Mislan asks.

"Placenta."

"Placenta!" the three officers repeat in sync.

"Yes, and by the size of it the fetus was between fifteen to twenty weeks."

"Is it in the womb, I mean the fetus?" Reeziana asks.

"Nope."

"Did she die from a botched abortion?" Mislan asks.

"I need to run some test but looking at the wound, I'm quite sure the C-section was done postmortem."

"You said the fetus was about fifteen to twenty weeks, could it survive a C-section outside the womb?" Rachael asks.

"No, unless it's a miracle."

"Doc, can you bag the masking tape? I've a million questions to ask but until you're done with the autopsy and get the test results, I think it's best if we leave you to do whatever needs to be done."

Dr. Matthew nods to his attendant. Taking the masking tape, the attendant goes to another room. He comes back carrying two evidence bags – the deceased's dress and the masking tape. He hands them to the inspector.

"Oh, one more thing," Mislan says to the pathologist, "can you do a parental DNA test?"

"I'll put in the request."

"Without the fetus can you do it?" Reeziana asks.

"Placenta is a rich source of DNA," Dr. Matthew says with a smile behind his facemask.

The officers thank the pathologist and leave, dazed from what they have just learned and witnessed. Outside the morgue, Rachael proposes that they go somewhere and talk. Mislan recommends the food court outside the hospital compound next to the open football stadium.

When he arrives at the food court, Reeziana and Rachael are already waiting for him by the roadside. He points to a table outside the food court.

"Let's sit there, I need a smoke."

"Are you not checking-in?" Rachael asks, referring to MySejahtera.

"We're not going in," he replies.

Taking their seats, Rachael goes to check-in and walks into the food court to order their drinks. Mislan lights a cigarette and offers the pack to Reeziana.

"Can we smoke here?" she asks.

"Look around."

Reeziana sees most of the customers are indeed smoking, inside and outside the food court.

"No one gives a damn anymore. The government that made the stupid rule is no more in power," she says, lighting up.

Rachael comes back carrying a tray with their drinks.

"You want anything to eat?"

"After what we just saw, no thanks," Reeziana jests.

"You smoke?" Mislan asks, holding his pack to Rachael.

"No," she says, looking at the tables around them. "Seem like everyone else does. I suppose after another year as IO, I will too," she declares with a chuckle. Taking a sip of her drink, she asks, "Is D9 taking the lead?"

"Looks like it," Reeziana answers for Mislan. "What's your theory?"

"Initially I thought she committed suicide but after Dr. Matthew's findings, my theory is busted," Rachael explains. "What about you?"

"My theory, the boyfriend or lover found out she was pregnant. She refused to abort and they got into a heated argument. He killed her and then cut the baby out to hide their affair," Reeziana answers.

"But she was like fifteen to twenty weeks in, why did they get into the argument now? There's no way she could abort the baby," Mislan refutes.

"Maybe initially, when it was discovered she was pregnant, she agreed with the boyfriend or lover to terminate it. Then she had second thoughts and decided to keep it without informing him. That could be the reason he killed her, she had passed the abortion stage," Reeziana theorizes.

"Cutting out the baby will not hide the fact she was pregnant, and Dr. Matthew said they can still do the parental DNA test," Mislan counters.

"Yes they can, but if the baby was born it would be much easier to identify the father. The deceased could've easily pointed him out."

"Mislan, what's your theory?" Rachael probes.

"Why do you call it a baby? I thought it's only a baby after it is born, otherwise it's a fetus," Mislan says.

"If I remember my Biology correctly, it's an embryo from the second to the eighth week, then a fetus until birth," Rachael explains. "But in conversations we refer to the fetus as baby. I mean, when you meet a pregnant woman, you don't ask her how many weeks her fetus is. It sounds so, I don't know, like icky," Rachael clarifies with a smile.

Mislan notices she does have a lovely smile, and smiles back.

"Yana's theory may be right," he says. "It may sound a bit extreme but if the birth of the baby would cause the father to suffer severe consequences, he might just lose his head and do her in."

"Severe consequences? Like?" Rachael inquires.

"Lose his job. No, no, like lose his political career," Reeziana offers.

"Or his wealthy wife," Rachael adds.

"Or wealthy future wife," Reeziana adds, laughing.

"Yana, you have a Facebook account right?" Mislan asks.

"Facebook, Instagram, Twitter, why?"

"When you're back at the office can you find out if the vic had a social media account?"

"Victim, now she is a victim and not a deceased anymore," Rachael states. "So now you've a good reason to lead the investigation."

"Your OC had already called my boss suggesting D9 lead the investigation. With this new discovery by medical forensics, I'm convinced she will agree."

"You don't sound thrilled," Rachael says.

"When there's a baby involved, it's never thrilling. This is not one but two murders."

"I wonder if the baby was a boy or girl," Reeziana ponders.

"Does it matter?" Mislan asks. "The fetus was not even given a chance to be born, to be a baby."

5

It is 4.15 in the evening when the officers leave the food court. Driving out of the car park, Mislan's stomach growls and he realizes he has not had anything to eat since breakfast. Hitting the main road to take the elevated highway home, he suddenly has a craving for claypot chicken rice. Making a detour, he heads to Wangsa Maju, the only place he knows that sells halal claypot chicken rice.

The AEON BIG shopping mall was initially called Alpha Angle when he and his ex-wife Lynn used to frequent it. She liked going there because the supermarket is well-stocked and there are a lot of food outlets. He did not mind going there because parking is free and he liked the claypot chicken rice.

Claypot chicken rice is a Chinese dish; he has not found or known of Malays or Indians selling it. Some shopping complex food courts do have claypot chicken rice and the municipal regulation mandates that all food courts must be halal. The tradeoff: The food court dishes are not as authentic or tasty as those in non-halal Chinese restaurants and roadside stalls. The proof: You will not find Chinese eating Chinese dishes at the food courts.

Entering AEON BIG, he heads straight to the food court next to the supermarket. The place looks different from what he remembers from his previous visits with his ex-wife. It looks brighter, livelier and busier. There are more stores and food outlets and they are more upbeat and trendier. Even the food court looks more hygienic and colorful. Mislan walks around the food kiosks, reading the display of dishes. The hot pan noodle and claypot chicken rice kiosk is the second one from the last. The two female workers are Indonesian and one of them is wearing the tudung. More likely to convince customers the dishes are halal.

Mislan order claypot chicken rice with salted fish and mushroom. He takes a seat at one of the colorful tables. An elderly man pushing an elderly woman in a wheelchair approaches the table next to his. Waiting for his order, he observes them. The man and woman are probably in their late fifties. The man removes a chair from the table and pushes the wheelchair in its place close to the table. He bends close to the woman's ear and then leaves her to check out the food kiosks. The man is clean-shaven, short-haired and smartly dressed. He walks upright and with purpose. *A retired civil servant or corporate man*, Mislan assumes.

Mislan notices the woman's head is lolled slightly to her left, her eyes fixed to a spot on the floor. Awhile later the man returns. He stops to look at the woman, takes a face towel from a bag behind the wheelchair and dabs her mouth. He whispers something to her and takes a seat next to the wheelchair. Mislan thinks he sees a tiny smile on the woman's lips. His order arrives and he senses the man turning to look in his direction. Mislan nods with a smile. The man reciprocates.

"Jemput makan," Mislan says, inviting the man.

"Bismillah. You come here often?" he asks, making small talk.

"I've not been here awhile, didn't know they had changed the name," Mislan answers with a smile.

The man smiles too. "My wife," he says, turning to look at the woman in the wheelchair, "she loves coming here. We used to come here two to three times a week after office."

Mislan looks at the woman inquisitively.

"Stroke, two years ago. She was a teacher but now she is on medical retirement," the man says with a smile, but the smile does not reach his eyes.

"I'm sorry."

Their order arrives and the man focuses on his wife. He spoon-feeds her and holds the straw to her mouth for a sip of water. Now and then he dabs her mouth with the face towel. All the time speaking softly to her.

Mislan finishes his meal, and says goodbye to the man and his wife. In the car he lights a cigarette, taking long deep drags. *How lucky the woman is to have a loving and caring husband. That is what a marriage vow is about: to cherish and to love in health and sickness.* It his case, the vow was long since discarded. What if it was him in the wheelchair? Who is there to care for him? No one. *I'll most probably be thrown in a welfare home and be forgotten.*

His mobile phone rings, it is Johan asking about the autopsy and Superintendent Samsiah's decision on them leading the investigation.

"Where're you?"

"Out for a drink with some friends, why?"

"Just asking. The pathologist didn't think it was suicide by hanging. He believes she was strangled. What's confirmed is that the vic was pregnant and the fetus was cut out of her."

"What?!"

"Remember the bandage on the abdomen?"

"The masking tape?"

"Yes. It was to conceal the C-section."

"Really! So we have a murder and a missing baby?"

"Two murders, the vic and her fetus."

"Sickening. Are we leading the case?"

"I've not briefed Puan yet, will do it tomorrow during the morning-prayer but my guess is we are."

"You want me to come in tonight?"

"No, I'm not going to the office. By the way Jo, can you get on social media and find out if the vic has an account? I've asked Yana to do the same if she is not busy. Since you're always on it why don't you try it too? You got her rap sheet right and a photo of her?"

"Yes."

"Tomorrow, I thought of going to Kuala Selangor after the morning-prayer. See if we can locate her family. Why don't you call Kuala Selangor police, see if they can extend us some assistance in locating the family."

"OK, will do that."

"Good, see you tomorrow."

6

The morning-prayer starts with the outgoing shift IO Inspector Reeziana updating on the last twenty-four hours call-out. She attended to three armed robberies but no firearms were involved. All cases are led by the district's investigating officers. Superintendent Samsiah asks Mislan to update them on the playground victim's autopsy.

Mislan gives them the preliminary findings by Dr. Matthew with Reeziana filling in the gaps of what he left out.

"Posthumous child," Samsiah says softly. "So, it's not suicide as initially suspected. Have you any theory on why the fetus was extracted?"

Mislan shakes his head. "What child did you say?"

"Posthumous child, a child born after the mother is dead. You said the fetus is between fifteen to twenty weeks, so there's the possibility the fetus was alive when it was extracted."

"Not according to Dr. Matthew," Mislan answers.

"Does he know for sure?" Reeziana asks.

"No, but he did say it would be a miracle."

Reeziana nods.

"Anyone has any theory?" Superintendent Samsiah throws it to the floor.

Reeziana puts forwards her theory of the boyfriend or lover killing the victim for fear their affair would be exposed if the baby was born.

"So he killed her and cut out the baby to hide their affair," Samsiah says. "Why is he so afraid of their affair being exposed?"

"Because he could be a prominent figure, or his wife is from a very wealthy family and he will lose it all," Reeziana suggests.

"Or he's a politician or prominent religious figure," Tee adds.

"Hmmm," Samsiah ponders. "Lan?"

"Yana and Tee could be right but let's not go there until we know more about the vic."

"I agree with Mislan."

"Puan, is it possible not to disclose to the press about the fetus? I mean, he can give a PC on the vic found at the playground but keep the missing fetus out."

"Any particular reason?"

"Just like to work on it without the press breathing down my neck. You know how the press and netizens are when a baby is involved."

"I don't think it's possible to ask him not to mention the fetus. If it's just a garden-variety murder, we've a lot of them. They're not front-page news. The fetus, that's the story and that's what he would tell the media to get on the front page," Samsiah says, referring to the Officer in Charge of Criminal Investigation (OCCI), who is a publicity junkie. "Lan, are you OK in leading this case?"

Mislan nods.

"I'll officially inform Brickfield. I'm sure they'll be glad to know it. By the way, Tee had applied for seven days' leave for Chinese New Year. So you and Yana will be on alternate days."

"When are we getting Kamil's replacement?" Tee asks.

"The request is being considered. With the disruptive political situation and never-ending pandemic, all districts are facing manpower shortage."

"If I'm back before the seven days I'll let you know and go back on rotation," Tee says.

"That's thoughtful of you but I'm sure Lan and Yana can manage. You and family enjoy the holiday. Chinese New Year comes only once a year," Samsiah decides.

"Puan, after this Jo and I are going to Kuala Selangor to locate the vic's family. Hopefully we get to learn more about her. Yana, you managed to find her social media accounts?"

"Not yet. I'll keep trying and let you know if I get anything."

"Thanks."

"Tee, if the standby detectives have spare time, you can ask them to check out D'Voice KTV in Jalan Putra, KL. The vic was working there as a GRO when she was picked up under section 15 DDA."

"I'll tell them."

"Thanks."

Kuala Selangor is about an hour's drive from Kuala Lumpur. The towns within the district are known for their seafood restaurants and sea produce.

Getting into the car, Johan asks which route the inspector prefers, through Sungai Buloh or Klang.

"Whichever is the easiest and fastest."

"Sungai Buloh but you have to pay the toll," Johan says, knowing how much the inspector hates paying toll which he deems the government's way of robbing the people. His argument: car owners are already paying road tax, so why the hell is the government imposing tolls for using the roads?

Mislan glares at his assistant and Johan laughs. They drive out of the city and hit the North-South Highway exiting at Sungai Buloh. Passing Sungai Buloh, the roads narrow to a single carriage. It is the federal road with no toll but the going is slow as the traffic is heavy and overtaking difficult. The scenery too changes as they travel from the concrete jungle to a greener landscape with rows after rows of palm oil trees. Brick shops and houses can still be seen but they are not congested as in the city. Once in a while, they come across cows or goats lazily grazing in the palm oil plantation along the road. They pass several stalls selling flowers or seasonal fruits and other village agricultural produce.

As Johan drives through small towns and villages, Mislan enjoys the escape from the hustle and bustle of the city. Lighting a cigarette, he ponders on the laidback and stress-free living in rural areas. Fewer materialistic wants and societal pressures. No wonder they live longer and healthier lives.

"I've asked Kuala Selangor to provide us with a guide to the victim's address," Johan says, distracting Mislan from his thoughts.

"We can just Waze the location, can't we?"

"We can but because it is in the village, Waze may not be accurate."

"You've the vic's address with you?"

Johan nods.

The dashboard clock shows 10.25 am as they pull into Kuala Selangor District Police HQ compound. Johan stops by the guardhouse, introduces himself and tells the sentry they are meeting Sergeant Fatimah, the assistant officer in charge of the station. The sentry points to a vacant parking bay and tells him to park there.

At the inquiry office, Johan asks for Sergeant Fatimah and they are directed to the back office. Sergeant Fatimah greets him warmly as Johan introduces himself and the inspector.

"Pleased to meet you, sir," Fatimah says without offering her hand. "Can I get you any drinks?"

"No thanks, perhaps some other time," Mislan answers. "We're in a bit of a hurry."

"OK, I'll get WPC Laila to follow you. She lives in that area," Fatimah says, leading them out of her office.

At the inquiry office Fatimah introduces Woman Police Constable Laila to the Special Investigation officers. Laila is not in uniform, but in a pair of jeans, blue polo shirt with a police logo on the left chest and Nike sneakers. She looks young, like she is fresh out of the police training center. She stands to attention when Mislan is introduced.

In the car, Laila tells Johan to head north across the Selangor River. Mislan notices makeshift sheds by the road selling salted fish immediately after they cross the Sultan Salahuddin Abdul Aziz Shah Bridge.

The bridge was built in 1979 across the wide Selangor River and named after the late Sultan of Selangor. Before that, crossing was done using a small, free ferry towed or pushed by a tugboat. It was operated by the local municipal but only in the daytime.

When he was stationed in Dang Wangi before being transferred to Special Investigation, Mislan heard stories from old-timers who were stationed in Kuala Selangor. Before the bridge was built, if there was a case after sunset on the opposite bank, the police had to drive almost forty kilometers through several small towns and palm oil plantations just to get to the other side of the river, to a town call Pasir Penambang. The good old days.

With Laila acting as their Waze, they easily locate the victim's permanent address at 41, Lubok Jaya. The address is a cluster of old low-cost single-story terrace houses built by the state government several decades ago. The houses look in dire need of maintenance and a fresh coat of paint. However, almost all the houses have ASTRO dishes on the roof. House number 41 is fronting the main road and is situated in the middle of the row of houses.

Johan makes a turn onto the inner road and stops in front of the house. The tiny front yard looks like it has not been weeded or tended to. No flower beds or potted plants. It is littered with used plastic bags and empty drink bottles. The front door is closed and there is no doormat, normally a common item for a Malay house. No car or motorbike, just a pair of Japanese slippers.

"You think anyone's home?" Johan asks doubtfully.

"Laila, can you find out?" Mislan says.

Laila steps out of the car and approaches the house. At the front door she calls out "Assalamualaikum." After several calls a woman opens the door. Laila speaks to her, turning to look at the Special Investigation officers waiting in the car. She is probably telling the woman those men are police officers from Kuala Lumpur and they wish to speak to her. Mislan sees the woman nod several time and Laila waves for them to come over.

She introduces the woman as Maimunah, the victim's mother. She is in her fifties, but looks much older. Her head is covered with white hair, she is short and rather large. Mislan fails to see any physical or facial resemblance between his victim and Maimunah. The victim possibly inherited her father's features.

After the introduction, the officers are invited into the house. The living room is tiny and barely furnished. A purple and yellowish crisscross-colored motif pandan mat is spread in the middle of the tiny living room in place of settees. A twenty-four-inch box television sits on a wooden coffee table pushed against the wall. That is all there is. There is no sign of a pet cat, another common feature in a Malay house, especially in the village. Maimunah offers to prepare drinks for the officers, which Mislan politely declines and invites her to sit on the mat with them.

"I'm sorry to be the bearer of bad news," Mislan begins as Maimunah takes her seat. "Your daughter Norita is not with us anymore."

Maimunah looks impassively at the inspector, saying nothing.

"Please accept our condolence for her passing," Mislan continues, puzzled by her lack of emotion.

Maimunah does not seem to be saddened or shocked. To Mislan she seems unmoved.

"I'm sorry to ask, you have a daughter by the name of Norita Mokhtar?" Mislan asks, thinking they may be speaking to the wrong woman.

"Yes, but since you just told me she is no more with us, I suppose I don't anymore," Maimunah drily answers.

By her nonchalant tone, non-emotional reaction and sarcastic response, Mislan suspects the mother-daughter relationships had long been severed.

"Again I'm sorry, may I ask where Encik Mokthar is?" Mislan continues.

"I don't know, hopefully dead too," Maimunah snaps.

Mislan looks at Johan, who raises his eyebrows on hearing the woman's answer. The inspector is aware he is talking to a very spiteful person and wonders if he could get any meaningful information out of her. He asks if they can be excused as he needs a smoke. Signaling to Johan and Laila to follow him, they step outside.

Lighting a cigarette, he asks Laila if she can speak to Maimunah and dig up information about the victim.

"I'm guessing the husband must have done bad things to her, and because of that she hates men. Maybe as a woman, she would be more willing to speak to you."

"Inspector Mislan probably reminded her of her husband," Johan pokes at his boss with a chuckle.

"Can't you force her to answer your questions, I mean truthfully?" Laila asks.

"She's not a suspect. She has no obligation to speak or answer any questions."

"You can beat it out of her," Johan jokes.

"I need to know, did Norita have a mobile phone and if she had one, what the number is. I also need to know if she was married, or had a boyfriend and where she was last working."

"OK."

"When was the last time she met or spoke to her? Where her last address is and whatever else you can pry out of the mother about her."

"You know, ask all the questions like you are interviewing your boyfriend's mother," Johan suggests. "You need to know everything about him, apply the same curiosity."

Laila laughs at the detective sergeant's suggestion.

"You think you can do it?" Mislan asks.

"I'll try my best."

Mislan beckons his assistant to follow him back to the car while Laila reenters the house. He asks Johan to start the engine and turn the air-condition on. He takes out his mobile phone to check the signal and makes a call.

"Rachael, can you talk?"

"Yes."

"Can you send one of the detectives to house number 79 and 87 to get a copy of the CCTV recording for that night?"

"The entire night?"

"From midnight till the body was found. Let me know when you have them and I'll get one of my detectives to collect them from you."

"What if the house owner refuses?"

"Get a court order."

Rachael sighs, knowing how sticky it could be especially if the owners are well-connected. Terminating the call, he makes another call.

"Kevin, did you get anything from the masking tapes?"

"Nothing much. Either it was wiped clean or whoever handled them wore gloves."

"But you did get something?"

"We took a swab of the tape and found traces of detergent."

"Detergent, you mean like for washing clothes?"

"More like washing dishes."

"Hmmh, what about on the inside?"

"Only traces of blood and tissue which I have to send for DNA. Don't get your hopes up, I'm sure the blood and tissue came from your victim."

"OK, thanks."

Johan turns in his seat to face the inspector.

"During my MPV days I was the bearer of bad news hundreds of times but never encountered anything like this," Johan says. "Why do you think she is not concerned about her daughter's death? I mean she didn't even ask when or what happened."

"I don't know. Hopefully we'll find out from Laila."

"And what she said when asked about her husband? He must have pissed her off real good."

"I guess."

"Probably took their life savings and ran off with a young woman," Johan says with a grin. "That would piss off anyone good."

They see Laila emerge from the house with Maimunah in tow. They chat cordially for a moment at the doorway. After a couple of minutes, Laila makes her way to the car.

"That was quick," Johan observes.

"Too quick," Mislan corrects him, not sounding happy.

Getting into the car, Laila tells the detective sergeant that he need not make a U-turn back to the road they came from. They can take the next junction left and hit the main road back to Kuala Selangor. Johan follows as directed.

"What did you get?" Mislan asks.

"She's a divorcee, no, not a divorcee, long-term separation if there's such a thing in Islam. Her husband, an Indian convert, was a drug addict. He disappeared six years back and has not been heard of since. They have two daughters, the deceased Norita was the eldest, and Norshida. Norshida is married and living in Melaka."

"What about the vic?" Mislan asks impatiently.

"Norita or Ita as she called her, moved to KL after she finished SPM. She worked as a waitress in several hotels of which the mother cannot remember the names anymore. She used to send her money but stopped doing so when the father went missing. The mother claimed Ita was daddy's girl and that was why she was not surprised to hear of her arrest for drugs a few years back, and now her death. To quote her, like father like daughter."

"Was Norita ever married?" Johan asks.

"Not that the mother was aware of."

"When was the last time she saw her daughter?" Mislan asks.

"About six years back, around the time the husband absconded."

"What about talking to her?"

"The last was two years back."

"You get her phone number?"

"Yes, but the mother doesn't know if she was still using the same number."

"Her younger sister, what's her name again?"

"Norshida."

"Yes, Norshida, you get her phone number and address?"

"Yes. She is a teacher."

"Good work," Mislan says.

Constable Laila passes the notes she took of the interview to the inspector.

7

When they drop off Woman Police Constable Laila at Kuala Selangor District Police HQ, it is almost noon. Driving back to the city, Johan suggests they stop for lunch at one of the small towns on the way. He claims that, unlike in the city, village restaurants cook authentic traditional Malay dishes. Mislan agrees. They stop at a small town called Ijok with only one row of shops. At the end of the row, there is a zinc-roofed extension which was turned into a restaurant.

It is still early for lunch by Malay standards and there are only two customers. The officers examine the dishes on display and place their orders. The dishes look delectable, especially the masak lemak which is thick and rich. Mislan once used Google Translate for the English term for masak lemak – the app got it wrong by making a direct translation: cook fat. If he is to translate the dish to English, he would call it yellow curry. To his delight, a small table next to the display is filled with a variety of ulam and sambal belacan.

Waiting for their orders to be served, Mislan tries the victim's mobile phone number given by the mother. He is not surprised when his call goes directly to voice mail, saying the number he had just dialed is not in service.

"Jo, can you call the vic's sister's number?" Mislan pushes Laila's note to Johan.

"Why not call her yourself?"

"You're better with women," he chuckles.

"She's married OK."

"I'm not asking you to date her, I'm asking you to call her for info on the vic."

Their orders arrive.

"Remember what they taught us during religious class in school? It's a sin to let food wait for us once served. I'm sure we don't need more sins than necessary, right? So. let's eat first," Johan quips as he stands to go to the sink to wash his hands.

Mislan asks the restaurant worker for fork and spoon as he does not want the smell of masak lemak to stick to his hands after the meal. Most Malay and Indian dishes tend to do that even after you wash your hands. Perhaps deliberately cooked that way to remind you of how delicious or yucky they were after you ate them. In this instance, it is clearly the former. To Mislan's surprise the lunch with drinks costs him only RM14.50; it would have easily been more than RM20 at any roadside stall in the city. And on top of that the restaurant operator gives him a 50 sen discount. Not out of kindness but usually because they do not have coins.

While he enjoys his nicotine dessert, Johan makes the call to Norshida. After three rings she answers. Johan puts her on speaker.

"Hi, Puan Norshida, I'm Detective Sergeant Johan from D9, Kuala Lumpur. I got your number from your mother, Puan Maimunah."

"Detective?! What's this about?"

"Puan, can you talk?"

"How do I know this is not a scam call? Since the MCO, I heard there're many scam calls from people claiming to be the police, inland revenue, court and what not."

"You can call Special Investigation Kuala Lumpur and check me out."

"Your name again?"

"Detective Sergeant Johan Kamaruddin from D9, Kuala Lumpur."

The phone goes silent and they hear soft tapping sounds like heels hitting concrete floor.

"She's probably in a classroom and is stepping out to have some privacy," Mislan says.

"Puan, you still there?"

"Yes, what is this about?" Norshida asks, sounding anxious.

"It's about your sister Norita."

"Is she in trouble again? If she is, I want nothing to do with it."

"I'm sorry to be the bearer of bad news, your sister is dead. Her body was found yesterday morning in Bangsar."

"Ya Allah," she cries.

"Puan please accept our condolence for your loss."

The silence returns.

Mislan whispers to Johan to ask Norshida to come to Kuala Lumpur Hospital to claim the body and make burial arrangements.

"What happened?" Norshida stammers.

"We're still investigating. Puan, we need for you to come to KL hospital for us to release the body. According to your mother, she does not know how to contact your father."

"Forget him. I'll come up and make the arrangements."

The officers detect bitterness in her voice.

"When? We need to be there for the release."

"I'll get permission from the school and leave immediately. It is 1 pm now and I should be there by 4. Where do I go?"

"The medical forensic department. We'll wait for you there. Again, please accept our condolences for your loss," Johan says, terminating the call.

"Told you, you're good with women," Mislan teases Johan.

They reach the office at 2.30 pm. The front desk clerk informs them Superintendent Samsiah wants to see them. They make a detour to her office. She beckons them in, pointing to the visitor chairs.

"How was your trip? Managed to sample the seafood there?"

"Inspector Mislan is allergic to prawn so we sampled the authentic Malay dishes," Johan answers, taking a seat.

"I didn't know that. Anyway, what did you find out?"

Mislan briefs her on their discoveries, which were nothing much or relevant to the investigation. They however managed to contact the victim's younger sister, who will be coming up to Kuala Lumpur to make the necessary arrangements for the body.

"That's good."

"We hope to meet up with her and see if she knows more than what the mother told us," Mislan says.

"They're siblings, I'm sure they kept in touch. Lan, he is asking about the progress of the investigation," Samsiah says. By 'he', she is referring to the OCCI, Assistant Commissioner of Police Burhanuddin Mohamad Sidek. "He claims he has been receiving calls from influential residents in Bangsar. They're annoyed, saying their upmarket neighborhood will lose value if it's considered an above-ground graveyard."

"Hitting their pockets where it hurts the most," Mislan sneers.

Samsiah smiles.

"Apart from what I briefed you, there's nothing new. Forensics found nothing much on the bandage or masking tape except traces of detergent. Dishwashing detergent. I don't even know if it's relevant to the investigation. Rachael said she will call me when she gets copies of the CCTV from the houses next to the playground. But I'm not putting any hope of getting anything from the recording."

"Why is that?"

"The CCTVs were probably installed to cover their driveways and not the playground. Even if they did, there is no playground lighting for it to capture anything visible."

Samsiah sighs. "I guess he has to bullshit his way through for the time being."

"He does it anyway even when he is provided with facts," Mislan says with a chuckle.

"OK, go home and get some rest. Sorry, I forgot you'll be meeting with the victim's sister later at 4. You're up tomorrow, right?"

"Yes, Puan."

8

Mislan and Johan arrive at the medical forensic department at 3.50 pm. Johan goes to check with the reception if a woman has inquired on the release of Norita Mokhtar's body.

"No," answers the man at the counter.

"The sister said she's coming to claim the body. We're seated over there." Johan points to the row of chairs and shows his police authority card. "When she arrives, please direct her to us."

"OK."

The officers watch as family members gather inside and outside the morgue lobby. Some are softly weeping, some talking in whispers and some just staring at nothing in front of them. Depressing.

At 4.10 pm, Mislan starts getting restless.

"Jo, can you call the sister and ask if she's coming?"

"Be patient. It's not advisable to rush a grieving person. Especially if they're driving," Johan quips.

"Just give her a call, will you," Mislan snaps.

Johan laughs, "This case must really be getting to you."

Just then a couple hurriedly walks into the lobby. From the woman's demeanor of looking at the people in the lobby, Mislan can tell she is the victim's sister. So too can Johan, who stands to greet her.

"Puan Norshida?"

The couple stops in their tracks and the woman nods.

"Detective Sergeant Johan, and this is Inspector Mislan, the lead investigator in your sister's case."

Norshida nods and introduces the man she is with as her husband, Zelmey Yusof.

"Puan, Detective Sergeant Johan will assist you in claiming your sister's body, then he and your husband can make the necessary arrangements. While they do that, can I sit with you to ask some questions?" Mislan says.

"About what?" Zelmey asks sounding concerned.

"Routine questions which will help us know more about the victim and possibly give us a lead in our investigation."

"But my wife doesn't know anything about her sister, she lived in KL and we're in Melaka."

"Sometimes we know more that we think. Until the questions are asked, we won't realize it. Jo, take them to the reception and make the necessary introductions. Then Norshida and I'll step outside to chat while you take Encik Zelmey to arrange for the hearse and what not."

"Sure."

The three of them move to the reception and Mislan retakes his seat. After a couple of minutes, Johan beckons to the inspector. When Mislan approaches, the detective sergeant tells him the receptionist has allowed him to use one of the counseling rooms at the back to talk with the sister.

"I'd like to see my sister first," Norshida says.

"Can she?" Johan asks the receptionist.

"She has been positively identified, right?" the receptionist asks.

"Yes, through fingerprints," Mislan answers.

"In that case, she can see her when the body is released."

"She came all the way from Melaka, can't we let her have a peek? Fingerprint technicians are known to make mistake, they too are human," Johan says. "Let's be sure she is who she is. Please."

"OK, take her to the cold-room," the receptionist says. "I'll tell them you're coming."

"Thank you. In the meantime, can you show Inspector Mislan to the counseling room? We'll be back in a minute."

Waiting in the counseling room, Mislan thinks of lighting a cigarette. *I'm sure the house guests will not mind or file a complaint, they're dead.* He looks up at the ceiling to see if there are any cameras, and spots none. *And no one is watching.* Before he can take out his pack, his mobile phone rings. An unknown landline number.

"Mislan," he answers.

"Inspector, hi, this is Dr. Matthew from medical forensics."

"Yes, doctor."

"I'll be going on a long Chinese New Year leave from the day after tomorrow. There're a few things about the autopsy on Norita Mokhtar I think you may like to know. The formal report will not be ready until after I return from leave."

"Great, I'm actually at the morgue to interview the victim's sister. Can I see you after I'm done with the interview?"

"Yes, I'll be in my office."

"Thank you."

Terminating the call, he hears a soft knock on the door and Norshida's face peeks in.

"Come in," Mislan invites. He sees the grief on her face and teary eyes and thinks about the emotionless face of her mother. "I'm sorry about your sister."

Norshida nods and takes a seat.

"I need to ask you about your sister, and hopefully it will lead us to what really happened and who did it," Mislan starts, trying to be as gentle as he can.

"I don't know much about her or her activities."

"When was the last time you saw her?"

Norshida closes her eyes searching her memory bank.

"I think it was two years back, just before the pandemic. We were in KL, my family and I. We met her for a drink at KLCC."

"The last time you spoke to her?"

"Maybe a week or two back when she video-called me."

"What was her mobile phone number?"

Norshida checks her mobile phone and reads out the victim's number. Mislan compares it with the number Woman Police Constable Laila got from the victim's mother – it is the same.

"Did she tell you where she was working, who she was seeing or where she stayed?"

"She did say she was working in a karaoke lounge in Sri Hartamas but she did not mention which KTV. Sorry, I don't know where she was staying."

"Did she say if she was seeing anyone special?"

"No. On Facebook she used to post photos with this one guy, but that was several months back."

"What's her Facebook account?"

"PinkyLady."

"And the profile photo?"

"A caricature of Pink Panther with a pink feathery boa," she says with a tiny smile of remembrance.

"No wonder we couldn't find her on social media. Is it the same on Instagram and Twitter?"

Norshida nods.

"Can you show it to me, her Facebook account?"

Norshida takes out her mobile phone and opens Facebook, searches for the victim's account and shows it to the inspector.

"Her privacy status is public. You can view it yourself," she says.

There are numerous posts of the victim with a man but as Norshida said, the last post was about seven months back.

"Did she break up with him because of a third person?"

"I don't know."

"Do you know if your sister was with someone else after she broke up with this guy?" Mislan asks.

"A month or two back, I can't remember exactly when, I did ask her what happened to the guy on Facebook. She said he's history and that she's going out with a judge. I asked why there're no posts of them on Facebook. She said he is a judge and married, so..."

"Judge! Do you know his name?"

"Salleh or something. I remembered her saying he was the judge who fined her when she was charged for drugs."

"A magistrate or a judge?"

Norshida looks at the inspector blankly.

"Is this judge on Facebook as friends with you or your sister?"

Norshida shakes her head.

"During her last call, did she say anything personal about herself to you?"

"Personal like what?"

Mislan thinks about how he should break the news to her. He knows there is no easy way of saying it. He gropes like a silly fool.

"Like she was starting a family."

"Starting a family?! She was not married!" Norshida says, staring intensely at the inspector.

"I mean, that she was carrying a baby."

"Pregnant?!"

Mislan nods. By her shocked response he knows she was not aware of it. "Yes, according to the forensic pathologist, about fifteen to twenty weeks."

"Where's the baby? Still inside her?"

Mislan shakes his head.

"The doctor removed the baby? Is the baby alive?"

"The pathologist said the baby could not have survived outside the mother's womb...."

"So the baby is dead and we'll be taking it with us for burial together with her?"

Before Mislan can answer, there is a knock on the door. Johan and her husband Zelmey enter. Norshida immediately springs out of her chair, facing her husband.

"Ita was pregnant and the baby was stolen from her womb!" she cries.

"What do you mean by stolen?"

"The fetus was removed from her by C-section," Mislan answers.

"Did she die because of the abortion?" she asks.

"That's not what the forensic pathologist said caused her death. He attributed the cause of death to asphyxiation."

"And what is that supposed to mean?" Zelmey asks.

"She was strangled."

"Because of the baby?" Norshida asks.

"We don't know yet," Mislan says.

"That's why you're asking me about the boyfriend. You think he killed her because of the baby," Norshida asserts.

"No. We need to know if she had a boyfriend and if the baby was his." Turning to his assistant, he asks, "Jo, all the arrangement made?"

"Yes, and Encik Zelmey has made arrangements with the hospital's hearse services for the body to be brought back to her hometown, Kuala Selangor."

"Good. I won't detain you any longer," Mislan says to Norshida, feeling uncomfortable answering her questions about the missing baby. "Should there be any development or if there's something more we need to ask, we'll get in touch with you. Thank you for your cooperation, and again please accept our condolences."

Leaving the counseling room, Johan asks where they are going. Mislan informs his assistant that they are meeting Dr. Matthew, who will give an informal update on the autopsy.

"That's thoughtful of him," Johan says.

"I think he knows we'll not be going on leave, so why waste the Chinese New Year break with idle time?"

Dr. Matthew is working on his computer when the Special Investigation officers knock on his open office door.

"Come in. Sorry my office is a bit of a mess. Please take a seat. Let me just finish this report and I'll get to you."

The two officers take their seats. Mislan gives the office a once-over. The pathologist's desk is covered with thick medical books, journals and printouts. It is messy but not as messy as forensic supervisor Chew's office. There is a small red clay teapot on a brown tray with two tiny blue porcelain bowls. *It has to be Chinese tea. The real tea.*

Dr. Matthew notices the inspector looking at the teapot and asks, "Would you care for some tea?"

"No thanks. I'm not cultured, I'm a coffee man," he answers with a tiny smile.

"I only drink tea here to calm my nerves, elsewhere coffee. OK, let me get my notes," Dr. Matthew says, turning away from the computer screen. "Aah, here it is."

He studies the notes as the two officers wait.

"First things first, the COD is confirmed as asphyxiation by strangulation. I've ruled out suicide by hanging. Apart from the inconsistent ligature marks to that of hanging, the bruising was not deep. The hyoid bone was broken, which is consistent with strangulation; no trauma to the cervical spines which is commonly associated with hanging. The trauma by the sudden drop in hanging cases usually would show on the cervical spines, the C1, 2 or 3. That's around this region," he says, indicating his neck area.

The officers nod.

"There are two light bruise marks on the back at the lower part of her neck, at the shoulder blades area. The bruising marks were made perimortem – at the time of her death. They're about 12 centimeters apart and I cannot figure out what could've caused them. It was like something was pressed or she was pressed against it."

"Pressed like how?"

"When she was strangled, something was on her back or was pressing against her back."

"Hmmm."

"The C-section or caesarean was not done clinically or professionally. It was not a clean single cut like in a surgery and there was no trace of antiseptic. It was done in multiple slices like one was cutting the stomach bit by bit over the initial cut, so as not to cut into the fetus. So you can take hospital or private maternity clinics off your list."

"That's helpful."

"I found a chemotherapy drug – alkylating agents in her system …"

"Meaning?"

"The biopsy indicates she had cancer, ovarian cancer. I think it was detected late and she was too far into her pregnancy for chemo treatment not to affect the fetus."

"If that was the case, why didn't she terminate the pregnancy?"

"Abortion is illegal here, unless if the pregnancy will cause harm to the mother. But then the process of getting it medically certified so that abortion can be legally done takes a long time."

"Can a woman with ovarian cancer conceive, I mean get pregnant?"

"If her eggs are not blocked from moving into the ovaries. Sometimes the surgical procedure done to remove the tumor causes scarring, blocking the eggs from moving to the ovaries. And some chemotherapy drugs can cause the ovaries to stop producing or releasing eggs. Otherwise, yes, a woman with ovarian cancer can get pregnant."

"Won't the chemotherapy drug harm the fetus?"

"It is safe if the pregnancy is in the second or third trimester. In your victim's case she was in her second trimester. I'm sure the oncologist would not have prescribed the drug if he or she felt it was not safe for the mother and child."

"Hmmm, learned something new today, thanks. Doc, she had a previous conviction for using drugs. Were any drugs detected in her blood?"

"No drugs but the blood screen did indicate her alcohol level was 0.15 percent which would have made her really drunk."

"She worked in a karaoke joint, maybe her alcohol tolerance is high," Mislan suggests.

"Maybe, but 0.15 is high even for someone who works at a karaoke joint."

"So she was out cold when she was strangled. That explains the absence of defensive wounds or bruises from struggle," Mislan says, nodding to himself. "Doc, can a baby be born after the mother is dead?"

"Well, it depends on the stage of pregnancy, if the fetus's organs are fully developed and the heart and lungs can function on their own, then yes, it is possible. In your case the fetus was between fifteen to twenty weeks, its heart and lungs were not fully developed to live outside the womb. Second, how long before the baby is extracted from the dead mother's womb. Because the mother is no longer breathing, the fetus will drown in the amniotic fluid if it remains in the womb. Why exactly do you need to know this?"

"Well, my boss moniker the case as Posthumous Child, so I was just curious if there is such a thing."

"In medical terms there is such a thing as posthumous birth. It is when a deceased, pregnant woman is buried with the fetus not removed from her womb. Gases will build up in the body through decomposition and the fetus is discharged through the weakest part of the woman's body, which is the vagina."

"Really!"

"Interesting, isn't it? So, posthumous child, that sounds intriguing. I suppose it is an apt moniker for the case."

"I think we've taken too much of your time. Thank you for the heads up. Gong Xi Fa Cai and be safe," Mislan wishes the doctor.

"Thank you. All the best in your investigation."

9

By the time the two officers leave the Medical Forensic Department it is 6.05 pm. Driving to the police contingent HQ, Mislan updates his assistant on the interview with the victim's sister.

"A judge in KL court?" Johan is surprised.

"She said it's the judge who presided over the vic's drug case. Section 15 DDA is not handled by Sessions Court. So I asked her if he is a magistrate. She said judge."

"To them they're all judges. That could be why the victim was only fined 500 and no jail time. He had a hard-on for her," Johan chuckles. "I'll check the court record and find out who the sitting magistrate on her case was."

"By the way, the vic's social media name is PinkyLady and her profile photo is a caricature of a Pink Panther with a pink feathery boa."

"Whaaat!" Johan exclaims. "No wonder I couldn't find it. I was searching for Norita, Rita, Ita, something that sounded like her name."

"Can you check it out? Her sister said her Facebook account is public."

"PinkyLady, hmmm, remember the Pink Lady massage joint in Hatyai?"

"What are you implying?"

"You know … she could be a working girl. She uses a name which men would associate with the Pink Lady in Thailand. Since the pandemic, I heard more and more of them are going online. No pimps, no hassle from the authorities."

"Known to those who have been to Hatyai and visited the Pink Lady."

"Thousands if not millions of men have been there."

"But not all of them have a mind like yours," Mislan says.

"You think so?" Johan challenges, grinning.

"Just check it out, OK?"

"What?"

"The vic's social media, Facebook, Twitter and whatnot."

Mislan's mobile phone rings; it is Inspector Tee.

"Yes, Tee."

"Lan, the standby detective checked out D'Voice karaoke and was told your victim left about two or three years back to follow a mummy to work at the Champion KTV in Sri Hartamas. The standby went to Champion KTV and it was confirmed."

"You got the address?"

"Google map it for location and direction."

"Thanks."

Mislan passes the information to Johan.

"You going up to the office?"

"No, I'm beat. I'll drop you off and go home. I suggest you do the same. We're on tomorrow."

"When the pathologist said he ruled out suicide by hanging because of the lateral and not upward abrasion mark around the neck, I don't buy it," Johan expresses his thoughts. "But then he supported his finding with other indications."

Mislan looks at Johan questioningly.

"Do you watch the TV series *Law and Order: SVU*?"

"Sometimes."

"I love the series, the older seasons. Especially the ADA lady, Alex. Tall and beautiful," Johan says, grinning. "Anyway, there's this one episode where a police officer and his partner who go around killing drug pushers. He did it because his brother died of an overdose but his partner did it because he was paid by the drug suppliers' competitor. When the one who killed them because of his brother was arrested, he refused to give up his partner. He committed suicide in his cell. He tied a rolled-up bedsheet or some cloth around his neck and tied the other end to the cell crossbar. Standing on his feet, he leaned forward and hanged himself. I'm sure the abrasion around his neck would be lateral or downward instead of upward."

Mislan laughs.

"You think when he leans forward he will die instantly? You don't die from hanging or in this case strangulation just like that, like blowing out a candle," Mislan says, snapping his fingers. "When he starts chocking and struggling for air, he would have stood up and called it off."

"But in the episode, he died."

"Jo, it's fiction OK. They can do whatever they want, like James Bond taking down a flying chopper with a .32 pistol."

"You're saying it's not possible? Even if one is set on committing suicide?"

"If one is set on suicide, he will jump from a building or blow his head off. Do something where there's no turning back or aborting. The person wants others to know it was a suicide."

After dropping Johan off in front of the police contingent guardhouse, Mislan heads home. His mobile phone rings; it is Superintendent Samsiah.

"Yes, Puan."

"Lan, I call to inform you the cat is out."

"Whose cat?"

"He gave a PC at 5.30 and the fetus story is out. Thought you should know."

"Thanks."

"I saw Jo at the office. Where are you?"

"Just about to reach home. Anything?"

"How did it go with the victim's sister?"

"Got some interesting info but have not followed up on it yet."

"Get some rest. We'll discuss it tomorrow."

Terminating the call, he knows the heat is on. The press and social media will be having a field day speculating on the missing fetus. Because the victim is a Malay and therefore a Muslim, the religious fruitcakes will also join the parade.

Reaching his empty apartment, Mislan heads straight for his bedroom, puts down his backpack and takes out his Beretta, placing it in the bedside drawer. He used to remove the clip, but since the failed attempt on his life he leaves the clip intact. It is also because his son Daniel is not staying with him; there is no one who will toy with his sidearm.

After taking a shower, he makes himself a mug of black coffee, sits at his workstation in the bedroom and switches on the TV. For the first time ever, he wishes he had a social media account. He googles 'PinkyLady' and what comes out are Pink Lady sites selling children's apparel.

He googles 'fetus at twenty weeks'. According to Google, the fetus is about the size of a bell pepper, whatever that is, and weighs about 300 grams. From crown to rump, it is about 15 cm long and you can cup it in the palm of your hand. It says the fetus will be fast-growing and the nerves connect the brain to the rest of its body. Mislan studies the image of a twenty-week fetus. It already has a human-like appearance except the head seemed to be rather big in proportion to the body. The mouth, ears, nose, limbs, fingers and toes are all there, formed.

He gasps. *The fetus has already resembled a human being. I can try to understand why the mother was killed, probably someone thought she did something inexcusable, but what did the unborn child do to deserve to die? What the hell is this world becoming?*

Logging off his laptop, Mislan lights a cigarette, pondering on what his case is all about. Taking out his notepad, he writes:

Posthumous Child

- *Murdered by strangulation around midnight to 1 am, Kevin & Dr. Matthew made same deduction.*

- *The vic placed at a playground, in Bangsar – why? There was nothing to indicate she was staying in Bangsar or close to it.*

- *The body carefully arranged in a fetal sleeping position, an arm to act as a pillow and another on her knee. Her dress & hair neatly arranged. Could it be a sign of remorse by the killer or someone who knew or had feelings for her?*

- *Her 15 to 20-weeks fetus was removed postmortem – rationale? To hide the fact the vic was pregnant? Perhaps but more likely not.*

- *The C-section was crudely done. In Dr. Matthew's opinion it was not done by a medically qualified individual. So a botched abortion is out.*

- *The bandage on the C-section was masking tape – was it an act of caring or was it to hide the wound or to stop the bleeding? It was done postmortem, so bleeding is not relevant. Or was it?*

- *The vic had ovarian cancer. Did the fetus die or was it deformed during pregnancy due to her taking chemo drugs and that was the reason the fetus was removed? Perhaps the father did not want the deformed baby to be born. Dr. Matthew said the cancer would not affect the fetus, but could he be wrong?*

- *Her blood alcohol level was very high, 0.15%. Did she intoxicate herself or was it forced down her throat? Dr. Matthew did not mention anything about throat trauma. So she drank herself blind.*

- *The mobile phone number provided by the vic's sister is the same with the one the mother provided. The number is not in service. Where is the mobile phone?*

- *The vic's sister said she was having an affair with a married judge. The judge was the same person that handled her drug case where she got off with a slap on the wrist. Need to identify this judge – a person of interest. Their affair started about six months back, could he be the father of her unborn baby?*

"Damn," he sighs, "so many question and no answers."

He makes a call to his assistant. Johan answers on the second ring.

"Yes."

"Jo, where are you?"

"At the office. Just finished viewing the tapes Inspector Rachael passed from the two houses on Jalan Tempinis 1."

"Anything on them?"

"Just approaching car headlights which stopped by the playground at 4.36 am and again at 4.55 am. No image of what the occupant was doing, too dark and too far away."

"Can you make out the car or its color?"

"Nope, too grainy and far."

"What about Champion KTV, did the detective manage to pay a visit?"

"Yes. Syed said it is an upmarket classy joint with GROs and private rooms. The victim worked there but lately she was not there regularly. Just came in when her regular clients asked for her."

"She slowed down. She was already pregnant. Did they get the list of her regular clients?"

"They requested but were not given. We'll have to pay them a visit. Syed said the manager was bragging that their clients are high net-worth individuals. The manager said, no warrant, get lost. Syed and Jeff didn't want to create a scene."

"Hmmm. His joint must be well-protected for him to be so cocky. I wonder by whom?"

"Brickfields police," Johan guesses.

"Perhaps more powerful than that."

"The judge that the sister mentioned?"

Mislan laughs.

"I heard ASP Ghani is arranging a few New Year eve raids. I think we'll be roped in as backup," Johan says.

"Who told you?"

"Inspector Tee."

"Is Puan still at the office?"

"She left about 30 minutes ago."

"OK, Jo, go home and get some rest. By the way, tonight why don't you check out the vic's social media? Maybe there's something there that can give us a lead in this crazy case."

"Will do. Want me to call you if I find something?"

"No, I just want to get some sleep. We'll talk tomorrow morning. Hey, can you get me nasi lemak, sambal sotong and telur mata? Thanks."

Before calling it a night, Mislan makes a call to his son, Daniel, or Kiddo to him. He is fourteen now, but his memory of Kiddo is when he was ten. The age he left to live with his mother. For years, he only talked over the phone with his son. All these years, not once did he see him. He used the nature of his work as an excuse but he knows it is not true. The truth is, he knows how selfish he can be. And if he is to see his son, he will want him back, to live with him. But any custody tussle with his ex-wife would only make the boy's life miserable. He cannot allow that to happen. Not again. Kiddo has been through a lot for a kid his age. The irony of it all, it was because of love – love for him by divorced parents.

He misses Kiddo, misses being a part of his growing up. Come to think of it, he actually does not know much about his teenage son: who his friends are, what music he listens to, what movies he likes, his favorite food apart from instant noodles when he was living with him, and all the things a father should know about his son.

Their telephone conversations are always brief and guarded. Sensitive to what is being said or asked.

10

Johan is already in the office when Mislan arrives. Inspector Tee has brought a carton of Mandarin oranges for the office, on the occasion of Chinese New Year. This is the time awaited with anticipation by civil servants, especially those in the enforcement agencies, for the 'angpow' – a Chinese tradition of giving money in small red packets. A tradition the Malays and Indians have no qualms adopting. For the Malays, the small packet is green with a yellow moon motif. For the Indians, Mislan has no inkling.

"Gong Xi Fa Cai," Mislan wishes Tee – May you have a prosperous New Year. Leave it to the Chinese to add wealth to their new year's greeting. Everything is money-related to them. "When are you going up to Ipoh?"

"After morning-prayer."

"Every year you go back to your wife's hometown for the big dinner?"

"What to do, she's the boss," Tee says with a laugh.

"Tonight is the big dinner … yee sang, the prosperity dish. Do you practice it?" Johan asks Tee.

Tee nods.

"So all family members will be there?"

"Yes, if they can make it. It's an old tradition strictly observed. And if your parents are old, you try to make it at all costs because next year they may not be around."

"Tonight there'll be a lot of raids by the districts," Johan says. "That's when most of the wanted guys will be nabbed. During the big dinner."

"They've wised up to our tactics, the wanted guys. We don't get as many as we used to. I heard Special Projects has a few targets lined up," Tee says.

"I heard too," Johan replies. "Puan wants us to be the backup."

Inspector Reeziana arrives, sees the box of oranges and asks, "Who gave that?"

"Tee," Mislan answers.

"You bought it or got it for free?" she jokes.

"Jo, did you manage to check the vic's social media?" Mislan asks.

"Yes, and there're some interesting leads we need to follow up on."

"Good."

The front office clerk announces the morning-prayer is starting. The officers grab their notepads and head for the meeting room.

"We'll discuss after the meeting," Mislan tells Johan.

Mislan's mobile phone rings; it is Audi the investigative journalist. He looks at it, surprised – not at her call but at how long she took before calling. He was expecting her to call last night after the OCCI gave the press conference.

"I can't talk, I'm in a meeting," he answers before Audi can say anything.

"Call me after the meeting. Got something juicy for you, bye," she says, terminating the call.

Inspector Tee briefs the morning-prayer of the call-outs he attended, which were not many as most city dwellers have left the city to go back to their hometowns. For the next few days until offices and shops open again, the city is going to be quiet. There will be a lot of drunk, disorderly conduct and driving under the influence but very little of the rest. The districts' general duty personnel and the mobile patrol vehicle (MPV) unit will have several busy days, and so will the hospitals' trauma and emergency centers.

As the pandemic measures are still in place, public gathering are closely monitored for adherence to the Covid-19 SOPs. After his briefing, Superintendent Samsiah releases Inspector Tee as he will be driving up north to his wife's hometown. They all wish him a prosperous New Year and safe journey. Turning to Mislan, she asks if he wishes to brief them on the postmortem findings and what he uncovered from the victim's mother and sister. Mislan tells her it may be a lengthy briefing.

"In that case, Ghani would you like to go first on your plans?" she asks the Special Projects officer.

"We've intel that said a group of out-of-town members of the recent goldsmith robbery in Cheras will be organizing a New Year dinner at an apartment in Pudu. The target location will be revealed before the raid. My men are staking out the place."

"This intel, how reliable is it?" Samsiah asks.

"I've worked with this CI before, he is reliable," Ghani answers. CI refers to Confidential Informant.

"You said you've worked with him before, what did he give us?"

"The loan shark murderer and the car dealer kidnappers."

"The standby detectives will be assigned to you for the raid. Only for the raid. Mislan and Jo will be your backup. Is that the only raid?"

"Yes."

"I thought you said there are two."

"The intel on the other one cannot be verified."

"Anything else?"

"The team will assemble here at 1900 hours for briefing."

After ASP Ghani leaves the room, Mislan asks why Reeziana and her assistant are not assigned as backup.

"Yana will be on tomorrow. She needs the rest," Samsiah explains.

Reeziana gives him a victorious grin. It is no secret that the investigators within the unit dislike teaming up with Ghani, who thinks he is the Grim Reaper.

"Get Pudu to assist," Mislan suggests, still trying to wiggle his way out of backing ASP Ghani.

"I've requested but they're short of manpower. They too have their own targets to secure. Does that answer your question?"

Mislan grins.

"You want to update us on your discoveries?" Samsiah asks. "Wait, can you call Jo to join us?"

Johan appears at the door, looking at the inspector with the expression of what-is-going-on. Mislan gives him a tiny smile and gestures for him to take a seat.

"We're going to discuss your case and I thought you should sit in," Samsiah says.

"The Posthumous Child," Reeziana says.

Referring to his notes, Mislan briefs them of his meeting with the victim's mother and then sister. He notes the dismay on Samsiah's face when he describes the detached reaction of the victim's mother. In the victim's mother defense, she says, people grieve in different ways. Mislan continues, updating them on Dr. Matthew's preliminary findings, cautioning them that things may change when all the test results are in.

"Something the pathologist said during the autopsy is interesting."

"That is?"

"I asked him why the ligature marks on the vic are not distinctive like we usually see on suicide or strangulation victims. His guess is the strangler used something like a folded handkerchief or bandana to strangle the vic. It is softer and wider, so the ligature mark would not be as distinctive as a rope's."

"And that tells you?"

"That the killing may not have been premeditated. A spur-of-the-moment thing."

"We'll keep that in mind. When will he get the results?"

"After Chinese New Year, that is if the labs are working during the festive break."

"Did you request for parental DNA?"

Mislan nods.

"Dr. Matthew would not have given you his preliminary findings if he's unsure of them. Let's go with it until we're told otherwise. Now, this judge the sister claimed the vic was having an affair with, has it been corroborated by any other parties?"

"A judge, interesting," Reeziana says. "Could he be the father of the baby?"

"We've not followed up on that lead. The sister said it was the judge that handled her drug case. If it's true, it would be a magistrate, not a judge."

"That was probably why she was only fined 500 with no jail time," Johan says. "Usually, they get at least two months in the can to detox."

"Her case was what, three years back? The magistrate could have been promoted to a judge ... Sessions Court judge," Samsiah says.

"So what you're saying is this judge who had the hots for the victim ... waited three years before he made a move on her," Reeziana challenges Johan's insinuation. "That's a hell of a long wait for someone with a hard-on."

"Maybe they met again by chance," Johan replies.

"Let's not speculate. I'll check with D5 and get the name of the magistrate that presided over her case," Samsiah offers. D5 stands for the Legal and Prosecution Department of the CID. "What about her social media, is there any mention of the judge or affair?"

"I checked her Facebook, Instagram and Twitter accounts as far back as six months. There was no mention of this judge or their affair. However, as the sister claimed, she stopped posting photos of her and this man named Ilyas about seven months back. Her Facebook profile relationship status – *It's complicated*, and no mention of who she was in a relationship with."

"It's complicated, that corroborates what the sister said," Reeziana points out. "It usually means a triangular relationship or there is a third party involved, like a spouse."

"Lan, what do you think?" Samsiah asks.

"She could be in a relationship with anybody as far as the status is concerned," Mislan says.

"Yes, but if it was a one-to-one relationship, why did she use the 'It's complicated' status?" Reeziana questions.

"What about this Ilyas, did you get anything on him?" Samsiah asks.

"Yes, he too has a Facebook account but it's only for friends, so I can't see any of his posts or his profile," Johan answers.

"Create a fake account and befriend him," Reeziana suggests.

"Isn't that illegal?" Samsiah asks.

"It's done all the time, no one cares," Reeziana says with a grin.

"I'll get IT to get into her account and find out who this Ilyas is. He could lead us somewhere," Mislan says. "Puan, I need to get the record of the vic's phone calls and text messages. Can you assist?"

"Which telco?"

"I'll get the standby to check with all the telcos and get back to you. We need to find out where she was staying. The standby detective checked her last known address, the occupant said she moved out two or three years back. No forwarding address. They also checked with Champion KTV where she worked but was told off by the manager."

"The KTV must have strong connections to tell our detectives off," Reeziana smirks. "Maybe you and Jo can pay them a visit. I bet you they'll be more accommodating."

Mislan grins.

"Careful, I don't want to get a call from you-know-who," Samsiah advises Mislan. "Let's work on what we have and see if we can wrap this up quickly."

"Puan, can you work your charm and get her court info from D5 as soon as possible? Really want to clear the judge mystery."

"Email me her rap sheet and don't forget the telco."

"With the victim's social background and social circles, you're going to have a rich list of potential suspects," Reeziana prompts.

"Let's put some hours on this and see where it leads us," Samsiah says, ending the meeting.

Back at the office, Mislan and Reeziana disappear through the emergency door for a quick nicotine fix. Johan has gone to the detective's room to get the standby to check on the victim's mobile phone service provider.

"Yana, what you said in there," Mislan says, "about the relationship status, is that true?"

"You mean about 'It's complicated'?"

Mislan nods.

"Women are not like men when it comes to relationships. Once a woman latches on to a man, she wants to tell the whole world. Unlike men, most of us are not players. A man would not want to announce his relationship with a woman and risk not being able to play around anymore. In your victim's case, she wants to tell the world that she is in a relationship but it's complicated and she cannot reveal who he is."

"Hmmm."

"Why are you asking the standby to find out her service provider? Isn't the service provider listed on her mobile phone?" Reeziana asks.

"Yes, but we do not have her mobile phone."

"Right, I missed that. Did you try calling the number?"

"Out of service or coverage."

"Have you wondered why she used PinkyLady as her profile name?"

Mislan looks at her probingly.

"I mean her account was public, which is rare unless she is someone with fans like a writer or singer or artist. Which we know she is not. And her profile name was PinkyLady. Does it not sort of imply something to you?"

"Like what?"

"Like, she may be a freelance working girl. I've come across a number of them. They don't directly advertise their services but use suggestive profile names."

"I know there's a massage parlor in Hatyai called the Pink Lady next to the hotel where we stayed."

"There you go. Men go to Hatyai for sex tourism, so they would know of Pink Lady. She just gave it a twist and called herself PinkyLady."

"So you think she was selling online?"

"I don't know, but you could explore it and see where it takes you."

"Your angle?"

"She got bumped when her lover found out about her selling online. He asked her to lose the baby because he doubted it was his. She refused and they got into a heated argument. He strangled her and cut out the baby to cover his tracks."

"The autopsy will still show she was pregnant and we can get the DNA."

"As you said, you don't think it was premeditated. He is not a career criminal. The killing was probably provoked by the discovery of her pregnancy and the ensuing heated argument. In his state of mind, I doubt he thought about medical forensics. That's why we always get them, they don't think things through before doing it."

Mislan gives her theory a slow nod, remembering Johan too thought the victim was selling online.

"My money is on the judge, if there is one. He's a judge and married...a lot to lose if the victim had the baby and made it public. And as a Muslim, which he most likely is, things couldn't get any worse for him."

"Is it enough for him to kill?"

"People have been known to kill for lesser reasons."

11

Stepping back into the office, Johan tells him the victim's mobile phone service provider is Digi. Mislan passes on the information to Superintendent Samsiah. He makes a call to Saifuddin of Crime Forensic HQ.

"Yes Inspector, long time no hear," Saifuddin answers.

"Sai, I need you to do something for me."

"Personal or official?"

"What's the difference?"

"If official, have to go through Chew as the super."

"Is hacking into someone's Facebook account personal or official?"

"Neither, it's illegal under the Communications and Multimedia Act."

Mislan laughs. "The account holder is dead, who's going to report it? Anyway, her account privacy is public. What I need you to do is go into her account and find out who her ex-boyfriend Ilyas is. His full name and particulars, I need to have a chat with him."

"If the account is public, just go to the friends list and click on this Ilyas' profile. You don't need to hack into his account."

"Jo did and said only his friends can see his profile. His contact number, workplace, school, hometown and what not."

"So you're not asking me to hack into a dead person's account but her friend's."

"You got it."

"Then this person is alive and can report it."

"*If* he finds out — but I'm sure you're good and will not be caught," Mislan says with a chuckle. "Anyway, who reports to the police or MCMC that his social media account was hacked? Unless of course it was used for illegal purposes, like a lonely-old-woman scam."

"Yea, right."

"When can I get his particulars?"

"Give me the dead woman's account. Will let you know by noon."

"Good man."

Terminating the call to Saifuddin, Mislan makes a call to Audi. His call is immediately answered.

"You sure take your time to call back," Audi says, sounding upset.

"What is juicy?" Mislan asks, straight to the point.

"Your victim, Norita aka PinkyLady."

"What do you mean?" he asks, playing dumb.

"You don't know!" she says, sounding surprised. "Wait a minute, the victim's mobile phone and social media are the first things you guys check. You're playing dumb with me, aren't you?"

Mislan can hear her laughing. He remains silent.

"It doesn't matter. You'll find out anyway. Your victim is a call-girl."

"So?"

"You don't sound surprised … you *do* know."

"Are you printing it?"

"What? That she was a call-girl?"

"Yes."

"It does make an interesting read, doesn't it? The headline – *Dead Call-Girl's Unborn Baby Ripped from Womb*," Audi says.

"Don't you people ever give the victim and her family any thought at all?"

"I'm *joking*. I'm not even selling newspapers, remember. Your press junkie OCCI said it was a botched abortion. Is it true?"

"I don't know, we're still investigating," Mislan lies.

"If it was a botched abortion, shouldn't D11 be leading the case? But D9 is leading, so it had to be more than a botched abortion." The D11 refers to the Sexual, Domestic Violence and Child Abuse Investigation Division.

"Because the victim is dead, we're leading the investigation," Mislan says, deflecting her suggestion.

"From the abortion?"

"Yet to be established. Lab technicians are on leave for Chinese New Year. We'll not definitively know until they're back at work."

Audi laughs. "Come on Inspector, don't give me that crap. Even I know the labs runs 24/7."

"I got to run, my boss just called me."

"Haven't you guys come up with new excuses to terminate calls?"

"It's not an excuse, that's why I've not coined new ones."

Mislan terminates the call, saying to himself, *Yana and Jo were right about the victim running an online sex service.* How could he have missed that?

It is mid-morning and Mislan is starting to get bored from not doing anything. He has several leads to follow but has to wait for more information on them. He has to wait for the IT technician to identify who Ilyas is. He has to wait for Superintendent Samsiah to get the victim's trial details and mobile phone record. That only leaves him with Champion KTV.

"Jo, want to go to Sri Hartamas?"

"What's there?"

"Champion KTV."

"It's only 11, I don't think they're open yet."

"We're not going there for karaoke."

"I know, but the staff won't be in until 2 pm."

"Shit," Mislan curses under his breath. "Maybe we'll get lucky and the staff are there."

"They won't be. I know they come in at 2 to get the place ready for the 4 pm happy hour. They used to start happy hour at 6 pm and close the joint at 2 am, but with the new pandemic regulations they close at midnight. So they start at 4 pm."

Mislan knows Johan is right; he is a social person and most probably frequents karaokes. He on the other hand is not a social person. Yes, he has been to karaoke joints but that was when he was with his ex-wife or Dr. Safia.

"OK, we'll go at 2."

"We have the Special Project briefing at 7," Johan reminds him.

"We'll be back by then."

"Jo, ask Syed or Jeff to standby. I want one of them to come with us."

"Why?"

"Point out the manager that shooed them."

"Oh boy. Are we looking for trouble?"

"If the asshole wants it."

The Special Investigation officers leave the police contingent at 1.50 pm with Johan driving. He cuts through Bangsar exiting at Mont Kiara. Detective Jeff sits in the back, guiding him to Modesto's. The Champion KTV is in the building close to it, occupying the ground floor. The façade and entrance to the joint looks grand and expensive. Mislan notices the parking lot next to it is empty.

"Jeff, can you check the place out if there's anyone?" Mislan instructs.

"It's New Year eve, I don't think they are open," Johan says.

"Check it out," Mislan insists.

Detective Jeff gets out of the car and heads for the entrance. He disappears from sight and a moment later reappears, shaking his head. Reaching the car, he tells the inspector it is closed.

"Shit," Mislan curses.

"Now what?" Johan asks the inspector.

"Go back to the office, what else."

Just as they are pulling out of the parking lot, Mislan spots a car pulling up in front of the KTV entrance. He tells Johan to drive up to the car. A Chinese man comes out of the car and Jeff excitedly says, "That's the manager."

"You sure?" Johan asks.

"Yes, the arrogant bastard."

Johan pulls up behind the manager's car. The manager stops in his tracks and turns to look at them.

Johan approaches the manager and introduces the posse.

"Sorry, we're closed. Come back tomorrow," he says mockingly.

"We're not here for karaoke," Johan says. "We're here to talk to you."

The manager recognizes Jeff and points to him, saying, "I already told him, no warrant no list."

"If you're closed, why are you here?" Johan asks.

"I'm checking the setting for tonight's gathering. We're having some of our regulars for a New Year celebration at 8."

"Eight, then we have time for a chat," Johan says with a tiny smile.

"About what?"

"About a murder," Mislan answers.

"I heard about it last night. I had nothing to do with it. She was just a hostess here."

"Hostesses or GROs are paid by the hour when booked, right?" Johan says.

"Yes, the mummy will record in the booking and verify the duration."

"May I see some ID?" Mislan asks.

"Why? I'm on private property. You've no right to ask me for my IC," he says defiantly.

"You're on private property which is freely accessible by the public. Either you show me your IC or my men here will let you try on our stainless-steel bracelet."

The defiance disappears from his face. Pulling out his wallet, he produces his identity card.

"Chong Loh Keng," Mislan reads out loud. "Mr. Chong, what do your regulars call you, Chong or Loh Keng?"

"Jimmy."

"OK, I'm not your regular and I prefer Chong. I'd like to see Norita's booking records and a list of her regular clients." Chong opens his mouth to object or say something but the raised palm of the inspector stops him. "I'd like to have them now. However, if you still insist on a warrant, I have no choice because of the long festive break but to station a patrol car with several uniformed personnel to stop and check every vehicle that your invitees drive for their identity."

"You can't do that, this is private property," Chong protests.

"Oh, but I can," Mislan says, smiling. "See that entrance to the parking lot? That is government road, a public area and that is where the patrol car and men will be stationed," the inspector says.

"Are you threatening me?"

"I don't make threats, I make promises. I'm thinking outside the box to get around obstacles," Mislan answers with a wide smile. "Then we'll see how many of your regulars will still want to attend your New Year party. Oh, the patrol car and personnel will still be there after the party, armed with breathalyzer."

Chong pulls out his mobile phone and makes a call. He steps away from the officers for privacy, speaking in whispers. Mislan hears him say "He can? … yes … you're sure … OK." He terminates the call and approaches the officers. His demeanor changes from arrogant to almost friendly.

Following the manager into the KTV lounge, the officers are impressed with the decor and fixtures. The open lounge is huge, a bar counter at one end and a glass display of a fully stocked bar behind it. The leather sofas look luxurious and comfy, with a large plasma TV mounted on every wall.

"We should check out the rooms, I'm sure it's more elegant than the lobby," Johan whispers to the inspector. "*This* is what a karaoke lounge should be."

Chong goes behind the bar counter, searching for something. He stands and makes a call, speaking in Chinese. Still talking on the mobile phone, he bends down to look under the counter. A moment later he puts the phone in his pocket and places a hardcover logbook on the counter. Mislan moves closer to him. Chong flips the pages, reads and turns the pages again. Johan asks if he can use the washroom.

"Go into one of the rooms or use the washroom at the end of the hallway," Chong says. "Here, Rita's booking record," he says, pushing the book towards the inspector.

Mislan examines the record. On the top, it has the hostess's name or nickname, the mummy or supervisor's name, phone numbers, then columns for date, time of booking, time the booking ends, name of the client and amount due. He flips to another to confirm all records are similarly entered.

"You don't computerize these records?" Mislan asks.

"We do later when we close the account for the day. The mummy writes in this book and certifies it every night before they end the day."

"These clients' names, are they real or nicknames?"

"Some real, some use nicknames."

"Why do you need to keep the clients' names?" Mislan asks, curious.

"Sometimes, when they drink too much they forget the booking and refuse to pay. If we keep records, we can show them proof and the GROs can also remind them of the happy night they had with her."

"Don't the clients clear their bills when it is closing time?"

"Some of our regulars do run a tab for a day or two. Only the regulars. So records help."

"What is the average bill?"

"For standard room with drinks promotion, 900 for two bottles of whiskey, that is not inclusive of pouring, ice bucket, food or the GROs. The GRO ranges from 45 to 60 per hour. What the GRO does with the client, they deal directly."

"Meaning offering sex services."

"Sex services, tender loving care, eating on their stomach or whatever the client wants are not my business. That's between them in a private room which they rent."

"So, the GROs do provide sex services?"

"How else could they afford the Honda, Toyota and the branded clothing they wear?"

"Since these records are handwritten, I need to take this book with me."

"I need the book for business."

"Start a new book, after all it's a New Year, a new beginning." Then Mislan adds, "Who is Rita's closest friend?"

"I don't know."

"Call whoever you called earlier about finding the book and ask."

Chong makes the call as told and tells the inspector it is Murni.

Mislan flips the pages of the logbook and finds Murni. "Do you know where Rita was staying?"

Chong shakes his head. "Check with the mummy handling her."

"You got her name and number?"

"Nelly, she's in the book."

12

On the way back to the office, Johan tells them about the private room he went into to use the washroom. It was fitted with two large plasma TVs, a stretch sofa that can easily accommodate ten to twelve people, two glass coffee tables, and a small bar by the side. It had a washroom, equipped with a dressing shelf, shower and towels.

"Wow," is all Detective Jeff manages.

"At almost 1K for two bottles of whiskey, what do you expect?" Mislan says.

"Shit, I can never afford that kind of entertainment," Johan sighs.

"That's not including the GROs and food or additional drinks and cigarettes."

"That's like burning money," Jeff moans.

"If you have loads of it, why not?" Johan says.

"Jo, can you call Murni, the vic's close friend, and arrange for us to meet?" Mislan asks.

"What about Nelly, the mummy?"

"I'd like to speak to Murni first."

"OK."

Mislan's mobile phone rings; it is Saifuddin, the IT technician.

"Yes Sai, I thought you said by noon. It's almost 4 and I had given up on you," Mislan jests.

"Sorry, took longer than anticipated. The name is Muhamad Ilyas Zulkifli, work as a barista at Starbucks 1 Utama."

"You got his contact number?"

Saifuddin reads out the number.

"Sai, you got his home address?"

"No. Inspector, from his social media posts, he broke up with your victim about six or more months back. It tallies with the same time your victim stopped posting about him. Since then, there are no posts of them together on either of their accounts. His current posts are with a new woman."

"That was what the sister told us. Thanks Sai."

It is already 4 pm and too late for the D9 officers to turn back and go to 1 Utama to have a chat with Mohamad Ilyas. They need to be back at the office for the 7 pm briefing by Special Project.

"Shall we stop and have a late lunch?" Johan asks.

The mention of lunch makes Mislan realize they have not eaten. He does not know what time the Special Project raid is going to be over and he does not relish the idea of getting into a shootout on an empty stomach.

"Yeah, OK."

Entering the Bangsar commercial hub, Johan makes a right at the traffic light at the junction next to McDonald's and then a left at the end of the road. He pulls into a parking bay after Subway.

"I don't feel like fast food," Mislan says as Johan cuts the engine.

"Who says we are? There is a wantan noodle restaurant on the next block," Johan says, pointing. "They also have nasi padang. I feel like wantan, you can have rice if you don't want noodles. The operator is Chinese but it is halal and the coffee is superb."

"If it's a Chinese restaurant, are you sure it's open?"

"I can see the tables outside, I'm sure it's open. Jeff, you OK with noodles?"

"I eat anything if it's free except stone and wood," Jeff answers with a grin.

"The girl selling the nasi padang is cute," Johan whispers to the inspector.

"That's the reason you brought us here."

"One of many," Johan admits with a smile.

There are several customers at the tables on the pavement. They sit at one of the tables and place their orders. All of them decide to have noodles.

"Amoi, not closing for New Year?" Johan asks the elderly woman at the wantan stall, bringing a smile on her face for being called amoi instead of ah soh.

"Closing soon, maybe you last customer," she replies.

Wantan noodles usually have sliced pork but as the restaurant is halal, so they use chicken instead. To Mislan it tastes just OK but the iced coffee is really strong and good.

At the office, Johan notices the inspector is behaving like a cat on a hot zinc roof. He keeps glancing at the wall clock and disappearing to the emergency staircase. Something is bugging him but Johan can't tell what. When the inspector reappears from the emergency staircase, he asks, "What's wrong?"

"We got several leads to follow up but this stupid Ghani's raid is…" Mislan lets his sentence hang.

"Calm down, will you? We can follow up on them after the raid or tomorrow."

"If the raid finishes early."

"It's Chinese New Year eve, I'm sure Murni and Ilyas will be up late, partying," Johan says, trying to pacify the inspector.

"Jo, have you called Murni?"

"Not yet."

"Call Ilyas first. Let's see what he's got to say before we talk to Murni."

"You think Ilyas is the unborn child's father?"

"I don't think so. They broke up six months ago. The vic's pregnancy was only twenty weeks max."

"I understand pregnancy weeks are only approximate, not exact."

"You're thinking Ilyas could still be a candidate for the child's father?"

"I guess."

"The more reason we should speak to him first."

"I'll call him and set the appointment at 10 pm, we should be done by then."

Assistant Superintendent Police Ghani of Special Projects and his team are already in the meeting room when Mislan and Johan arrive. They are all wearing ballistic vests and eager for action. Ghani is seated at the head of the table where Superintendent Samsiah normally sits when chairing the morning-prayer. On the whiteboard is a sketch of the target surrounding area. Just as he is about to start, Samsiah appears at the door. Ghani jumps out of the chair, offering it to her. She waves off the offer and stands by the door. She gives Ghani the nod to go ahead.

"My informant said the leader of this group is known as 'Dai-gaw' which means 'big brother'. The 'big' here actually means 'fat' as it is disrespectful to label him fat. He is from Johor and is suspected to be linked to several gold shop robberies in Penang, Kedah and here. He has never been arrested so we don't have a photo of him. His group does not belong to any known gang or secret society. So he is not on D7's radar." The D7 refers to the Vice, Gambling and Secret Societies department.

Pointing to the sketch, Ghani continues, "The target is a unit on the first floor of a low cost-apartment block, on Jalan Chin Chin. This is a Chinese area. Upon exiting our vehicles, we've to move fast to the target. With everyone carrying a mobile phone, the occupants will know of our presence within a couple of minutes."

He pauses to look at Samsiah. No indication that she is going to say anything.

"We'll knock once and announce our presence. Before they can react, we'll ram the door open. I'll lead the entry. There's no back exit, the only way out is through the front door. Any questions?"

"What's my role?" Mislan asks.

"You and Jo come in last, just in case we need backup."

"How many of them inside?"

"My CI doesn't know exactly but I'm anticipating at least five to six. That's the number involved in the Cheras robbery."

"Why are they not going back to their hometown for the big dinner?" Samsiah asks.

"They are being hunted by Johor, Perak, Penang and Kedah police. So they felt it is safer if they stay put here in KL."

"They're being hunted here too," Mislan says.

"Yes, they are and I don't know why they felt safer here. Maybe you can ask them after we take them in," Ghani says mockingly. "Any other questions?"

"If they're who Ghani claims they are, they'll be armed. Lan, Jo, please get your vests. Remember I hate dead heroes," Samsiah says. "Be careful, and good luck."

The raiding party leaves the police contingent HQ in two unmarked vehicles. It is 7.20 in the evening and the last of the daylight still lingers in the sky. Driving along Jalan Pudu, they turn right onto Jalan Chin Chin. The area is rather shabby, with rundown flats, shop-houses and illegal brick wall extensions of houses with zinc roofing. Mislan notices some of the women walking up and down the road look like fair skin foreigners, Thai, Filipino, Vietnamese or Laotian. Hard to tell unless you speak to them. The leading vehicle pulls up to a faded yellow four-story apartment with the second vehicle close behind. Instantly all surrounding eyes turn to look at them with a few of them making a hasty retreat, disappearing between the clustered houses.

Ghani is the first one out of the lead vehicle, barking, "Go, go, go!"

The rest of the team jump out of the vehicle, running after him. By the time Mislan exits the second vehicle, Ghani and his team have already turned the corner of the apartment and are out of sight.

"Shit," he cusses under his breath, running after them. Turning the corner, he spots the last man in the team turning into the stairwell. *I should give up smoking*, he says to himself as he makes a dash for the stairwell. Climbing up the one flight of stairs he is panting.

By the time he reaches the first floor, the apartment grill door of the targeted unit is already pried open and a member of the raiding team is swinging the battering ram. One swing and the thin plywood door with its flimsy lock bursts open. Ghani and the five raiding members rush into the apartment shouting repeatedly, 'POLICE, GET DOWN ON THE FLOOR!'

As instructed, Mislan and Johan take their positions outside the apartment. To their surprise, there is no gunshot, very unlike Ghani's raid. Instead, they hear a commotion, clanking sounds of plates and chopsticks hitting the floor, chairs tumbling, shouting and swearing in Chinese. They also hear the sounds of children crying and a woman screaming obscenities. Johan turns to look at the inspector.

Mislan takes a peek into the apartment and sees a terrified looking family. A man spreads his arms wide to protect his family; he squats in front of a woman and three crying children who crouch on the floor besides the dining table.

He signals for Johan to follow him inside. The raiding team members are searching the two bedrooms for anyone hiding.

Ghani turns to look at Mislan and Johan who are standing in the doorway stifling a smile. He stares at them as if daring them to say something. Mislan turns on his heel and goes out to the front walkway, followed by Johan. The walkway is crowded with curious onlookers from neighboring units. Telling them to stand back, he lights a cigarette and turns to look at Johan; they both smile from ear to ear.

X

Back at the office, Mislan and Johan have a good laugh about the blundering raid and the priceless expression on the faces of Ghani and his assistant.

"Did you notice the way he stared at us?" Johan says. "I think if we so much as smiled he would've cut us to shreds with his MP5. I'd love to sit in when he explains it all to Puan. I think we're going to get a call-out for a dead CI tonight."

"Jo, did you manage to call Ilyas?" Mislan asks, changing the subject.

"Yes, he's on afternoon shift and will be done by midnight."

"We talk to him after that."

"He sounded a bit reluctant, saying he dare not drive around after midnight."

"Tell him it's OK. If he's stopped by the police, ask him to give you a call. Wait, it's only 8.10 now, we can drive there and talk to him."

"I'll give him a call."

Leaving the police contingent HQ at 8.30 pm, Johan again drives to Bangsar then to Taman Tun Dr. Ismail, or TTDI. From there he drives to Lebuh Bandar Utama and to 1 Utama shopping mall. The journey is about 14 km and takes roughly 20 minutes. Starbucks is on the ground floor of the old wing. They are now in the police district of Petaling Jaya, under the Selangor Police Contingent. Since they are not there to conduct any raid or arrest, there is no reason for them to inform Petaling Jaya Police of their presence.

The place is packed with customers, mostly teenagers. *Where the hell do they get the money to spend on expensive drinks?* Mislan asks himself. Most of them are either on their mobile phones or laptops. *Why even come out with friends to an overpriced outlet if you are going to be glued to your phone?*

They approach the serving counter and instantly recognize Ilyas from their victim's Facebook posts. He is working the drinks dispenser or maker or whatever it is called. He is wearing an apron with the familiar green and white long-haired woman with a crown – the Starbucks logo. Johan approaches the order taker, introduces himself and tells her he needs to talk to Ilyas. The girl calls for the supervisor.

"I'm Detective Sergeant Johan and this is Inspector Mislan," Johan introduces themselves to the supervisor. "We need to talk to Ilyas."

"Is he in any kind of trouble?" the supervisor asks, concerned.

"No, he's not. We just need to ask him some questions about a person he knew."

"But as you can see, we're very busy now."

"It'll only take a few minutes. I'm sure you can get one of your staff to replace him."

The supervisor turns to the order taker. "Julie, go replace Ilyas. I'll assist here."

"Thank you."

Ilyas comes around the counter, saying, "There's no empty table."

"It's OK, we'll go out to the front by the open carpark," Johan suggests.

Ilyas is in his thirties, of average height and build. He seems nervous but tries to look casual. When they reach the open carpark,

Mislan leans against a car and lights a cigarette. Seeing him do so, Ilyas lights one too.

"I'm Detective Sergeant..."

"I heard you talking to Julie," Ilyas says, cutting Johan off mid-sentence. "What is this about?"

"Do you know a woman named Norita Mokhtar?" Mislan asks.

"Yes, but that was quite some time back. Why?"

"The two of you were...?"

"We were together but as I said, that was some time back."

"Together, boyfriend girlfriend, a couple?"

"Couple."

"When was the last time you spoke to or saw her?"

"I don't know, when we broke up?"

"When?

"Six, seven months back. Why? What is all this about?"

"Didn't you heard Norita is dead, murdered?"

He looks only mildly shocked. "Oh my god, when?"

"Didn't you watch the news?" Johan asks.

"No. Who watches the news anymore?"

"Do you know she was pregnant?"

"What? No! She never told me."

"Well, she was, and there is a possibility she was carrying your baby," Mislan says.

"No way. We broke up what six, seven months ago. I'm sure if she was pregnant then she would have told me, milked me dry."

"What do you mean by milked you dry?"

"She is, what do you call them... Gillette shaver, a gold digger. Everything must be branded, breakfast at La Bodega, Guess T-shirts, you know the sort of thing."

"Why did you break up?"

"I found out she was selling online."

"Selling what?"

"Selling her services," Ilyas sneers. "The bitch was hooking behind my back."

The two officers look at each other.

"By her social media name PinkyLady, I'm sure you would've guessed," Mislan says.

"It used to be RitaM. She must have changed it after we broke up. I mean, what is there to stop her from advertising what she was offering?"

"Do you know where she lived?" Mislan asks.

"She used to stay in Kota Damansara, D'Rimba, where she rented a room. But after we broke up, I don't know if she still stayed there."

"Are you willing to give us your DNA sample?"

"What for?"

"So we can confirm that you're not the father of the child."

"Sure. When?"

"Here, now. Jo here can punch you on the nose and we can swab your blood off his fist, or you can pull some of your hair strands from the root and put them in this evidence bag," Mislan says. "That way you don't need to go to the office for a buccal swab."

Ilyas grips a few strands of his thick black hair and pulls them out. Showing them to the inspector, he asks, "Is that enough?"

Mislan examines the hair, making sure it has the root. "Yes, thank you."

"Anything else?" Ilyas asks, turning to look at Starbucks.

"One more thing, did you hear Norita saying anything about going out with a judge?"

"As I told you, the last time I saw or talked to her was when we broke up months ago."

"So that's a no. Oh, sorry, do you know the apartment number of her rented room?"

"I think it was B04-11B."

"That would be block B, level 4, apartment 11B," Johan says.

"And the name of the main tenant?"

"I don't know, never met her."

"Thank you."

13

X

Driving back to the city, the two officers discuss the interview they had with Ilyas. They agree that he seemed truthful, and the fact that he willingly gave his DNA sample supported their assessment of him.

"Yana did suspect the vic was providing sex services online," Mislan says.

"She did? How did she know?"

"Her profile name and her social media status is public. Audi said the same thing too."

"Audi the journalist?"

Mislan nods. "What do you think?"

"I told you, I know a lot of them are going online now, especially with the pandemic and the MCO. Like most businesses, they too heeded the government's call to go online," Johan says with a smile.

"How do you think Ilyas found out about her offering happy ending services?"

"I don't know. Why didn't you ask him just now?"

"Give him a call later and ask him, will you?"

Johan nods.

"The manager, Chong said the GROs do provide other services apart from being a singing companion. But he claimed that's between the GROs and the clients. Nothing to do with the KTV."

"That's common. Why do you think they put a shower in the private rooms? I think the mummy is also involved. They are the ones who whisper in the customers' ears what the GROs are offering. In some cases, it's the customer that makes a special request to the mummy for a GRO that offers such services."

"They take a cut."

"So I hear."

"By going online, she gets rid of the intermediary. Keeps all her earnings to herself. Could that have been the reason she got killed?"

"By who? The mummy?" Johan answers with a smile.

"Jo, call the vic's friend Murni and set a meeting. I'm sure she can tell us more."

"About the mysterious judge?"

"Hopefully."

"You want to meet her tonight?"

"If possible, otherwise tomorrow morning."

"I'll give her a call now."

Terminating the call, Johan tells the inspector that Murni is out with friends. She said to meet her at Tapak Urban Street Dining on Jalan Ampang.

"That's the one next to Corus Hotel?" Mislan asks.

"Yes, she said to call when we arrive and she will find us."

"It's almost 10, we can have our dinner there."

As it is the eve of a holiday, the place is packed with merrymakers. The open carpark next to it is full, so Johan has to use the car jockey service. Approaching Tapak Urban Street Dining, they can smell fried food and hear the merry hum of conversation and laughter in the air. Johan gives Murni a call, telling her they are waiting at the entrance.

Tapak Urban Street Dining or just Tapak to those that frequent there, is an open parking lot during weekday office hours. In the evening it is transformed into an alfresco food court, with colorful food trucks selling Western, Malay, Chinese and Indian cuisine and fast food. It is the place for the young to chill and while the night away. The food and drinks are not cheap like that of roadside stalls operated by the makciks, but the place does have an upbeat ambience.

Johan spots a woman in her early thirties – short hair, fair, sexy, in jeans and a pink Hard Rock Bangkok T-shirt – approaching and he nudges the inspector

"That must be her," he says.

Mislan turns to look. "She's beautiful."

"Gorgeous."

The woman, who is not wearing a facemask, steps up to them and introduces herself without proffering her hand.

"Hi, how do you know it's us?" Johan asks.

"Who else could you two be? The police look is so apparent," Murni says with a giggle.

"And I thought only the illegals can spot police from a mile away," Johan jests with a wide smile.

"We are seated over there," Murni says, pointing to the middle of the crowded dining area.

By the size of the large crowd and the sitting proximity, there is no way the MCO social distancing is being observed. The Covid-19 Omicron tally is increasing daily, reaching the tens of thousands. Mislan figures the government has run out of ideas and willpower to take further stringent measures. The people are tired, they need their lives, and more importantly their livelihood, back. 'Live with it or die' is the dictum the government is adopting.

The word 'we' said by Murni is not to the liking of the inspector. He wants to talk to her privately, to ask about the victim's personal life. He spots a group of customers standing to leave.

"Can we sit by ourselves?" Mislan says, pointing to the table where the customers are leaving. "Jo, go grab the table before someone takes it."

"Why?" Murni asks, puzzled.

"I need to talk to you in private, about Norita."

"Oh," she says, sounding concerned.

"Can you tell your friends you're joining us for a little chat?"

"Sure."

Murni disappears into the crowd to inform her friends, and Mislan joins Johan at their table.

"What do you want to eat?" Johan asks.

Mislan surveys the food trucks close to them. "Get me a burger special and an iced coffee."

"Set?"

"No, just burger."

While Johan goes to get their orders, Mislan sees Murni walking towards their table.

"I'm sorry to disrupt your evening with friends," he apologizes.

"No problem," she says, taking a seat. "We've no other plans."

"Can I get you anything?"

"Just mineral water, thanks."

Mislan messages Johan and asks him to get a bottle of mineral water for Murni.

"I heard over the news she passed away, something to do with a failed abortion. Is it true?"

"We're still looking into it. How well did you know Norita?"

"I guess you can say we're close but not like BFF or something like that."

Johan returns with their orders. Mislan observes smilingly as Johan uncaps the mineral water bottle and hands it to Murni. He knows his assistant is trying to charm this attractive woman – love at first sight, or infatuation at first sight.

"You want something else?" Johan asks Murni.

"Thanks, I just ate."

"You can share mine if you like."

Murni shakes her head with a smile. Mislan takes a bite of his special burger, which is beef burger wrapped in egg, and continues with his interview.

"You knew she was pregnant?"

"Yes, she told me about it two or three months back when she missed her period for the second month."

"Did she tell you who the father was?"

Murni shakes her head. "I did ask her, but she said the father didn't know about it yet, so she wouldn't tell me."

"Meaning?"

"If the father did not want the baby, she might have to terminate her pregnancy."

"She didn't, so you're saying the father agreed to have the baby?"

"I don't know. We never talk about it after that."

"Did she have a steady boyfriend at that time?"

"I know she broke up with her boyfriend but that was months before she told me she was pregnant. I also heard she was having an affair with a married man but she did not tell me who."

"Did she mention a judge?"

"Not to me."

"What about her regular clients, was there a judge?"

"There's this one customer, we all call him Tuan, but I don't know if he's a judge. He always booked Rita."

"Can you describe him?"

"Mid-forties, dark skin, about your height and build, and wears glasses."

"You know his name?"

Murni shakes her head, "I think the boss knows him. Every time he comes, the manager will personally greet him. Mummy Nelly will always take care of him."

"Norita was under mummy Nelly's supervision?"

"Yes."

"What I'm about to ask you is a little sensitive, I'm sorry but I need to ask."

Murni looks intensely at the inspector, her big eyes narrowing and her forehead creasing.

"Was Norita providing side services to her customers?"

"By side services you mean sex?"

Mislan nods.

"Yes. Most of us do. That's how we make a living. We don't have bookings every night, and lately with the pandemic SOP we don't get many customers. We have commitments, rent and car installment to pay, food to eat and whatnot. I'm sure you can understand that. We are not government servants that get paid no matter what the pandemic situation is," she says pointedly at the two policemen.

"I do understand and I'm not here to judge you, her or anyone. I'm here to find the truth and hopefully get closure on her death."

"I'm sorry," she says, "it's just that… oh, never mind."

"Did you know she was offering her services online?"

"I suspected, but we never talked about it."

"What made you suspect?"

"She did tell me the pandemic hit her hard, financially. KTVs were closed and her savings had dried up. That was when I think she started doing it online. For your info, even the drug syndicates are selling online, delivered by the food delivery guys like Grab or FoodPanda."

Johan smiles at Murni's comments. He remembers Inspector Reeziana telling them about it.

"Do you know where she was staying?"

"Kota Damansara, D'Rimba but I can't remember her unit number."

"Was she renting the whole apartment?"

"No, she rented a room. The anchor tenant is a woman, Siti. She works at Wawa KTV."

"That's the one behind Shangri-La Hotel, right?" Johan asks.

"In Regency," Murni answers.

"Thank you, you've been very cooperative. I'm sorry if I in any way offended you with my questions," Mislan says, standing.

Johan immediately hands Murni his calling card. "If there's anything else you remember that can help us in our investigation, please give me a call."

"If there is nothing else I remember, I can't give you a call?" Murni says teasingly.

"Of course you can," the detective sergeant answers, beaming at the prospect. "And sorry to pull you away from your friends."

X

In the car driving back to the office, Mislan mocks his assistant about his attempts to charm Murni.

"She just lost her best friend, I'm just being sensitive and polite," Johan says, grinning.

"Yeah right, and you are looking for a new companion."

"Sheer coincidence."

Mislan laughs.

"Whatever, she's gorgeous."

"And high maintenance. With your salary, you can only maintain her for a couple of days before you go broke. Jo, we need to talk to this judge."

"I thought Puan is getting the court records from D5."

"She is, but tomorrow and the day after is a holiday."

"Then we just have to wait."

"I don't like waiting. We need to visit the KTV again. Murni said the manager and mummy Nelly know the judge."

"I'll check the bookings book if Nelly's phone number is there."

"It is," Mislan says.

"Why do you always ask me to make the calls?"

"As I said many times, you are good with women. They hear your voice and they'll agree to anything you ask," the inspector says, pulling Johan's leg.

"Then after they see me?"

"Their hearts melt like butter in a hot pan," Mislan says.

"Murni's didn't," Johan replies disappointedly.

The inspector laughs.

Reaching the office, Mislan checks with the front desk detective if Superintendent Samsiah left anything for him. The detective replies no and jokes, "Expecting angpow?" It is almost 11.40 pm and in twenty minutes, the Chinese New Year firecrackers will start. Firecrackers were banned several years back but in welcoming the Lunar New Year, the authorities close one eye, or in this case deafen an ear. It is a cultural thing. The MCO SOP has been relaxed a little to accommodate family reunion dinners, which is also a Chinese cultural tradition.

Mislan puts his backpack at his desk, walks to the pantry and takes an orange. Seated with his feet resting on his desk, he starts peeling the orange. He makes a call.

"Gong Xi Fa Cai," he wishes.

"Inspector, thank you," Chew of Forensic answers.

"Can you talk?"

"Yes, what's up?"

"I got a witness to pull out his hair, can you do a DNA test?"

"With the roots intact, yes."

"When will you be working again?"

"Tomorrow."

"No leave?"

"Got an urgent case Bukit Aman is working on. No choice, got to come in tomorrow."

"What time will you be in?"

"A little late, around 10 or 11."

"OK, I'll get one of my men to pass it to you. Thanks."

"No problem."

"Hey, again Happy New Year."

"Thanks."

Taking the evidence bag containing Ilyas's hair from his backpack, he passes it to Johan.

"Mark it with our case number and pass it to Chew tomorrow. He'll be in around 10."

"I called Nelly but the call went to voice message. I left a message for her to return the call."

"Maybe she's busy. Remember the manager said they're holding a party for their regulars tonight? Try again after midnight, the party should end by then."

"OK, will do. When I was in MPV, we were sometimes assigned to assist in KTV raids by Immigration and JAKIM. You know what surprised me? Almost all the GROs were Malay. You do get some non-Malay but they're from Sabah or Sarawak."

"Your point being?"

"Nothing, just saying."

14

The shift ended with no call-out. The incoming shift's Inspector Reeziana and Sergeant Reeze walk in together chatting and laughing. Reeze is telling her he stopped at the detective room and was told of the Special Project's blundered raid. Seeing Mislan and Johan at their desks, Reeziana jokingly asks, "How many killed?"

"You should have seen the expression on ASP Ghani's and his lapdogs' faces," Johan says. "Priceless."

"You should've taken their photos!" Reeze says.

"He was just waiting for an excuse to cut us down with his MP5."

"How long since he last drew blood? A year? It's bad for his reputation," she says with a laugh.

Mislan goes to the pantry to make coffee and asks if they want any. They all decline, aware that he makes the thickest, most undrinkable black coffee ever: two spoons of coffee powder and one of sugar.

"How was your snooping?" Reeziana asks.

"A lot of new info but nothing solid to work on. By the way Jo, after your visit to Forensic are you up to going to Kota Damansara?"

"I thought of arranging a meeting with Nelly."

"Good, have you given her a call?"

"Too early, she's probably still sleeping. I'll call her on my way to Forensic and set the meeting at 11."

Mislan glances at the wall clock. 8.15 am. "In that case, I'll go home and shower first."

"Who is this Nelly?" Reeziana asks.

"The mummy or whatever they are called," Mislan answers.

"How is she involved?"

"According to the manager, the vic was under her supervision. I'm guessing she would know who the vic's regulars are. We got the booking register but most of them are using nicknames and initials."

"That makes sense. If the book falls into the wrong hands, it can be used to blackmail them."

"Like they care."

"They may not, but their wives would."

"Hmmm, that could also be a motive I have to look into. In every murder there are three elements: means, motive, opportunity."

"We know the means – strangulation, motive still unknown, opportunity, well the victim was a call-girl so opportunity was abundant," Reeziana deduces.

"Apart from trying to hide a scandal, what other motive could there be? I mean, OK, to silence her – but why remove the fetus?"

"The pathologist says the victim was undergoing ovarian cancer treatment."

Mislan nods. "Perhaps that could be the motive, the baby was deformed from the chemo drugs she was prescribed. Or it was already dead in the womb."

"But Dr. Matthew said the drug would not affect the fetus. If the doctor is wrong, then all the more reason the fetus shouldn't be removed. If the fetus was intact and actually deformed or dead, it could be used to say she committed suicide after knowing it. The depression would make her kill herself," Mislan argues.

"But it was not suicide, the pathologist can prove that."

"I know, but all the killer needs to do is create reasonable doubt and he may get away with it. Get an expert to say it is possible to commit suicide by hanging yourself while standing firmly on the ground. Like Jo said he saw on *Law and Order*."

Reeziana laughs, turning to look at Johan who is chatting with Reeze at his desk.

"Jo, you really believe a person can hang himself while his feet are firmly on the ground?"

"Didn't you hear Inspector Mislan? Anything is possible," Johan laughs.

"Yes, on TV."

"OK, last twenty-four hours no call-out," says Mislan. "Heard a lot of sirens but no call-out. I better go home and shower before meeting the mummy. Jo, call me once you speak to her."

Stepping out of the shower, his mobile phone rings. It is his assistant.

"Yes Jo."

"I think Nelly the mummy's phone is switched off. I called her twice and it goes straight to voice message."

"Where are you?"

"Forensic."

"Is Chew there?"

"Don't know, I'm just parking the car. The parking lot is almost empty. Are you sure they're working?"

"I don't know if the lab is open but Chew said he's coming in, some urgent case. Jo, keep calling the mummy, I think she is sleeping off last night's yam seng with the regulars."

"OK."

"Call me whatever the outcome."

"Will do."

Mislan puts on shorts and a T-shirt, and goes to the kitchen to make a mug of coffee. Suddenly he feels hungry and realizes he has not had breakfast. He boils water in a small pot, places two eggs in it and toasts two slices of bread. After about two minutes he takes out the eggs and cracks them into a small bowl. Sprinkling a few drops of light soya sauce and white pepper, he mixes them. He spreads butter on his toast, tears it into bite-sized chunks, dips them into the bowl and eats.

After washing the bowl and placing it on the drying rack, he takes his coffee mug and heads for the bedroom. Sitting at his workstation, he reviews his case notes. He keeps asking himself, *Why was the fetus removed?* Reeziana did put up a strong case for the motive but he feels there has to be a more compelling reason. Granted that in a moment of rage, one would take another person's life, but cutting out a baby from a womb – that's something else. Imagine cutting a woman's stomach and scooping out the baby, all eerie-looking and bloody. It is even worse if the baby is yours. No, something more evil or sinister must be the motivating drive.

He Googles for cases of fetuses stolen from the womb. Wikipedia has a definition – fetal abduction. It is where an at term pregnant woman's fetus is extracted by crude Cesarean section. It is also termed 'fetus-snatching'. It goes further to state that fetus abduction is mostly perpetrated by women. *That's interesting,* Mislan thinks. There were 18 cases recorded in the United States between 1983 and 2015.

Nothing is said about what the fetuses were used for. The term 'an at term pregnant woman' tells him it had to be a baby-for-sale racket. In his case, the fetus was only 20 weeks old and had no possibility of surviving outside the womb. The motive of child abduction is ruled out.

He lights a cigarette, pondering. A crime needs three elements – means, motive and opportunity. He has figured out the means and opportunity but he can't put his finger on the motive.

His mobile phone rings; his assistant again.

"Yes, Jo."

"Still can't get through to the mummy. What do you want me to do?"

"Why don't you come over to my apartment and we go to Kota Damansara, D'Rimba. Maybe the anchor tenant is home and we can check out the vic's room."

"OK, will be there in thirty."

In the car driving out of Bukit Antarabangsa where Mislan lives, Johan asks the inspector if he knows how to get to D'Rimba Apartment. Mislan shakes his head.

"Do you know how to get to The Curve?" he asks Johan.

"Yes. Is D'Rimba near there?"

"Could be, Kota Damansara is next to The Curve, right?"

"I'm not familiar with the area," Johan admits.

"Once we get to The Curve, I'll Waze D'Rimba."

"Why do you think Nelly switched off her phone?" Johan asks.

"I don't know, maybe hungover from last night. I'm guessing the drinks were on the house, so you know how they yam seng when the drinks are free. Jo, did Chew say when we can get the DNA result?"

"I didn't ask. Why, you had something planned?"

"No, just asking. Before you picked me up, I was Googling. You know our case is unique, but the theft of a fetus is not. Such incidents happened in the US."

"Serious?!"

"The statistics are for 1983 to 2015, eighteen cases. Nothing more recent."

"That's 18 cases in 32 years. Not even one a year. What about here?"

"I searched, nothing. No reported case."

"Did you find out what they did to the baby… fetus?"

"Don't know, Mister Google didn't say. Anyway, Wikipedia said the reported cases in the US are of pregnant women at term. I guess it had to do with baby snatching for sale. It also claimed that fetus abduction is mostly perpetrated by women."

"No shit!"

"It makes sense, doesn't it? A woman pretending to sympathize and care for a pregnant runaway kid. Then when the kid is due, she performs an illegal C-section, steals the baby and sells it."

"But in our case, it is not full term, it's a fetus, and our victim is not a runaway kid."

"That's what's puzzling me."

Johan makes the turn to The Curve shopping mall. Mislan calls up Waze on his mobile phone and keys in D'Rimba apartment. Waze tells them to take Jalan PJU 7/3, then Persiaran Surian. The area is saturated with high-rise apartments. When they hit the roundabout on Jalan Kenyalang, Waze tells them they have arrived at their destination. The road leading into D'Rimba apartment is a restricted road and non-resident vehicles are not allowed in. They are required to park along the roadside.

Johan drives up to the guardhouse, introduces himself, shows his authority card and is waved in to the vsitors' parking. D'Rimba comprises several low-rise apartment buildings spread over a large area of green landscape with trees. It has a huge swimming pool, children's playground, and a gazebo. Mislan supposes that is how the apartment got its name D'Rimba (D'Forest).

"B04-11B," Mislan says.

"Block B," Johan says, pointing to a building with obvious signage.

"Let's go."

"I don't think they have elevators," Johan says, grinning at the inspector. "We have to climb stairs to level four."

"In that case, why don't you go up first? If the tenant is home, you give me a call. That way I don't have to waste energy climbing the four flights if she's not home," Mislan says with a smile. "I'll wait for your call, there," he says, pointing to the gazebo.

"You should come with me, you need the exercise."

"Yea, like I need a boob job," Mislan replies, laughing.

Johan walks to Block B and Mislan to the gazebo. Sitting on the edge of the concrete floor, he lights a cigarette and watches Johan disappear into the apartment building. Halfway through his cigarette, his mobile phone rings, it is Johan asking him to come up.

Struggling up the four flights of stairs, stopping to catch his breath at every landing, Mislan finally reaches the intended floor. His assistant is nowhere to be seen. Resting against the guardrail catching his breath, he sees Johan stepping out of one of the apartments, looking at him with a mocking grin. He frowns at Johan.

"Over here," Johan says. "Just a few more steps."

The panting inspector sees a woman appear next to Johan. She too is grinning at him. Johan says something to her, they laugh and the woman disappears.

Taking off his shoes in front of the door, Mislan steps into the cool, welcoming apartment. The woman comes out from the kitchen with a glass of iced water for the inspector.

"Thanks," Mislan says.

"Cik Adibah, this is Inspector Mislan the lead investigator," Johan introduces. "She's the anchor tenant. Our victim rented that room," he says, pointing to a door.

"Just call me Siti," she says.

Siti Adibah is in her late thirties or early forties. She is slim, about 1.6 meters tall, fair, wears her hair long below her shoulders, has big clear eyes and a lovely warm smile. She is in pajama pants with a worn, oversized T-shirt and she is definitely braless.

The living room is quite spacious, furnished with simple but tasteful furniture. No framed pictures on the wall, which is typical of a bachelor pad. The balcony overlooks the swimming pool. There is no television, so Mislan assumes they probably have TVs in their rooms.

"How long have you been staying here?" Mislan asks, making small talk.

"Almost two years now, just as the pandemic started."

"Before here, where were you staying?"

"Singapore, I worked there for almost six years."

"What made you decide to move back here?"

"Homesick I guess," Siti says with a lovely smile.

"Sorry to ask, are you married?"

"Was, no children," she answers, looking at the inspector inquiringly.

"Just curious," Mislan says. "Norita, how long had she rented a room from you?"

"Let's see… Rita came in June so that would be eight months."

"Have you heard what happened to her?"

"Yes, from the news. What actually happened? The news said it was a failed abortion."

"That's what we're here to find out. How close were you with her?"

"I bumped into her now and then, but we were not close. She worked at Champion and me at Wawa. In the daytime we slept and in the evening we went to work."

"Did she bring friends or a boyfriend to her room?"

"I suppose she did but I didn't see or ask her. After all, it was her room, she was a grown woman and it's none of my business."

"Did you know she was expecting?"

"No! She didn't mention anything to me."

"I'm sure you'd notice her stomach."

"How many week was she pregnant?"

"Fifteen to twenty weeks," Johan replies.

"Twenty weeks, well if she knew how to dress, I don't think you'd know she was pregnant."

"May we see her room?"

"I don't know if I should let you. Don't you need a warrant or something?"

"This is your apartment and if you allow us, there's no need for a search warrant," Mislan says. "Anyway, we're not taking anything. We just need to see if there's anything that could tell us who the father of the child is. By the way, we met her younger sister Norshida. Perhaps you should give her a call to come and collect Norita's belongings."

"I'll do that, thanks."

"Can we?"

Siti looks at the inspector, unsure of what is asked.

"See the victim's room."

"Eh sorry, yes, I guess."

The victim's room is the middle of the three-room apartment. It is about four by five meters, which is quite big for an apartment's middle bedroom. The room has no attached bathroom; this is common in most apartments, where only the master bedroom has an en suite bathroom. The occupants of the other two rooms share a common bathroom. The first thing the Special Investigation officers notice is the mess. Dresses, pants, blouses and handbags were thrown on the unmade bed. In one corner there is a standing hanger rack that is overloaded with clothing. A dressing table littered with cosmetics and a towel rack loaded with T-shirts and jeans. A single bed pushed against the opposite wall with several pairs of high heels under it. The window has no curtains; there is a ceiling fan but no air-conditioner or television. The room smells of soiled clothing, dry sweat and old perfume.

Is this how she lived or did someone go through her room looking for something? Mislan turns to look at Johan and the anchor tenant standing in the doorway with shock on their faces.

"Did someone do this or was her room always like this?" Mislan asks Siti.

"I don't know, never been inside her room. What are you looking for?"

"The question is, *how* do we look for what we're looking for?" Johan replies.

"Jo, look for her phone, laptop or diary if you can find them. I'll check her luggage and pants, maybe there is something in them."

Johan comes into the room, careful not to step on the things scattered on the floor. Mislan checks the luggage – nothing. While he pats the pockets of jeans, Johan examines the handbags.

"Anything?" Mislan asks.

"Condoms and KY."

Siti, standing in the doorway, giggles.

"Siti, do you know if Norita has another place?" Mislan asks.

"You mean another place where she stayed?"

Mislan nods.

Siti shakes her head.

After 10 minutes of futile searching in the stuffy room, the inspector and his assistant give up. Stepping back into the living room, they inhale deeply to clear their lungs of the stale air from the room. Taking a sip of the water which Siti brought earlier,

Mislan asks if he can smoke. Siti goes to the kitchen and comes back with a glass of water for Johan and an ashtray.

"Did Norita ever tell you about a client, a judge?" Mislan asks her.

"As I said earlier, we didn't talk much. We bumped into each other when we went to the kitchen or when she used the washroom."

"That's a no. What about car, does she have one?"

Siti shakes her head.

Before leaving, Johan gives her the victim's sister's mobile phone number and asks for hers. The officers thank her for her cooperation and leave.

15

By the time the Special Investigation officers leave D'Rimba apartment it is past noon. Mislan asks Johan to try and call Nelly again, saying, "She's probably up by now." Johan does and after four rings she answers.

"Who's this?" she asks, sounding tired.

"Detective Sergeant Johan from D9. I left you a message to return my call."

"What's this about?"

"We're investigating the death of Norita," Johan says, substituting the word *murder* with *death* so as not to scare her.

"The news said she died because of a screwed-up abortion," she says dismissively. "What has it got to do with me?"

"Miss Nelly, it's best if we talk in person. Can we meet?"

"I'm staying in Kosas."

"That's in Ampang, right?"

"Yes. I'm going to Ampang Waterfront for lunch. Maybe we can meet there."

"We're on our way back from PJ. It will take us about 30 minutes or maybe a little more to reach the Waterfront. Is it OK with you?"

"Yes, give me a call when you reach there."

"Thanks, will see you in 30 minutes or so."

Nelly is in her early fifties. Her thin hair, which she wears shoulder-length, is dyed blonde. She is petite so she looks younger than she actually is. A pear-shaped face, sunken cheeks, thin lips and pencil-line eyebrows; fair-skinned but she does not look Chinese or Malay. Her eyes are red, probably from lack of sleep or too much drinking. She spots the Special Investigation officers standing at the entrance of the café with eyes roaming over the dining area, and waves at them. After the introduction, she asks if they'd like something to eat. The half-eaten chicken rice in front of her looks good.

"I only come here for the Hainanese chicken rice," she says.

The two officers order the same. Waiting for their food, Johan makes small talk with her. She tells them she is staying about two kilometers down the road in Taman Kosas. She is an Iban from Sarawak, divorced and living with her son.

Taking out his digital recorder, Mislan places it on the table, saying, "Do you mind me recording our conversation?"

Nelly shakes her head. "Is this about Rita?" she asks.

"Yes, she was under your supervision?" Mislan asks.

"She and a few others."

"So you know most of her regulars?"

Nelly nods. The officers' orders arrive and Nelly gestures for them to eat.

"It's tastier when eaten warm," she recommends. "When it's cold and does not taste so nice then you'll say that I lied," she jokes.

The Hainanese chicken rice is really tasty. To Mislan the Chinese make the best chicken rice, period. It is after all their invention.

"Are you aware that Norita or Rita was pregnant?" Mislan asks with his mouth full.

"Yes, she told me about two months back. She asked if she could come in only when her regulars requested for her."

"What about Chong the manager, he knew too?"

"Yes, I had to seek his permission, otherwise Rita might have been terminated for not coming to work."

"I thought GROs are not wage earners," Johan says.

"They're not. Their income is through bookings, but Chong wants all of them to come in. He said the more girls they have, the more attractive the lounge is. The girls that do not have bookings can always join those booked to entertain the customers."

"But they won't get any payment because they were not booked."

"No, but they can get tips from the customers," Nelly explains. "Sometimes 50, sometimes more. If they butterfly in several rooms that can be quite a lot."

"Butterfly?" Mislan asks.

"Meaning they pop into one room, sing one or two songs then pop into another room, we call that butterflying. They can do it because they are not booked."

"I see."

"So the manager agreed?" Mislan asks. "I mean to Rita not coming in every night."

"Yes."

"Do you know if she was having an affair with one of her regulars?"

"They all do."

Mislan looks at her surprise.

"Why are you surprised?" Nelly asks. "The girls are in their late twenties or early thirties. You think they want to be GROs until they become old maids? They know the men who come to

KTVs that have GROs are looking for fun. Fun their spouses cannot provide, and they have money. You put money, fun and women looking for retirement security, what do you have – affairs."

"I won't argue with that. Do you know who Rita was having an affair with?"

Nelly shakes her head. "No."

"Ohh, I'm sure you heard something," Mislan says, gazing at the mummy's face. "She or the other girls must have talked about it."

"I heard gossip but I'm not really sure from who."

"What did the gossip say?"

"That she was having an affair with a big-shot but they never mentioned a name."

"Could it be a judge?"

Nelly gazes blankly at the inspector.

"One of her regulars is a judge, right?" Mislan asks.

"Which one?"

"I don't know, but I heard every time he comes to the KTV your manager and you greet him at the entrance."

"You mean the Tuan," Nelly says. "He is a judge? I thought he is from the police."

Mislan looks at Johan. "What makes you think he is a police officer?"

"His arrogance and the manner he spoke and acted."

"What is his name?"

"I don't know, I call him Tuan and so does everyone else."

"Was he having an affair with Rita?"

"Maybe. He only booked her and I saw them leaving the KTV together many times."

"You maintain a booking register, right?"

Nelly nods.

"What name do you record when he booked Rita?"

"As I said, I thought he was a police officer because he never paid for the drinks and girls. He always came with others, businessmen or corporate people. They did the booking and paid for the room and girls. Even the tips. So I recorded the bookings under them, the hosts and not him."

"Can you describe this Tuan?"

"Early or mid-forties, about your height, dark skin, looks like mamak, crewcut hair and a jerk."

"Hmmm."

"Is this going to be long? I need to go back and get ready to go to work."

"A bit more. Was Rita providing extra services?"

"You mean, sex?"

Mislan nods.

"Most of them do."

"At the KTV or outside?"

"Sometimes there in the washroom, sometimes outside. Depends on what the clients want. Outside may cost them more."

"OK, thank you. We'll contact you again if there are any other questions." Standing to leave, Mislan says, "Oh, one more thing, when was the last time you saw Rita?"

Nelly gives the question a little thought. "Three days ago, the Tuan and his group came and booked her."

"Did they leave together? I mean the Tuan and Rita?"

"Yes, with his group."

"What time was it?"

"Around 11 plus, I think."

X

Leaving the Ampang Waterfront, Johan asks if they are headed for the office. Mislan tells his assistant that since they are close to his apartment, it is best to drop him off.

"Jo, you going back to the office?"

Johan nods.

"Can you check the booking register, see if our vic was booked three nights ago as Nelly said?"

"Three nights ago was when she was killed."

"Yes, if it's true then the last person she was seen alive with was the Tuan or judge, if that's who he is."

"So he's our prime?"

"For now, until something else comes up." Mislan groans, "Tomorrow's still a holiday, no chance of getting the vic's phone record."

"Who do you think has her phone?"

"Probably the killer, together with all her other personal belongings, IC, bankcard, and whatnot. I forgot to ask Nelly how she was paid, I mean her bookings."

"Why?"

"If it was bank-in then we could get her bank account number. We can ask the bank to put a high alert if anyone tries to withdraw money from her account. Can you call Nelly and ask? Another thing, I noticed a CCTV camera at the entrance. Ask Jeff to pay them another visit and get a copy of their recording from a week back."

"The manager will shoo him away like the last time."

"After our last visit, I don't think he will."

"No matter, I'll go with Jeff."

"In that case, you can ask the manager about the GROs' mode of payment for their bookings. No need to ask Nelly."

"Will do. This judge, are you sure he exists? I mean both Murni and Nelly said they're not sure. Maybe the vic's sister was wrong."

"Maybe. I guess we have to wait until the offices are open to know for sure."

"In the meantime, what do we do?"

"Nothing we can do."

16

The next morning when Mislan arrives at the office, Inspector Reeziana and her assistant are at the pantry having breakfast.

"You're early," Reeziana greets.

"What are you guys having?"

"Reeze bought mee goreng from Kampung Baru. You want some?"

"No thanks. I thought of buying something on the way but most of the stalls are closed."

"Chinese celebrate New Year and Malays don't open for business – because the Chinese are the ones supplying the fresh produce."

"I thought those days are long gone. Nowadays the supermarkets are open."

"Still the same, supermarkets don't get their supplies and jack up the prices. Buying from them, the stalls cannot make any margin and will lose their customers. So it's better for them to close their stalls until the wet markets reopen," Reeze rationalizes.

"The Malays control the government, the Chinese control the economy," Mislan says.

"And the Malays thinks they are in power," Reeziana laughs.

Johan arrives carrying a plastic bag.

"What have you got there?" Mislan asks.

"Roti canai, the nasi lemak stall is closed."

"So, what did you find out about the victim and her side business?" Reeziana asks.

"Nothing much. Apart from her sister's claim that she was having an affair with a judge, no one we talked to can verify her claim. All they heard was the vic was having an affair but they don't know for certain."

"Maybe your victim was jerking her sister around. You know, telling lies to make her think she was doing great. Her sister is a teacher and she was well, a GRO, so she made up stories to make her sister envious. Sisters do that you know, compete with each other about who is doing better."

"What's so good about having an affair?" Mislan asks. "It's not like she was *married* to a judge or something like that."

"Who knows, maybe she was looking to be his second wife?" Johan interjects with a grin. "If he is a Malay, he can have four wives."

"Yeah, look at how many of our MPs and politicians have second and third wives. Polygamy is encouraged by our fruitcake preachers," Reeziana sneers.

"I don't know," Mislan says. "I just have to wait until tomorrow when Puan gets hold of the records from D5 and the telco."

"Lan, if this judge thing is true, I'm sure the case will be explosive," Reeziana says. "I suggest you do it right, right from the beginning."

"We are," Johan states, glancing at his lead investigator.

"I hope you are," Reeziana says.

"Yana, a woman-thingy question. Can a woman who is 20 weeks' pregnant hide it?"

"You mean the bulging stomach?"

Mislan nods.

"Yes, if she knew how to dress to hide it. Because at 20 weeks the baby bump is just appearing, and you don't walk funny yet," Reeziana says giggling.

"Funny, how?"

"Swaying right and left like a seasick sailor. Next time you see a pregnant woman, especially those that are in their advanced stage, watch how they walk. Like a robot that cannot bend its knees."

"What about having sex?"

"What about it?"

"I mean surely the partner will notice the bulge."

"I'm sure he will, but having sex during pregnancy is safe as long as you don't ride her like a rodeo cowboy. Google it. Do you know there are men who like having sex with pregnant women?" Reeziana notices Johan cringe like he bit into something sour, and says, "You don't believe me, Google that too." Picking up her backpack she says, "OK, that's all for today's sex education."

After Reeziana and Reeze leave, Johan Googles men who like having sex with pregnant women. He is surprised by what he reads, and calls out to the inspector.

"It's true. They even have a term for it, pregnancy fetishism or malesiophilla or maieusophoria. It says here, pregnancy is seen by individuals or cultures as an erotic phenomenon."

"Why are you surprised by what men like to have sex with? Do you know that men are paying 20 to 40 thousand US dollars to buy sex dolls? A man's primary objective in life is to find that one perfect partner with whom he can enjoy the greatest sex whenever and however he wants."

Johan laughs.

17

By 7.15 the next morning Mislan is all freshened up, anxiously waiting for the morning-prayer. The last two days had no morning-prayer due to the public holiday. He is especially eager to know the result from the Legal and Prosecution department and telco company. Earlier Johan had gone to get breakfast and he made two mugs of coffee for them.

Inspector Reeziana arrives and joins them at the pantry. She looks like she is bursting to tell him something.

Staring at her, he asks, "What?"

"You read the Selangor D9 case on the cigarette warehouse robbery where the security guard was killed?"

Mislan nods.

"Last night, I went out with a couple of Selangor D9 guys. They told me they collared two of the perpetrators. One of them offered to deal, claiming he knows the shooter of a police officer."

Mislan gawks at her.

"Selangor D9 contacted Bukit Aman and he was taken away by them."

"Did he say where the shooting took place?"

"No. According to my friends, he refuses to say anything unless there's a deal on the table. That's the reason Selangor contacted Bukit Aman. Thought you'd like to know."

"Thanks."

"Maybe Puan can find out more."

Mislan nods.

The failed attempt on his life was almost two years ago. A year after the shooting, he was able to move on. He eventually stopped having nightmares and managed not to think of it anymore. It was never forgotten but he succeeded in storing it in his brain's memory drawers. He refused to let the incident dominate his thoughts.

That is, until now. Until Reeziana told him about the arrest of the cigarette warehouse perpetrators. Now he is consumed by the thought of closure. His memory drawer is opened and its contents brought to the forefront, to his brain's RAM. He is certain the nightmares will return. The feeling of being helplessly slumped in a pool of his own blood will return.

If what Reeziana says is true and if the information about the shooter is genuine, he wouldn't want Ghani to lead the raid. He needs the shooter alive. He needs to know who put out the hit on his life.

Sulky ASP Ghani is already in the meeting room when Mislan and Reeziana enter. Putting on blank faces, they take their seats. They know today's focus will be on the failed raid by Special Projects. Mislan notices Ghani stealing looks at them through the corners of his eyes. Looking for an excuse to create a scene and escape facing Superintendent Samsiah for his screw-up. *Well, he is not getting it from us*, Mislan says to himself.

Superintendent Samsiah enters the meeting room and greets all present, but her eyes are fixed on Ghani.

"Lan, you want to start?" she asks.

Mislan informs them there was no call-out the entire shift. "I guess people are exhausted from too much eating and drinking. Not to mention being stuck for hours in the traffic jams coming back from their hometowns."

"Yana, what about your shift?"

"One homicide. A restaurant owner was whacked on the head by a disgruntled customer. The customers disputed the bill, claiming they were cheated. The owner confronted them and they got into a heated argument. One of the customers hit him on the head with a beer bottle. The owner fell to the floor, cracking his skull. He was 66. District is handling the case."

"Were the customers still there when the police arrived?"

Reeziana nods. "They've been taken into custody."

Turning to ASP Ghani, she asks, "Explain what went wrong."

"I don't know. I tried contacting my CI but he is not answering my calls."

"You said your CI is reliable and that you put eyes on the target. I'm sure your stakeout would've noticed there were no movements. The coming and going of men that fit your suspects."

No reply from Ghani.

"The way I figure it, either your CI fed you lies or your stakeout was not watching the target. That was what went wrong."

Again, no response from Ghani.

"I heard from upstairs that the family is planning to take action against the police for breaking into their home while they were having their reunion dinner, traumatizing his family, especially the children. Not to mention embarrassing them in front of their neighbors."

The room goes silent.

"Tell me if I'm wrong in my assumptions about your CI and stakeout," Samsiah continues.

"There could be a third possibility," Mislan offers.

All eyes turn to him.

"And that is?" Samsiah asks.

"There could be a leak in our unit," Mislan answers.

Instantly he feels Ghani's burning stare on him.

"How dare you make such an allegation," Ghani says, his face flush with anger.

"Mislan was not making any allegation, he was stating a possibility," Samsiah says. "I want a full report on the raid. I also want you to list down all your failed raids, who were involved, who were privy to the information, and your CI's details. I want it by this afternoon." Samsiah looks intensely at her head of Special Projects. "I want you to prepare the list yourself without help from your assistant or men. Do you understand?"

Ghani nods without saying a word. Superintendent Samsiah excuses him from the meeting to do what needs to be done. Standing to leave, Ghani cannot resist giving Mislan another deadly glare.

After ASP Ghani leaves, Superintendent Samsiah asks for Johan to join them. When Johan takes his seat, she asks Mislan to update her on his case. Mislan tells them about his visit to Champion KTV, his interview with Ilyas and Murni, the visit to the victim's room, the interview with Nelly and the CCTV Johan obtained from the KTV.

"You two have been busy," Samsiah says.

"You said you did not find anything in the victim's room," Reeziana interjects, "it was in disarray. Could it be possible that someone had gone through her room looking for something?"

"I didn't say it was in disarray, I said it was messy," Mislan corrects her.

"It was not like someone had turned everything inside out looking for something. Like Inspector Mislan says, it was untidy, dresses and blouses thrown on the bed and towel rack. She was just untidy and disorganized," Johan says.

"But Yana could be right," Samsiah suggests. "You both found nothing, no phone, laptop, tablet, diary, photos, nothing. It's a little strange to me that a woman does not have any of those things, especially photos, in her room."

"Not so strange, Puan. Nowadays no one keeps printed photos anymore. Everything is in their mobile phones," Johan explains.

"Well, maybe you're right Jo. I'm not in the mobile phone age. I still think about printed and framed photos," Samsiah says with a chuckle. "So, no one knows who this judge is?"

"As I said, Nelly called him Tuan and thinks he is a jerk of a police officer. Murni didn't know either," Mislan answers. "We viewed the CCTV from Champion but they only have one camera at the entrance. According to Nelly, the victim left with the Tuan and his group on the night she was murdered. But we're unable to identify her leaving because the camera captured them from the back."

"Let's get Nelly to come in and identify this Tuan or judge. I'm sure she can identify the victim even from the back by her clothing," Samsiah says.

"Puan, when can we get the report from D5 and the phone company?" Mislan asks.

"Hopefully today. Anyway, the D5 record would not have a photo of the magistrate. You still need Nelly to identify him through the CCTV. In the meantime, after we get the D5 report, I will try and find out more about the magistrate – where he's based and if we can get a photo of him."

After the morning-prayer, Mislan goes to Superintendent Samsiah's office. Knocking lightly on the door, he asks if she can spare a minute. Samsiah beckons him in. Holding the doorknob, he gestures if he may close the door. She looks at him quizzically and nods. Something seems to be bothering him and weighing heavily on his mind. She knows it can't be his case because they had just discussed it and things are moving along.

"Puan, did you hear anything from Bukit Aman D9?" he asks.

"About…?"

"Did you read about the cigarette warehouse robbery in Selangor where a security guard was killed?"

"I read the summary. What about it?"

"Yana told me she went out with a couple of Selangor D9 guys and they told her they arrested two of the gang members. One of them claimed he has information on the shooting of a police officer and wanted to deal. Selangor called Bukit Aman and they took him away."

Samsiah now knows what is weighing heavy on her investigator's mind.

"Did he say where the shooting happened?"

"Yana said he refuses to say anything else until he is offered a deal."

Samsiah makes a call and a moment later Reeziana knocks on her door. She tells her what she told Mislan earlier.

"Did they mention which case, your friends?" Samsiah asks.

"Sorry, I didn't ask," Reeziana answers apologetically.

"Who from Bukit Aman took him?"

She shrugs. "Actually, I didn't make any connection until this morning when I saw Lan at the pantry."

"It could be any case," Samsiah deduces. "Could be the recent case in Taiping or the one in Penang. Let me talk to Selangor before calling Bukit Aman."

She sees the pain in her investigator's eyes. Although he acts like he has moved on, she knows it's not easy.

"Whatever it is, Lan, you know you will not be involved," she reminds him.

He looks at her and sighs deeply.

"Don't get your hope ups, this may not even be related to your case."

Mislan nods.

18

Nelly comes to the office at noon and together with Johan they view the CCTV recording from Champion KTV. She points out the Tuan on the computer screen as he enters the KTV. Johan freezes the frame and sends it to the printer. When the image frame of the group leaving appears on the screen, she points out the victim. Johan freezes the frame showing a group of people from the back.

"How do you know it's Rita?" he asks.

"She was wearing a black dress, like that," Nelly says, pointing to the back of a woman among the men.

"Other girls might have been wearing black too."

"Yes, but look, her size is small with long hair."

Johan prints the photo of the group leaving with their victim. He thanks her for taking the time to come in.

Giving the two printouts to the inspector, he tells him that Nelly made positive identifications of the Tuan and the victim.

"Jo, I also need the photo of our vic when she arrived at the KTV," Mislan tells his assistant. "The time and date will show that she was there when he was there."

"Anything else?"

"That's all for now."

Armed with the three photos, Mislan and Johan go to Superintendent Samsiah's office. She is on the phone and signals for them to come in, pointing to the visitor chairs.

"Thanks... that's very helpful... yes, still the same number... thanks," Samsiah says, putting down the phone. "That was DSP Gill from Legal and Prosecution. He said the magistrate Sallehnor Muhammad presided over your victim's case. He was promoted to Sessions Court judge a year back. Gill will get one of his men to get a photo of him and send it to me. What have you got there?"

"The vic's sister was right. She said the name given by the vic was Salleh or something," Mislan says, showing the photo of a man entering the KTV. "Nelly identified him as the Tuan or the judge to us."

The man looks forty plus, his features akin to an Indian Muslim or mamak. His hair is cut short, he wears glasses, is of medium build and was wearing a blue sport shirt and dark pants.

"This is the vic entering the KTV and this is where the vic and four other men are leaving the KTV."

Samsiah scrutinizes the photos. "How does Nelly know it was the victim? The photo is from the back."

"The dress, her body size and hair," Johan replies.

"And the judge?"

"The blue sport shirt."

"There could be many other customers wearing blue sport shirts," Samsiah rebuts. "I can accept she might recognize the victim even from the back as they work together, but the judge I'm not so convinced."

"I checked the GRO booking register. It tallied, the vic was booked that night. The thing is, it was not recorded under the judge's name but under Gary Liu. Nelly said the judge always came in a group and he never paid for the room, drinks and girls. The name of the person making the booking is the one recorded because he will be responsible for settling the bill," Mislan explains.

"And we have the victim and the judge in the KTV on the same night around the same time," Johan adds.

"They could be in the same KTV but different rooms," Samsiah shoots down their circumstantial evidence. "You need to identify this Gary Liu and get him to put the judge and victim in the same room and that they left together. Remember, he is a judge, he knows the law. You need direct evidence."

"Puan, what about the phone records?"

"I'll get them by this evening. By the way, why are you two still in the office? Go home and get some rest."

Leaving Superintendent Samsiah's office, Mislan tells Johan to go home, shower, change and meet him back at the police contingent HQ at 5 in the evening.

"Where are we going?" Johan asks.

"Karaoke."

"You're kidding me."

"I'm serious. Better dress to impress because you'll never know if we bump into gorgeous Murni," Mislan jests.

"Yea, right."

On his drive home, Mislan receives a WhatsApp from Superintendent Samsiah. It is a photo of the judge Sallehnor Muhammad with a text saying – *It's him*. He lets out a sigh of relief, "Yesss," and makes a call to thank his superior.

"Lan, I need you to be careful. Find out all you can to connect him to the victim before you take any action," she reminds him.

"I will, Puan."

"Keep me posted on your every move."

"I'll be going to the KTV later to find out more on this Gary Liu."

"OK, tread carefully. I don't want the judge making complaints and allegations. Not just yet."

"I hear you."

19

As Mislan approaches the police contingent HQ, he gets a call from Johan anxiously asking where he is. Pulling up to the guardhouse, he spots his assistant standing at its front. Johan is dressed smartly with his pastel-colored long-sleeve shirt, dark pants and black leather shoes. Mislan bets he is even wearing clean socks. When Johan steps into the car, he smells of cologne.

"Woah," Mislan teases, "you smell like a desperate gigolo."

Johan laughs.

"Did you fall into a bathtub filled with cologne?"

"Can it, will you?" Johan tells the inspector.

"Now my car will smell of your cologne for weeks," Mislan says, laughing.

The road is expected to be jammed with after-office traffic. Johan suggests they head for Bangsar and cut to Sri Hartamas.

"It's jammed everywhere. We'll just go with the flow. Don't worry, Murni will be there no matter what time we arrive," Mislan says. "By the way, Puan confirmed the Tuan is our judge. Here." He passes his mobile phone to his assistant.

"You think he did it or paid someone to do it?"

"I don't know – but for now, he is our prime suspect."

"You mean our *only* suspect," Johan corrects him.

"You don't think the vic's ex-boyfriend could've done it?" Mislan probes.

"Nooo, he is ex, why should he care who the victim was going out with or if she was pregnant? Anyway, he willingly gave his DNA sample. When are we getting the DNA result?"

"I haven't checked with Chew. We need the parental DNA result from Dr. Matthew before we can compare. That'll only happen next week after he comes back to work."

"Are we getting the judge's DNA sample?"

"Puan says not to make any move until we have evidence to link him to the vic."

"Getting his DNA will be dicey. I'm sure there will be a lot, I mean a *lot* of heat from upstairs."

"That would only prove we're on the right track."

"In your experience, have you known of a judge being arrested for murder?"

Mislan shakes his head. "There's always a first time."

"Me too – corruption yes, murder no. But as you say, there's a first time for everything. They're human after all, and as humans we all have our weaknesses."

"In your case, gorgeous women," Mislan says.

"In your case, nasi lemak, sambal sotong and telur mata kerbau," Johan joins the inspector in his laughter. "Ohh, I forgot cigarettes and black coffee."

Mislan drives to the half-full parking lot. The parking attendant asks for RM10 and hands him a parking ticket. Johan tells the attendant they are on police business. The Indian or Bangladeshi attendant furrows his forehead and stares at them, narrowing his eyes. When the officers do not make any move to pull out their wallets, the attendant relents and waves them on.

Stepping out of the car, Mislan tells Johan that Superintendent Samsiah says not to do anything to spook their suspect.

"I think he already knew from our first visit. Remember the manager making a call when we met him? I've a strong feeling he called the judge to ask for advice," Johan says.

"I think so too, and after we left he would've told him we were asking about the vic. If he was having an affair with her, he would put two and two together and know we are on to him. That's if he *was* having an affair with her. Let's just tread carefully. No loose tongue to impress Murni."

At the entrance, the officers introduce themselves and ask to see the manager. The receptionist cum greeter makes a call on the intercom and tells them Mr. Chong will be along shortly. From the entrance, they can hear songs being played from inside the lounge. Chong comes to the entrance, his expression not welcoming.

"What is it this time?" he asks curtly.

"We need to speak to you," Mislan says.

"What about?"

"We can speak to you outside here and let your staff hear, or somewhere private like your office or back at our office," the inspector says firmly. "Your choice."

"Come to my office," Chong yields, leading the way.

Chong's office is at the lobby, behind the bar counter. On entering the office, the officers are hit by the smell of burning incense. The wall of the small office is lined with figurines in all shapes and sizes. A few of them look like an elderly male with a big tummy and one of a standing toddler. All of them are shawled with bright yellow cloth and the toddler figurine has bright red cloth wrapped around its waist. There are at least four of them. Each has a plate of fruit, a tiny glass of red liquid and red holder with burning incense. *This place must have a lot of divine help*, Mislan thinks to himself. His eyes start watering from the smoke and smell.

"Do you have some other place we can talk?" Mislan asks.

"What's wrong with here?"

"My eyes are sensitive to smoke," Mislan says, feeling uncomfortable with the staring figurines and the smell of incense.

"We can use one of your karaoke rooms," Johan suggests.

"Will this take long?"

"Not if you answer truthfully."

"Follow me," Chong reluctantly says, leading the officers out of his office.

Chong leads them along a dim hallway and opens the first door on its left. Mislan notices the door label: **VIP 1.** The room is easily double the size of his master bedroom. One side of the wall is lined with a plush leather stretch sofa facing two huge plasma TVs mounted on the opposite wall. In the middle of the room are three glass coffee tables with four wireless microphones in two holders. Just by the door is a serving table, and on the opposite side a washroom. The room can easily fit 20 people with the word *expensive* written all over it.

Chong takes a seat and again asks the purpose of this visit. Mislan switches on his digital recorder, placing it on the glass coffee table. Chong eyes the recorder uneasily but says nothing.

"I understand you have a regular by the name of Gary Liu," Mislan begins.

"Yes."

"What is his full name?"

"Liu Tak Chin, known as Gary Liu to us."

"What is his occupation?"

"Why are you interested in him?" Chong asks defiantly.

"As this is an ongoing investigation, I'm not able to reveal anything to you at this point of time. Just answer our questions and we'll be out of here."

Chong's mobile phone rings. Standing, he pulls out his phone from his trouser pocket, saying, "I have to take this," and steps out of the room.

Mislan takes the opportunity to ask Johan to look for Nelly.

"What for?"

"Ask her apart from her ability to recognize the vic by her hair, dress and size, how else can she identify her from that night."

"Like what?"

"Did she see them leaving together, bump into them or did the vic tell her she was leaving with them?"

"OK, got you," Johan says.

Johan leaves the room and soon after Chong returns.

"I was told I don't have to talk to you," he says boldly.

"In that case, turn around," Mislan instructs. "You're under arrest for withholding information about a crime under investigation."

The inspector takes out his handcuffs, pushes Chong against the wall and yanks his right hand behind his back.

"No, wait, you cannot arrest me."

"Like hell I can't. You know what's the problem with advice from a friend? It's not him that is being arrested."

"OK, OK, I'll tell you."

"Tell me what?"

"Anything you want to know about Gary."

Mislan releases his grip on Chong and instructs him to sit.

"Gary operates his own business."

"What business?"

"Importer and supplier of whiskey, wine, beer, et cetera. Sometimes when he has stock he supplies cigarettes too, but only sometimes."

"He's a regular here?"

"Yes, we get our drinks supply from him."

"When was the last time he came here?"

"CNY eve, when we held the party."

"Before that?"

"Maybe three days before CNY."

"He came alone?"

"Gary never comes alone. He always entertains clients or friends."

"Who did he come with that night?"

"His usual group."

"They are…?"

"Tuan, Wong and Andrew."

"Who is this Tuan?"

"I don't know. They call him Tuan so I call him Tuan."

"And you never asked?"

Chong shakes his head. Mislan knows he is lying.

It's impossible he was not interested in knowing who this Tuan is. Tuan is a Malay title usually given to a person of authority. A person who can cause him trouble or assist him when he gets into trouble with the authorities. Certainly a person he would want to befriend and provide favors to.

"How did you get to know this Tuan?"

"Gary introduced him to me the first time they came."

"Where is Gary's office?"

"Jalan Pudu."

"His contact number?"

Chong checks his mobile phone and gives the inspector Gary's number.

"The last time Gary came here, three days before CNY, who paid the bill?"

"Gary, he always pays the bill."

"Cash or card?"

"I think the bill was almost 2K and he paid by card."

"I'll need the receipt for that night. When Gary and his group left, did Rita follow them?"

"I don't know, I was entertaining Dato' in another room," Chong says, emphasizing the word *Dato'* to impress the inspector. Hoping that would keep him at bay.

"Do you know what time they left?"

"I was told around 11 pm."

"Are you a shareholder or just an employee here?"

"I own a small share."

"What about Gary Liu?"

"He's also a shareholder, why?"

"Nothing, just my curiosity."

Just as the inspector and Chong stand to leave, Johan enters. Mislan gestures for the detective sergeant to follow them to Chong's office. After getting the receipt, Chong gladly walks the officers out. At the entrance, Mislan thanks him for his cooperation.

"Inspector, if you want to relax, happy-happy come here. Everything on the house," Chong offers.

20

In the car Johan, tells Mislan that on the night in question Nelly walked the group to the main door.

"But she was not on the CCTV," Mislan says.

"Yes, because she stopped at the main door and the camera is facing outward. Remember what Murni told us? The manager always greets him and Nelly takes care of him. So, she was the one who closed their bill and walked them to the main door."

"That's good. She can put them together the night the vic was killed."

"But Nelly did not see who the victim left with. I mean, she did not follow them to the carpark."

"Who else could she have left with?"

"There were four men. She could've gone with any of them."

"But she was having an affair with the judge, surely she would go with him."

"That's circumstantial, and Puan says we need direct evidence."

"The person who can tell us who the vic left with is this Gary Liu."

"You got his contact number?"

"The manager gave it when you were out looking for Nelly. What took you so long to locate her?"

Johan grins.

"You went looking for Murni. Did you find her?"

"Room 6, Nelly took me to the room. She says hi to you."

"You said that just to please me."

"No, she really did."

Dropping Johan off at the police contingent's guardhouse, Mislan tells him he is going home. He suggests Johan do the same as they are on duty tomorrow. Just then, he gets a call from Superintendent Samsiah.

"Yes, Puan."

"Lan, I got the victim's phone record after you left. I passed it to Yana."

"Thanks, Puan."

"OK, see you tomorrow."

"Jo, Puan said she passed the vic's phone record to Yana. If you're not doing anything tonight, maybe you can run through it. I'm feeling exhausted. Age must be catching up with me," Mislan says.

"Will do. What about Gary, are we not meeting him today?"

"It can wait until tomorrow."

Mislan is having coffee at his bedroom workstation when the 7.45 pm news comes on the television. He hears his case mentioned and turns to watch. It is a recorded broadcast from Kuala Selangor, his victim's hometown. Standing in front of the mother's house, the reporter interviews the mother and younger sister. The mother claims she was not told by the police that her daughter was murdered. She says the victim was a good daughter and a caring person bla, bla, bla, while wiping crocodile tears from her cheeks. She wails, how could anyone brutally murder her daughter and unborn grandchild. She urges the police to bring the perpetrator to justice so their souls can rest in peace.

The reporter turns to the victim's sister, saying, "You said your sister was going steady with a prominent person. Do you know who this prominent person is?"

"She told me he's a judge but I was never introduced to him."

Mislan stares at the TV in disbelief.

"When did you know your sister was pregnant?"

"At the morgue, when I went to claim her body."

"The morgue informed you?"

"No. When we were waiting at the hearse for my sister's body to be brought out, we overheard one of them there saying to his friend … *this is the case where the baby was stolen*."

"I also understand your sister's baby was not handed by the morgue to you for burial?"

"When I asked the morgue attendant, he said it's a police case."

"Did you ask the police about the whereabouts of the baby?"

"By then the police had already left."

"May I know why you invited us for this interview?"

"I want answers. Who murdered my sister and where is her baby?"

"Thank you."

Turning to face the camera, the reporter says the police gave a press release three days ago saying it was a case of illegal abortion went wrong. It is however clear from the victim's mother and sister that Norita was murdered and her unborn baby stolen from her womb, a hideous and barbaric act.

"Ohh fuck," Mislan cusses.

Just then, he gets a call from Superintendent Samsiah.

"Lan, did you watch the news?"

"Yes."

"Is it true what she said?"

"Which part?"

"The mother claiming she was not told her daughter was murdered."

"I can't remember, but I did tell her the vic was dead and the case is being investigated."

"What about the baby?"

"I told the sister that the vic was pregnant and the fetus was missing. Not to the mother. I also told her that we're still investigating."

"Was Jo with you when you told her?"

"I can't remember. Maybe he wasn't because I told him to assist the husband in claiming the vic's body."

"Check with Jo and let me know. I'm sure tomorrow will be a hot day in the office."

"Sorry."

"It's not your doing. Good night."

"Good night, Puan."

He calls Johan.

"Jo, when I told the vic's sister the fetus was missing, were you already in the room?"

"I came in when you were telling her the baby was stolen from her womb. Why?"

"Thank god. In not so many words, she just told the world she was not informed by us of the missing fetus."

"Check your digital recorder," Johan says, because he knows the inspector always records his interviews for reference.

"The recorder will not tell if you were in the room or not."

Johan laughs. "Yes I was, and I can swear to it."

"Thanks. Where are you?"

"At the office, going through the vic's phone records with Reeziana."

"OK, see you tomorrow."

He makes a call to Superintendent Samsiah, informing her that Johan was already in the room when he told the sister of the missing fetus.

He makes a call to Audi, the investigative journalist. She answers on the first ring.

"Yes, Inspector, how may I assist you?" she answers with a soft chuckle.

"Did you catch the 7.45 news?"

"I did, and…?"

"Both of them were lying."

"Since when do you care about people lying?"

"Since they're trying to get me into trouble."

"What were they lying about?"

"The mother, when I went to tell her of her daughter's death, she was not bothered, not a single question as to when or how. The tears on camera were crocodile tears."

"People do tend to get a little dramatic when they know they're going to be on TV. Just look at our politicians," Audi explains, not hiding her laughter.

Mislan just has to laugh with her. "The sister said she was not informed of the missing fetus, that's a lie. Jo can vouch I told her."

"Jo will swear to anything for you," she states. "Sorry, that was uncalled for. Don't worry about what she said, it will pass. About the prominent person being a judge…is it verified?"

"We're still digging. Anyway, since the sister is proven to be a liar, that tells you not to believe what she said."

"But somehow you are digging."

"Like you, I need to follow up on all leads."

"How deep have you dug?"

"Looks like not deep enough."

"Meaning, you still can't prove anything."

"For now."

"I get first call on it, right?"

Mislan laughs.

"Come on, we're a team."

"I paid my dues, we're even."

Audi laughs.

21

The morning-prayer starts with Inspector Reeziana updating the team on her twenty-four hours shift. She attended to three call-outs. The first was a stabbing where a food stall operator on her way to the cash deposit machine was robbed of her daily collection. She suffered massive blood loss and died before the paramedics arrived. A witness recognized the assailant and the district investigating officer is handling the case. The second call-out was supposedly an armed robbery in Kepong but the victim did not actually see the gun. The victim claimed the perpetrator pointed the gun at him while it was concealed in the pocket of his track-top. The third was a report of a kidnapping, but several witnesses claimed they saw a teenage girl walk into a car which then drove off. The case was reclassified as a runaway.

"Ghani," Superintendent Samsiah says, looking at the head of Special Projects. "I've read through your report on failed raids and your CI. See me after this."

ASP Ghani responds with a nervous nod.

"Lan, see me with Jo after Ghani."

Back in their office, Reeziana asks Mislan why Superintendent Samsiah seems to be brisk and cold this morning.

"How would I know?" he answers. "Maybe something is not right at home."

"Puan? She never mixes home and office. Did you do something to agitate her?"

"Why do you always think it's me?"

"Because you've made it into a fine art," Reeziana says, smiling.

"Jo, Puan wants to see us after Ghani."

"Trouble?"

"There you go again. Nooo, she just misses you."

"If it's me she misses, why are *we* supposed to see her? Shouldn't it be just *me*?" Johan jests.

"Don't you start," Mislan says.

"Why are you extra grumpy this morning?" Reeziana butts in.

Just then the office line rings, requesting for Mislan and Johan to the office of Superintendent Samsiah.

The two officers update her on their visit to the Champion KTV and the interviews conducted with Chong and Nelly.

"So, Nelly can positively testify that the victim left the KTV with the judge although she was not captured in the video?" Samsiah reaffirms.

"Leaving the KTV, but not who she left the carpark with," Johan corrects her. "By the time they walked to the carpark, Nelly had already gone back inside."

"Hmmm, there's still the probability she left with one of the other three men."

"But she was having an affair with the judge, surely she'd not go with one of the three men. Not with him there with her," Mislan argues.

"What we think is not evidence," Samsiah reminds him. "Talk to this Gary and see what he has to say."

Samsiah's landline phone rings. She holds up a finger to indicate she needs to take the call. Putting down the phone, she says, "It's starting."

Mislan raises his eyebrows questioningly.

"OCCI want to see me in ten."

"Shouldn't you be going?"

"He can wait. Jo, were you in the room when Lan told the sister about the missing baby?" she asks, looking intensely at the detective sergeant.

"I just stepped into the counseling room where the interview was conducted and I heard Inspector Mislan telling her the baby was missing."

"And what was the sister's response?"

"She was shocked, stood up and told it to her husband."

"Did Mislan tell her mother the daughter was murdered?"

"Inspector Mislan told the mother her daughter is dead. The mother didn't seem to care, didn't ask any questions. In fact, she was not even willing to talk to us. We had to ask WPC Laila to interview her alone."

"Don't go out until I return," Samsiah says, standing up to leave.

X

Back at the office, Mislan asks Johan what he and Reeziana got from the victim's mobile phone records.

"Nothing much, except she got a lot of calls especially in the evening and late night. I'm guessing she was not a morning person."

"Nature of her work... sleep in the daytime, wide awake at night. Do you know any of her callers?"

"Nope, except for Nelly."

"What about text messages?"

"We need a court order for text messages."

Mislan nods.

"Some of the names she saved are nicknames or initials. Can't figure out who they are."

"The regular numbers, get one of the standbys to call and find out who they are. What about the judge?"

"Didn't see Judge or Salleh, Nor, Darling, or Sayang listed on her contact list. She must have used a code for him. I have to wait until we get the text messages to figure it out."

"I hope Puan gets the court order soon," Mislan says.

"The last call she received was at 10.01 pm but she did not answer it, no talk time recorded, and the last call she accepted was at 5.10 pm from Nelly. That was on the day she was killed."

"That must be Nelly informing her of the booking made by the judge."

"From then on, no outgoing calls and all incoming calls were unanswered. She was probably with the judge and not taking calls."

Mislan and Johan are again summoned to Superintendent Samsiah's office. She looks tired after the meeting with the OCCI. Taking their seats, Mislan asks what happened.

"The usual witch hunt nonsense."

"About the lies by the vic's sister?"

"That and our 'lack of integrity' in dealing with the case. He claimed, and you know the creditability of his claims, the family is looking at suing the police for withholding information, thereby causing them emotional trauma."

"What?!" Mislan exclaims.

"The mother didn't even care about her daughter's death," Johan sneers.

"I want to lodge a report against them for making false accusations," Mislan says angrily. "It's time we teach the public that civil action is a two-way street."

"Calm down, both of you. I know you record all your interviews."

Mislan nods.

"Make a copy of the interview and I'll pass it to Amir."

"But the recording will not prove that Jo was in the room with me."

"Does it matter? It proves that you informed her and she responded. That will clear your name."

"I'll do it by today. Puan, can I?"

"Can you what?"

"Make a police report against them."

"If you want to prolong the matter. Lan, you know when we take civil action against a member of the public the whole nation will stand behind him or her. Not because they believe he or she is in the right, but because they're against us. The public notion of us is – because of a few bad apples the whole orchard is rotten. So, you think about it long and hard."

Back at the office, Mislan makes a call to Gary Liu. The call is not answered and it goes to voice message. Waiting for Gary to return the call, he uploads his interview with the victim's sister and emails it to Superintendent Samsiah.

His office phone rings and Johan answers it. Cupping the mouthpiece, he tells the inspector it is Gary Liu. Mislan picks up the parallel phone on his desk.

"Mislan."

"Hi, Inspector how are you, what can I do for you?" Gary says like they are old buddies.

"Mr. Liu, I would like to meet you in regard to a case I'm investigating," Mislan says formally. "Will you be in the office?"

"Yes of course. For my friends in the police, I'm always available," Gary says, followed by phony laughter.

"May I have your office address?"

Gary recites his address.

"We'll be there in 15 minutes. Thank you," Mislan says, putting the phone down.

In the car, he tells Johan the address. Leaving the police contingent HQ, Johan makes a right and Mislan tells him he is going in the wrong direction.

"It's easier to go there through this road," Johan says. "We'll cut back just before the petrol station and we're there."

Mislan keeps quiet, for he knows his detective sergeant is well versed in all the back roads and shortcuts from his MPV days. After several right and left turns, behind and beside buildings, through narrow lanes, Johan pulls by the roadside. Mislan looks at him questioningly.

"We're here. There's no parking along the main road," Johan states.

"Where's the office?"

"On our left."

"Are you sure my car is safe here?" Mislan asks, concerned.

"As safe as any old car anywhere else in the city," Johan jests.

"Just so you know, this old car has served me well."

The officers walk the fifty meters to the address given by Gary. It is a three-story shophouse and Mislan is convinced there will be no elevator and somehow, the office will be on the third floor. To his delight, Gary's office is on the ground floor, which is also his beverage shop and showroom. After introducing themselves to the front staff, they are told to wait while he informs the boss.

A moment later, a beer-bellied Chinese man in his fifties appears from the back office with a booming "Hello my friends." He proffers his hand but the inspector politely offers his knuckle for a fist bump – the new norm for shaking hands .

"Sorry, sorry, no more handshake I forgot," Gary says, grinning. "Come, we can talk in my office."

Gary's office is large, complete with a sofa set and a large plasma TV on a show cabinet filled with liquor bottles. It looks more like a place to entertain than an office. On one side wall is a full display of liquor, wine and beer while on the other is a minibar with stools and a fridge. Next to his work table are two figurines, one of a child and another of a shirtless, sitting, smiling pot-bellied male. The toddler figurine is shawled with a bright red cloth and its waist is wrapped with a bright red cloth. Similar to what he saw in the KTV manager's office. Both figurines have fruit and drink offerings in front of them. The difference between Gary and Chong's offices is that the incense in Gary's office is all burned out. *These must be figurines of prosperity deities,* Mislan says to himself.

The officers are ushered to the sofa. As soon as they take their seat, Gary asks if they'd like a drink.

"Whiskey, beer?"

Mislan declines for both of them.

"A little bit, I'm sure it's OK," Gary insists.

"No thank you."

"OK, Coke, coffee or tea?"

"No thanks, we just had our breakfast," again Mislan declines. "We need to ask you a few questions."

"Yes, anything. I always help the police. I've many friends in the police and every time I help them."

"When was the last time you went to Champion KTV?"

"CNY eve, they had a party."

"Before that?"

"Let me see..." Gary seems to be thinking hard. "I think one week before that, yes one week."

"And between that and the CNY party, you did not go there?" Mislan asks, staring at him unblinkingly. He notices Gary flinch and thinks to himself, *Why is the guy lying? He must know this fact can easily be verified. Perhaps Chong had called to warn him after our last visit.*

"Now that you mention it, yes I went there again three or four days before CNY. Why do you want to know? Did something happen?"

"You went there alone?"

"With some friends."

"They are?"

"Wong, Andrew and Tuan."

Mislan wastes some time asking about Wong and Andrew, just to cloud his actual target. When he feels he has wasted enough time on them, he asks about the Tuan.

"Why do you call him Tuan, what is his name?"

"Everyone calls him Tuan so I call him Tuan," he answers evasively.

"But he's your friend. As friends, I'm sure you know his name."

Gary remains silent.

"Tuan is from the police?"

Gary stands and says, "I think you've asked enough questions. I've got work to do."

"Mr. Liu, you can sit down and answer my questions or my detective sergeant here will make a call to our Customs counterpart to conduct a check on your imported liquor."

"I have friends there too," he declares boldly.

"In your business, I'm sure you have, but our friends are not your friends," Mislan says with a grin. "By the time our friends complete their inventory you'll lose a few days of business – that is, if they don't find anything worth taking you to court for."

Gary reluctantly sits.

"Tell me this Tuan's name?"

"Salleh."

"And he is from which government agency?"

"Judge."

"Did you, Wong, Andrew and Salleh go to Champion KTV three nights before CNY?"

"Yes."

"Did you or any of them book GROs?"

"We each booked one."

"Their names?"

"Mindy, Lina, Helen and Rita."

"Who partnered with who?"

"Mindy with me, Lina with Wong, Helen with Andrew and Rita with Tuan."

"How do you know Salleh?"

"Chong introduced to me. He said in my business, maybe one day I can use his help."

"That night when you left the KTV, did the mummy escort you out?"

"Mummy Nelly always greets and escorts us out. Two of the girls were under her care."

"Did any of the girls follow your group from the KTV?"

"Rita. She is Tuan's girlfriend."

"So Rita went into Salleh's car?"

"Yes."

"Where did all of you go after the karaoke?"

"We went for supper at Sri Hartamas food court."

"Then?"

"Chong joined us."

"Oh, did he?"

"He sometimes joins us for supper."

"Then?"

"I left because I got severe stomach ache or food poisoning."

"Who did Rita leave with?"

"I don't know, because I left earlier than them."

"Don't start lying to me."

"I'm telling you the truth, you can check with the clinic I went to for treatment," Gary says, challenging the inspector.

"Which clinic?"

"Tung Shin emergency. Why are you asking me all this? You think we have something to do with her death?"

"Do you?"

"*No!* Your boss said it was a failed illegal abortion. Why are you investigating us? You think we arranged for her abortion? That's ridiculous, why should we?"

"As a favor to Salleh," Mislan says, and gets a vile stare from Gary. "You knew she was pregnant," he states rather than asks.

"Yes, Tuan told us."

"What did he tell you?"

"That Rita was pregnant."

"When did he tell you?"

"Two, three months back, I cannot remember exactly when. He told all of us when we went for dinner."

"Did he tell you who the father was?"

"No. He just told us she was pregnant and that she only comes when he booked her."

"Did she ask for help to do the abortion?"

"Not from me."

"What about to the rest, Wong, Andrew, Chong or Salleh?"

"I don't know. You'll have to ask them."

After several more questions, Mislan ends the interview. Walking out through the showroom, the officers are stopped by one of the staff. The staff picks two gift paper bags and hands them over.

"What are these?" Mislan asks.

"Boss asked to give, New Year."

Mislan peeks into the paper bags and sees a bottle of Chivas Regal and a carton of Marlboro Lights.

"No thank you," Mislan says, and leaves the showroom.

22

Back in the car, Johan asks where they are headed. Mislan tells him to drive back to the office. The inspector looks disgruntled. He lights a cigarette and stares out the window at the massive MRT construction with its road diversions and traffic jam.

"Something bothering you?" Johan asks.

"Gary said Sallehnor the judge was introduced to him by Chong."

Johan nods.

"If I remember correctly, Chong said he didn't know Sallehnor, Gary was the one who introduced them. One of them is lying. I need to listen to Chong's interview to be certain."

"Why do you think Chong or Gary lied?"

"That's what I need to find out. Jo, after you drop me off can you check with Tung Shin on Gary's claim that he went there for treatment?"

"You think he lied about that too?"

"I doubt it. Just need to confirm that he does not know who our vic left with after supper."

"You want me to check with Wong and Andrew?"

"We'll do that later after lunch."

"You want me to get lunch?"

"Might as well," Mislan says, pulling out his wallet.

"What do you want?"

"I feel like having mutton curry. You know the Fayas Curry House, Pudu?"

"Yes, I used to go there too. What do you want?"

"Mutton, fried fish and vege."

In the office, Mislan takes out his digital recorder and listens to his interview with the Champion KTV manager Chong. He jots down verbatim the questions asked and the answers given by Chong on the Tuan or judge.

"Who's this Tuan?"

"I don't know. They call him Tuan so I call him Tuan."

"How did you get to know this Tuan?"

"Gary introduced him to me the first time they came."

Then he does the same with Gary Liu's interview on the same matter.

"How did you come to know Salleh?"

"Chong introduced to me. He said in my business, maybe one day I can use his help."

"Shit," the inspector says. *I should've interviewed Gary before interviewing Chong. Then I would've nailed the lying son of a bitch's ass,* he says to himself, annoyed. He sees Superintendent Samsiah entering the investigator's office.

"Puan," he greets.

"You look agitated," she remarks. "Something wrong?"

"I just came back from interviewing Gary Liu. He said something that contradicts what Chong the KTV manager said in his interview." He shows her the notes he made from the interview recordings.

Samsiah reads the notes and says, "One of them is lying."

"My money is on Chong."

"Based on?"

"Just a gut feeling. Something about him calling to get advice the first time we went there, and the same on our second visit."

"You think he called Sallehnor?"

Mislan nods.

"If he's not close with Sallehnor, he wouldn't have called him or the judge wouldn't have answered his calls. Gary on the other hand did not make any calls when he was interviewed."

"Makes sense."

"According to Gary, Chong joined them that night after they left the KTV. Chong failed to mention that too."

"Did he?"

"I'd like to take him in. I think he was lying to hide something. I'm sure he knows more than he is telling."

"Put that on hold for a while. The reason I came is to inform you that Sallehnor's lawyer has called the OCCI and they're coming in to clarify his position."

"When?"

"At 2.30. You're not invited."

"Why not?! I'm the lead on this case."

"He wants D5 to be present."

"Puan, I'd like you to hear what Gary Liu said in his interview. It'll give you a picture of what happened that night after they left the KTV."

Samsiah pulls up a chair and Mislan plays the digital recorder. Johan arrives with their packed lunch and heads for the pantry.

"So Gary confirmed that the victim was Sallehnor's girlfriend and that on the night in question they left for the food court together."

Mislan nods.

"But he doesn't know who she left with from the food court."

"Jo, did Gary check out at Tung Shin?" Mislan asks.

"Yes, he was there at 11.28 pm complaining of severe stomach ache," Johan replies from the pantry.

"That clears Gary," Samsiah states, "and leaves us with Wong, Andrew, Sallehnor and Chong."

Mislan nods.

"The other thing that tells me Chong was lying, he claimed not to know the judge's name. People in his business like to drop names, I don't buy it if a judge was introduced to him and he does not memorize the name. Do judges carry name cards?"

"I don't know, why?"

"If they do, I'll bet a month's salary Chong would have kept it in his office. We just left Gary's office. I don't think he called the judge to give him a heads-up. Chong on the other hand could've called him yesterday, giving him ample time to arrange for a friendly lawyer to set the meeting with the OCCI."

"There's also the possibility he saw the news and decided to make the arrangement."

"Possible."

"I suggest you have your lunch. I will try and make a case for you to sit in the meeting but don't hold your breath."

"Thanks."

"By the way, the info on the shooting, it's not related to you. Just got a call from Bukit Aman."

Samsiah sees the disappointment on her investigator's face.

X

While having lunch, Johan asks the inspector why Superintendent Samsiah came to the office. Mislan tells him the judge and his lawyer are coming to see the OCCI at 2.30 pm. Johan raises his eyebrows.

"And you're not sitting in?"

"By invitation only," Mislan says. "D5 is invited but not me."

"D5? Is he making an admission?"

"I hope so but I doubt it. He'll probably come up with some cock and bull story. The OCCI will swallow it whole and get his face on the news."

"I'm sure Puan and D5 will not allow that to happen."

"I have a feeling this case is coming to an abrupt end," Mislan says.

Mislan's office landline rings and it is Superintendent Samsiah asking for him and Johan to come to her office. Putting down the telephone, he glances at the wall clock – 3.10 pm. *That was quick.*

Signaling to Johan, he says, "Puan wants us."

Walking to her office, Mislan braces himself for the worst. He knocks on her door, and Superintendent Samsiah beckons her two anxious officers in.

"What did he say?" Mislan asks, taking his seat.

"Did he admit killing her?" Johan butts in before she can answer the first question.

"I was hoping he would but no, Jo, he didn't," Samsiah answers with a tiny smile.

"What did he say?" Mislan asks.

"If both of you stop badgering me with questions, then maybe I can tell you what happened and what he said."

"Sorry," both Mislan and Johan say in unison.

"I'm giving you the gist of it. He admitted to knowing the victim, short of saying he was having an affair with her. He did however admit to having *paid* sex with her several times. Around four months back, the victim told him she was pregnant with his child. He told her she can't have the baby, suggested for her to terminate her pregnancy and that he would take care of all the expenses. She refused and said she wanted to have the baby. He asked Chong to talk some sense into the victim. He said Chong even offered her ten thousand to agree but she still refused."

"*Paid* sex. How convenient, knowing she was providing such services," Mislan sneers.

Samsiah smiles at the inspector's statement.

"By asking the vic to terminate her pregnancy, he admitted to being the father of the baby?" Mislan says.

"He said *she* said it was his baby," Samsiah corrects the inspector. "And you shouldn't interpret it as an admission."

"If it's not his, why ask her to terminate the pregnancy?"

"To avoid speculation and unnecessary innuendo."

"He can be charged for abetting if the vic did terminate her pregnancy," Johan says

"But who is to know? Was he willing to give us a sample of his DNA?" Mislan changes the subject.

"No, he was not."

"Shit," Mislan cusses, instantly rewarded with an admonishing glare from Superintendent Samsiah. "Sorry."

"About the night in question, he admitted to going to the KTV and booking the victim. After the karaoke, he and his group together with the victim went for supper at Sri Hartamas food court. Midway through their supper, Chong joined them. After supper, he asked if Chong could send the victim back because he needed to get some rest for a big case he was hearing the following day. That was the last time he saw the victim. The next day he heard the news of her unfortunate death."

"According to his story, Chong would be the last person to be with the vic when she was alive," Mislan says with a sigh. "Again, how convenient. As a judge, he is aware that in theory the last person with the vic alive is always a suspect."

"He may be telling the truth," Samsiah suggests. "His story can easily be verified by his other friends that night."

"If it's true, what motive could Chong have to kill her?"

"Maybe he paid Chong to do it, or get someone to do it," Johan suggests. "Chong runs a karaoke joint and usually karaoke operators have, you know, colorful friends."

"That could be an angle to examine," Samsiah says, raising her eyebrows at Mislan. "To firmly tuck the judge into his back pocket. A very powerful friend to have."

"Puan, I'd like to pick Chong up as a suspect. Work on him for a few days. I'd also like to get a court order for the judge to give a sample of his DNA. Since he did not admit to the unborn child being his, I think we need to be certain. I already have the vic's ex's DNA sample, now I need his."

"I'll get D5 to work on the court order. As for Chong, I suggest you verify with the others if he was the one the victim left with on the night in question. At the same time, dig up anything you can on him before picking him up."

"Can I also have Chong's phone record and location for the night in question?"

"Give me the details and I'll get D5 to get an order for it too."

"Did he give any reason why he come to see us?" Mislan asks.

"He said after the news aired that a prominent person, a judge, is involved, the media, especially social media is full of speculations. Very soon, his name will pop up. Before it does and we go after him, he wanted to clear the air. He said he is married and a sitting judge. The allegations of him not only having an affair but being involved in the death of the woman would be detrimental to his marriage and career."

"Do you believe him?"

"What I believe does not matter, what we can prove does."

23

Mislan sits dejectedly at his desk. Getting the court orders for Sallehnor's DNA sample and the phone record and location will take time. That is if the court grants the requests. He ponders on the briefing given by Superintendent Samsiah. Assuming what Sallehnor had told her was true, why did the vic want to keep the baby? Was she so sure that the baby's father was Sallehnor? By having his baby, would she stand to gain from it? She was a Malay Muslim, and having a child out of wedlock is not acceptable, in fact illegal under Syariah law. She knew it and so did he. If she named him as the father of their illegitimate child, his marriage and career were as good as over. Was the fear of that happening, enough to push him over the edge to get rid of her and his unborn child?

Johan and Detective Jeff have gone to verify Sallehnor's claim that the victim had left with Chong on the fatal night. Soon, some of his questions will be answered.

Mislan reaches out to a colleague in D7 – the Vice, Gambling and Secret Societies department. Passing on Chong's full name and IC number, he asks his friend to run a check on him.

He then gets a call from Johan, informing him that Andrew, one of the men at the supper with the victim, confirmed the victim left with Chong. According to Andrew, Sallehnor asked if any of them could assist sending the victim back and Chong volunteered.

"Did he see the vic get into Chong's car?"

"Yes, they walked together to the carpark. He and Chong assisted the victim to the car as she was tipsy and unsteady. Do you still need me to check with Wong? His office is in Klang and that will take me another two hours to get there and back to the office."

"Not necessary, Andrew's verification is enough for now. Jo, remember I asked you to find out from Nelly how the GROs are paid?"

"Sorry, it slipped my mind. I'll call her now."

Terminating the call, Inspector Mislan is at a loss. His prime suspect with a solid motive to kill is fast fading from his suspects list.

His office landline rings and it is his colleague from D7. To his dismay, his second suspect Chong is not a known active member of any secret society, or has any link with one on police record.

Mislan is at his private smoking area when Johan comes back to the office. Seeing the inspector not at his desk, the first place he checks is the emergency staircase landing. He finds Mislan sitting on the floor, leaning against the wall with his hands resting on his raised knees. He is staring blankly at the wall in front of him.

"You OK? What's going on?" Johan asks.

Mislan does not respond, nor does he turn to look at his assistant. Johan sits beside his lead investigator.

"What's going on?" Johan asks again. "Why are you acting like a trishaw puller who just lost a passenger?"

"I think we're looking at this case with blinkers on," Mislan says more to himself.

"What do you mean?"

"The vic was pregnant, the sister claimed she had an affair with a judge, and the fetus was stolen from her womb."

Johan nods.

"We immediately jumped to the conclusion the judge killed her and got rid of the fetus to hide their affair, to save his marriage and career."

"That is the most logical theory."

"Because of that, we failed to examine other possibilities. We put on our blinkers and conducted our investigation with tunnel vision. When the judge came up with a solid alibi, we were screwed."

"What about Chong? He was the last person to be with the victim alive."

"He is not a known active SS member, no police record."

"That just means he is not on D7's radar," Johan argues. "I'm pretty sure some of the SS members go his place to enjoy themselves. He might have gotten to know them there. Anyway, you can't open an entertainment outlet without paying them for protection."

"We need to dig deeper into Chong's background. Who he associates with, his other businesses if he has any and how tight he is with this Sallehnor. Do you know anyone at Sri Hartamas station that you trust?"

"No one that I can think of. What about Gary? I noticed how scared he was when you said you have friends in Customs. Maybe we can squeeze him to spill on Chong."

"He's a stakeholder in the KTV with Chong."

"But we're not after the KTV. By the way, before I forget, the GROs are paid by checks."

"The vic must have a bank account to deposit the checks. Unless it was a cash check, which I don't think the KTV would issue. Jo, can you get the standby to check with the banks if she had an account?"

"The bank won't release that information."

"Just to know if she had an account, I think they would. Once we know which bank, we'll write formally to request for details."

"I'll ask them to try."

"Check with CIMB or Maybank, those are the two most likely banks for her. A lot of ATMs around and I suspect she was the kind that spent money like water."

As she normally does before calling it a day, Superintendent Samsiah pops into the investigators' office. She finds her lead investigator Mislan and Johan at their desks looking glum.

"Somebody we know died?" she asks.

"Puan, sorry I didn't notice you coming in," Johan says, standing.

She waves for him to sit. "Why the dark clouds over your heads?"

Superintendent Samsiah leans against an empty desk next to his. Mislan tells her of his burst theory and striking his prime suspect off his list.

"Perhaps you're right, you've not given any other possible motive a thought," Samsiah agrees.

"What other possible motive is there?" Mislan asks.

"In my opinion the stolen unborn baby is a critical part of the case but it may also have misled you. Let's say if the victim was not pregnant, would you still consider the judge your prime suspect?"

"He would still be on the suspect list but may not be the prime."

"There you go."

"You're saying we should focus on the victim's killing, and forget about the stolen baby?" Johan asks.

"I'm not telling you to forget about the stolen baby. What I'm saying is, what if there was no baby in the picture? Only the victim. Your investigation would examine a wider scope than just center on the judge killing her to hide their affair."

Mislan and Johan slowly nod their agreement.

"What about this Chong fellow?"

"Because he was the last to be with the vic alive, he is now a prime."

"And his motive would be as we discussed? A favor for the judge so that he can own him?"

Again, Mislan and Johan nod.

"There you go again, back to the judge. You can't get him out of your equation. For all you know, he has nothing to do with the victim's death." She pauses, looking at her investigators. "Look, if Chong killed the victim, he would surely tell the judge. No sense in you doing a huge favor for someone if that someone does not know of the favor. Then he would not be obligated to you."

"What if he's waiting to tell the judge of the deed after things settle down?"

"Possible, but unless Chong is a man of strong willpower and self-control, he would've told the judge. Is he?"

"What?"

"A man with strong willpower and self-control?"

"I don't know."

"I think he's not. You said he called the judge when you first went to talk to him. That to me indicates that if he had done a huge favor for the judge, he would have told him so. He would want to start reaping the fruits of his labor."

Mislan and Johan give Superintendent Samsiah's observation a hard think.

"During the meeting how did you read him, the judge?" Mislan asks.

"Either he's a good actor or he doesn't know about the killing. And I'm more inclined toward the latter." Samsiah pushes herself off the desk and picks up her carry bag. "Use tonight to think of what we discussed, expand your scope. I'm sure Jo has many theories that can be kicked around. Good night. I'll see you tomorrow."

24

The morning-prayer starts with Mislan updating the team on his shift. Surprisingly there was only one call out, in response to an armed robbery. It was later established that no firearm was used in the robbery, and the case is being handled by the district. Superintendent Samsiah announces that Inspector Kamil's replacement will be reporting today and she will be mentored by Reeziana.

"Why me, why not Mislan?" Reeziana asks, not pleased at having to babysit a rookie.

"We want her to learn the tricks of the trade, not learning tricks," Samsiah answers. "Furthermore, she would be more receptive and open to you as a woman than to a man. A little background on Hartini, she hails from Johor, joined the force three year ago, stationed in Ipoh as an IO. She is not a rookie and please welcome and treat her as a colleague ."

Mislan grins at Reeziana.

Superintendent Samsiah turns to ASP Ghani. "See me after this meeting," she says, and excuses him. After Ghani leaves the room, she asks, "Lan, you'd like to share any new thoughts over the quiet night?"

"The whole night I've been Googling cases of stolen fetuses. Apart from the 18 cases reported in the US from 1983 to 2015 which I read earlier, I couldn't find any other cases. There are more recent cases mainly in South America but it was related to baby or fetal snatching for sale, or stolen by crazy women. All the reports are of fetuses at full term pregnancy. In my case the fetus was between 15 to 20 weeks and there is no possibility of it surviving outside the mother's womb."

"I too did some research, but my area of research is closer to home," says Samsiah. "I'm Kelantanese, and growing up I heard stories of fetuses being stolen for the purpose of black magic. It was said that the women targeted are those carrying their first baby. That's why the Kelantanese believe not to tell others of your first pregnancy because your baby might be a potential target. The Kelantanese call the stolen fetus, after certain rituals performed to appease the sprits, anak kerak."

"Serious!" Reeziana exclaims.

"Google it," Samsiah says. "In Thailand, Cambodia, Laos, Vietnam and the Philippines this is a practice. It's so infused into their culture that it has become a household divinity. I don't know what they're called in the other countries but in Thailand it's Kuman Thong, the Golden Sanctified Young Boy or in short, the Golden Boy and Kumari Thong the Golden Girl. If you Google Kuman Thong, you can find a lot of literature on it."

The room falls silent. All eyes are on the head of Special Investigation.

"Your case has gone supernatural," Reeziana tells Mislan in mock horror. "The Kuman – what was it, Puan?"

"Kuman Thong."

"Right, the Kuman Thong chaser!" Reeziana says.

"I'm not saying your case has anything to do with black magic or the supernatural. I'm just highlighting to you, a possible motive for fetal snatching. I leave it to you to do more research."

"You and Jo better start wearing talismans to ward off any curse or spell the killer may cast on you," Reeziana jests. "On second thought, can you get one for the office too? Just to be sure we're all protected from whatever spell's cast on you."

"Funny," Mislan snarls.

After showering and making himself a mug of coffee, Mislan sits at his workstation and Googles a*nak kerak*. It is claimed that anak kerak is a form of spirit akin to toyol, but it is more powerful. Toyol is an undead infant in Indonesian and Malay folklore. It can be invoked by a bomoh or dukun who is a shaman through black magic. Toyols are used by their owners to rob people. As a kid, Mislan had heard stories of toyol and it is said they were bought from the holy land of Mecca.

However, he had not heard of anak kerak and is surprised there was a movie made of it in 2017. The belief is deep-rooted in Kelantan. It is said that anak kerak is a fetus of six to seven months that was killed in the mother's womb. The preferred fetus to be most potent will be from a first pregnancy. The fetus is dried by a shaman and then black magic rituals, chanting and worshiping are performed to turn the murdered child's spirit into a powerful entity. The spirit is used for evil purposes like causing illness and mishaps to the owner's adversaries.

Lighting a cigarette, Mislan wonders how easily people believed in all this hocus-pocus. How on earth could a person even think of killing, much less doing it to an innocent unborn baby. How heartlessly must a person be to rip out the fetus from its mother's womb. Pure evil.

He remembers as a small boy he had watched a Malay movie where a Sultan's pregnant consort or a pregnant palace maid ate his jackfruit without his permission. He sentenced the woman to death and the baby was cut out of her womb. He vividly remembers in the movie the baby was holding the flesh of the jackfruit. Then something bad happened to the Sultan, he can't remember what.

He Googles Kuman Thong and numerous sites appear. He randomly clicks on one and reads. It is exactly what Superintendent Samsiah said. Unlike anak kerak, the practice and belief of Kuman Thong is widespread and deeply embedded in the Thai Buddhist societal fabric. The owners and worshipers of these divinities believe they will enjoy protection, blessed with wealth, good health and happiness.

It is said that the practice and belief originated in the 19th century based on a famous Thai poet's account of his own experience. However, the Thai Buddhist authorities do not sanction such a belief and deem it to be black magic.

It is also believed that worshipers have to feed the golden boy with food, red sweet drinks and so on. Another site says that a monk can transfer the spirit of a golden boy into a life-size boy figurine made from wood, clay or porcelain. These figurines are called Luk Thep or baby angels. Unlike anak kerak, there is no explanation given as to how old the fetus must be, or the method of extracting it to make Kuman Thong.

Mislan keys in '*crimes associated with kuman thong*'. Several sites appear. He clicks on one and reads: *In 2012 a British citizen of Taiwanese origin was arrested in Bangkok airport for trying to smuggle out six dried fetuses. According to him he paid 200,000 baht each for them and he can sell them for six times more.*

Checking the going exchange rate, the current rate is RM25,000 per fetus. *People have been killed for much less*, he says to himself. He then reads: *In 2011 it was reported that a man in Laos murdered his pregnant wife for the fetus to be used as Luak Lord.* Mislan assumes Luak Lord is similar to Kuman Thong. And from another site: *In 2010, the Thai police found the remains of more than 2000 fetuses believed to be from illegal abortions hidden in a temple in Bangkok.*

"Holy shit!" he exclaims. "2000 plus, that's a lot of Kuman and Kumari Thongs."

He continues scrolling the site headings and sees some sites are from the Philippines, Cambodia, and Vietnam. *People are mad. Just plain nuts.* His eyes tire and his brain is horrorstruck. He logs off and crawls into bed.

Sleep eludes him. His mind is actively trying to put the pieces of his investigation together. To identify any other possible motive for the victim's murder and the fetus removal. He toys with the scenario that the victim was not pregnant – what would he be looking at to find the murderer? Jealous boyfriend, rejected advances, pissed off wife if she was having an affair with the husband. He would look into her business activity if there is anything to see – a dissatisfied or conned or crazy jilted client – her financial status and her enemies if any. Who would want her dead, and why?

Superintendent Samsiah was right. He did not look into all aspects of the victim – victimology. He was conducting his investigation in a rabbit hole. The three components he was taught about crime: means, motive and opportunity. He knows the means, now he has to find the motive and opportunity.

He needs to know more about his victim. If she was operating her sex services online, he needs to know the site. He had already Googled the name Pinklady but came up with nothing. Perhaps she was using a different name for her website. He makes a note to get the IT technician Saifuddin to do a more extensive search, maybe even on the dark web. Most of all he'd like to get hold of her mobile phone, which he knows will reveal most of what he needs to know.

25

The next morning, Mislan walks into the office closely watched by Reeziana and the newbie Hartini. He puts his backpack at his desk and goes over to the pantry to make a mug of black coffee. Reeziana gestures to Hartini to join her at the pantry.

Mislan acknowledges them and asks the newbie how her first day at Special Investigation was. Hartini says it was fine, she learned a few new things from Reeziana.

"Everything OK with you?" Reeziana asks.

He nods, looking at her inquiringly.

"You looked like you've not slept the whole night. The bags under your eyes are as big as my thumb," she says, holding her right thumb to him. "Where did you go last night? Out hunting for ghosts and spirits?"

"Nowhere, I was home doing some research."

"Can anyone verify that?" Hartini jokes, getting a glare from Mislan.

She doesn't know that Mislan is divorced and living alone. A touchy fact he does not wish to be made known, much less discuss with someone he had just met yesterday for a few minutes. His glare shuts the newbie up from joining their conversation.

"On?" Reeziana interjects to distract him from Hartini innocent jest.

"Puan said not to be distracted by my vic's pregnancy and the stolen fetus. To expand the scope of investigation and look at other possible motives."

"What did you find?"

"People are crazy, and will go to any and I mean any extent to get rich."

"That goes without saying. Humans have always and will always be greedy. We cheat, rob, murder, plunder, you name it and we will continue doing so."

Johan arrives empty-handed and joins them.

"No nasi lemak?" Mislan asks.

"The stall is still closed."

"You spoiled your boss," Reeziana mockingly admonishes the detective sergeant. "See now he expects you to bring him breakfast daily. When you don't, he gets all grumpy."

"Where is Reeze?" Mislan asks about Reeziana's assistant.

"Out buying breakfast."

"Can you call and ask him to get something for me and Jo?"

"What do you want?"

"Anything but roti canai from a mamak restaurant."

Mislan lights a cigarette and Johan immediately tells him to put it out: "Puan is already in the office. I came up with her in the elevator."

Mislan puts out his cigarette and inserts it back into the pack.

"Austerity drive," he says, smiling. "After Puan told us about anak kerak and Kuman Thong I did some research. You'll be shocked to know that people actually believe and worship such entities. And the money they're willing to pay for it, shit, twenty-five K. That was back in 2012, by now the going price will be higher."

"Serious?" Reeziana is stunned. "Pay that much money for something like that?"

"If they believe it can make them rich..." Johan says. "How do you think the Nigerian, Hong Kong or whatever other scammers make their money? They make you believe you won a lot of money but to get the money you have to pay for the bank charges or tax or delivery. If you believe them, you get scammed. The key word here is 'believe'."

"I thought they scam lonely spinsters with marriage proposals," Mislan says.

"One of the many scams. Even that hinges on belief. The spinster believes the man is a handsome professional in love with her," Johan stresses.

Sergeant Reeze arrives carrying a plastic bag filled with breakfast.

"Back to your case, you think the victim was murdered because of the baby?" Reeziana asks. "I don't know, but the anak kerak or Kuman Thong seems a little bit far-fetched to me."

"Maybe not that far-fetched," Johan disagrees. "With the prolonged pandemic, businesses are closing down and people are desperate. They'll do anything to make a living and I heard apart from facemasks and gloves, bomohs are in great demand to get supernatural help."

Reeziana laughs. "Looks like we too need one to help solve this case."

"We'll make him an honorary detective," Hartini suggests, unable to refrain from joining the conversation.

The officers have a good laugh at the possibility.

"Jo, what about the vic's bank account? Did the standby manage to get the info?"

"Sorry, yes. She had a savings account with CIMB."

"Good, after the morning-prayer I'll prepare the request letter to the bank for her account statement."

Inspector Hartini is given the honor of updating the team on her shift call-out. She and Reeziana attended to two call-outs. The first was for a dead body in an abandoned house in Kampung Baru. According to the people there, the house is vacant and frequently used by drug addicts as a shelter and hangout. For the time being, the case is classified as sudden death from overdose until otherwise informed by the pathologist. District is handling it. The second call-out was for a suspected child kidnapping. An eight-year-old girl went out with her father and did not return home. The parents are divorced and the father has visitation rights. It is believed the father abscond with the girl. D11 was called and they are handling the case.

"How did you find your first day here?" Samsiah asks.

"Interesting and I have a good mentor," Hartini replies.

"By next week you'll be flying solo."

Hartini nods.

"Ghani, I've forwarded your request to personnel for action," Samsiah continues. "For everyone's info, Ghani has put in his request for transfer. I've given my blessing. I'd also like to state that upon his transfer, the Special Project section will be dissolved. All detectives shall be put on roster. That'll give the duty IO more bodies to hit the pavements."

All heads turn to look at Ghani who seems to silently disagree with Superintendent Samsiah's decision. He is excused from the meeting.

"Lan, did you read about what I told you yesterday?" she asks.

Mislan replies with a non-enthusiastic nod.

"You don't seem convinced it could be a possible motive?"

"Jo is."

"But not you?"

"I'm keeping an open mind," he replies unconvincingly.

"May I know why?"

"If our case is in Kelantan, perhaps it's more probable."

"But not here in KL? Do you know that KL is flooded with Kelantanese people?"

"I do."

"And you don't think they'll bring along their superstitions and practices here?"

Mislan purses his lips.

"We also have a large number of Thai and Pattani people here. If you take into account the Cambodians, Vietnamese and Laotians, that could be a huge number. On top of that, you add some local Buddhists who might believe in such a divinity too."

Mislan remains silent.

"Have I made my case?" Samsiah asks, smiling.

Changing the subject, Mislan asks if the court orders have been obtained.

"D5 said we'll get them by today. I'll personally handle Sallehnor's for the DNA sample. I don't want any untoward incident or allegation. I'll get D10 to accompany me."

"Thanks."

Back in the office, Mislan calls Chew from Forensics to ask about Ilyas's DNA.

"I've run it through the database, not a match with the parental DNA uploaded by the hospital on your case."

"GH has uploaded my case's parental DNA result?" Mislan is surprised.

"Yes. And your donor is not the child's father. Sorry."

"Don't be, I never thought he was," Mislan says. "Hey Chew, have you heard of Kuman Thong?"

"Ku what?"

"It's a Thai spirit, Kuman Thong means golden boy. Something to do with Buddhist prayer or belief."

"Sorry, Inspector," Chew apologizes with a chuckle. "You know I'm not a good Buddhist and don't know much about it. If you want, I can ask my mother."

"It's OK. I try someone else."

Terminating the call, he makes another call.

"Yes, Lan what's up?"

"Tee, are you free to talk?"

"Yes, I'm already back home. Anything?"

"Tee, you know anything about Kuman Thong?"

"You mean the kwai chai?"

"What is that?"

"Boy devil in Cantonese. It's something like Kuman Thong in Thailand. Why are you asking about it?"

"So the Chinese believe in it too?"

"Some but not all."

"What can this kwai chai do?"

"Protect you, make you prosper, hurt your enemies, all that crap. Why are you asking about this?"

"Do you believe in it?"

"No. You've not answered my question. Why are you interested in this mumbo-jumbo?"

"Just curious. When are you starting work?"

"Day after tomorrow. Don't give me the 'curious' answer OK. You're never curious about anything unless it involves your case. Shit! Your pregnant victim's baby was stolen and you think it had something to do with black magic."

"Tee, got to go. Thanks, and we'll talk when you are back."

"Lan, Lan!" Tee says but the call is already terminated.

Superintendent Samsiah calls to inform him that D5 has already gotten the court orders.

"Since I'm going to see Sallehnor, I suggest you serve the telco with the order," she says.

"No problem, I'll come over," Mislan says.

Samsiah is preparing to leave when Mislan knocks on her door. She beckons him in and hands him the court order for the phone service provider to produce a copy of his victim's mobile phone record which includes the location, text messages as well as incoming and outgoing calls. Walking with her out of the office, Mislan informs her that the vic's ex-boyfriend's DNA did not match the fetus's parental DNA.

"You don't sound surprised by it."

"No."

"What if Sallehnor's DNA doesn't match?"

"Then my investigation is screwed."

"And why is that?"

"Because I don't know where to begin with this supernatural motive. I talked to Tee, he said some Chinese do believe in it. They call it kwai chai in Cantonese, devil boy."

"Dig deeper into her friends and social group and if possible her business clients."

"You mean her sex business?"

"Yes. There may be some dissatisfied or possessive clients or some clients that she conned. They may have reason to want her dead."

X

Mislan calls his assistant, asking his whereabouts. Johan says he just got the victim's bank statement and is on his way back to the office.

"I've got the court order for the telco. You want to come along?"

"Yes, give me ten and I will wait for you downstairs. Why don't you borrow a helmet from one of the standby detectives? Better for us to go there by bike, there's no parking there."

"OK, will meet you downstairs."

After borrowing a helmet, Mislan takes the elevator to the ground floor. Johan who is waiting on the motorbike at the carpark footpath waves at him. Leaving the police contingent HQ, the two officers head to Low Yat Plaza in Bukit Bintang where the telco customer service office is.

The counter staff asks the officers to take a seat while she goes to the back office to consult her superior. After several minutes, a woman in her late thirties comes out and tells the officers they will have to go to the head office in Shah Alam to serve the court order. Her statement displeases the inspector.

"Look Miss..." Mislan pauses, not knowing the woman's name.

"Mrs. Gan," the woman says.

"Mrs. Gan, with all the technology your company claims to have as a service provider, you cannot get in touch with your head office from here?"

"Of course I can," she answers defiantly.

"Then, can you call and inform them of the court order?"

"I did, and they said for you to go to the head office."

"Who did you speak to? Give me his name and contact number, I'd like to speak to him," Mislan says a little louder than necessary.

Other staff and customers turn to look in their direction.

"We're investigating a murder and your company is being uncooperative."

"Shall we go to my office to discuss this?" Gan suggests, noticing the customers' interest in their exchange.

Gan leads the two officers to her office. She makes a call to the head office and passes the phone to the inspector.

"This is Inspector Mislan from D9 KL, who am I speaking to?" Mislan inquires firmly.

"Ragu, from the legal department. How may I assist you, Inspector?"

"I have a court order which I served to Mrs. Gan for the detailed record of my victim's mobile phone."

"I understand, she told me."

"She said I need to go to Shah Alam to serve it. The court order says the company or its agents. Is she not one of the company's agents?"

"Yes she is, but not of the level that is authorized to deal with legal matters."

"And you are?"

"Yes, I am."

"Look here, it's not mentioned in the court order that an agent of the company has to be of a certain level to deal with legal matters."

"I understand, but that is our company's policy."

"The court or the law doesn't give two hoots about your company's policy. If she refuses to provide me with the mobile phone record, I will put her under arrest for refusal to comply with a court order."

"May I speak to Mrs. Gan, please?"

Mislan passes the phone to a terrified-looking Mrs. Gan. With a trembling hand she reaches for the phone, avoiding eye contact with the inspector or the detective sergeant. Mislan hears her mutter 'yes…yes…OK…yes' and then she replaces the phone.

"I'm sorry for the misunderstanding and inconvenience. Please wait a minute while I print out the records," she says, braving a smile.

"Thank you," Mislan says.

Leaving the customer service office, Mislan tells Johan to scrutinize the victim's mobile phone record and make a list of anything interesting that could give them a lead.

"Where will you be?"

"Who is on standby?"

"I saw Syed at the detective's office. I saw some of ASP Ghani's men too."

"I need Syed to pick Chong up. He lied to us and that's a good enough reason for him to win a couple of days' stay in our hotel at the taxpayers' expense. Don't you agree?"

"You cleared it with Puan?"

"No need to bother her with it. She's got more important things to think about," Mislan says with a sly smile.

"Why don't I go with Syed?"

"I need you to focus on the phone records. We're running out of leads. Hopefully you'll find a fresh lead there."

26

Back at the office Mislan, scrutinizes the victim's bank statement. The account received numerous online transfers – on average about three times a week. Most of them in small amounts of RM300 to RM350. Every middle of the week there was a check deposit, the amount varied from RM200 to RM500. Mislan deduces the RM300 to RM350 are transfers made by her business clients and the checks are from her booking as GRO. She had a balance of RM2,104.40 in her account. Every three to four days there was a withdrawal of RM500 via ATM.

There is no record of a large amount deposited into her account. The suggestion that the victim may have blackmailed the judge is not supported by her bank account. There was also no record of withdrawal on and after the date she was murdered.

The judge did say that Chong offered RM10,000 for the victim to terminate her pregnancy. The inspector supposes the money was not paid as she refused the offer. Again the judge was telling the truth, at least about the victim refusing the offer.

He is hitting a dead end with the bank statement and hopes his assistant has better luck with the mobile phone records.

"Jo, anything interesting?" he calls out from his desk.

"Still reading the WhatsApp chats. I believe most of them are with her clients. They're enticing and intimate. This woman really knows how to give a man a hard-on."

"Don't tell me you're having one reading her chats?"

"Listen to this – *I can sneak into your office, get under the table and take you in my mouth while you pretend to work. You can come all over my face, how's that for office thrill?*"

Mislan laughs. "Focus on her social chats. We need to identify her friends and talk to them."

"How would I know who they are if I don't read all her chats?"

Mislan picks up the office phone and calls the front desk, asking if Superintendent Samsiah is back in the office. The front desk tells him, no. He wonders what is taking her so long to get the judge to give his DNA sample. Did he object to giving the sample? He can't, there is a court order. Maybe being a judge himself, he will challenge the court order. Can he? Curious to know about the delay, he thinks of calling her to ask but decides against it. He is sure she can handle any challenges thrown at her by the judge. He will ask her when she comes back.

Detective Syed informs Mislan his suspect, Chong, is in interview room 1.

"Did he protest?"

"I think he dropped five names. I told him I don't recognize any of the names mentioned. He made two calls before we managed to put the cuffs on him," Syed chuckled.

"What were the names?"

"All have Tuan like Tuan Zainal, Tuan Goh, Tuan Salleh and two or three more that I can't remember."

"Must be men that frequent his place. He didn't happen to mention their positions?"

"No, just Tuan this and Tuan that."

"OK, lodge the arrest report and link it to my case. Tell standby to be with him." As the detective is leaving, Mislan says, "Syed, leave his cuffs on."

Taking out his digital recorder, Mislan calls to his assistant, "Jo, you want to join me?"

Johan looks at him, saying, "I'm not done yet."

"The phone record is not going anywhere. You can continue after the interview."

Chong glares intimidatingly as the two officers enter the interview room. His face is flush with anger and his unblinking eyes are fixed on them.

"This is harassment!" Chong hisses.

"This is investigation," Mislan cuts him off and takes a seat. Placing the digital recorder on the table, he says, "You lied and withheld crucial information on a murder probe. That gives me a reason to arrest you. You can verify it with Tuan Sallehnor."

Chong blinks rapidly, feigning shock at hearing the inspector's allegations against him. Finally he asks, "What lie, what information?"

"That Gary introduced the judge to you, knowing it was the other way around."

Chong remains silent, but Mislan can see a glimmer of fear in his eyes.

"You withheld crucial information, that you were the last person to be with Rita on the night she was murdered."

Chong's eyes widen on hearing the inspector's accusation.

"You conveniently left out the part where you joined them at the food court. Jo, what is the medical term used for such behavior?"

"Memory glitch."

"Yes that's it, memory glitch," Mislan says with a smile.

Chong inhales deeply several times, refraining from responding. His face contorts in anxiety.

"We know that you joined the group at the food court and you volunteered to send Rita home. I've three witnesses who can testify to it. The thing is she never did make it home. You were the last person to be with her alive, and you know what that means in a murder investigation?"

"You're a prime suspect," Johan answers for him.

Mislan watches the suspect's face, searching for telltale signs. There is a look of submission on his face.

"Where did you take Rita to from the food court?" Mislan presses on.

"Yes," Chong admits with a sigh. "I did volunteer to send her home but on the way I stopped at the KTV to keep the day's collection in the safe and get my things from the office. When I came, out she was already gone."

"What a tale," Johan mocks.

"I told her to wait in the car while I went to the office. I swear over my mother's grave."

"If you went back to the KTV, I'm sure Rita would've followed you in."

"She was tipsy. She drank too much. It's always the same when she and Tuan were together."

"But she was pregnant. Pregnant woman are not supposed to consume alcohol," Johan states.

"Not supposed to, but she did. Who was I to stop her?"

"What about her lover, the judge, I'm sure he would not have allowed her to drink," Mislan points out.

"He wanted her to drink. He said maybe the drink would end the pregnancy."

"You mean kill the baby?" Mislan snaps.

Chong cringes but says nothing.

"You know what? You've just admitted that you and the judge conspired to terminate her pregnancy, to kill the baby. My theory is after your persuasion and offer of compensation failed, you murdered her and got rid of the baby."

"You're crazy, why would I do that?"

"Because you promised the judge you'd take care of it," Johan suggests.

"To make sure the judge owes you a favor, a huge favor," Mislan adds.

"I never promised Tuan I'd *kill* her. I promised him I'd try and *talk* to her. You people are crazy."

"Are we? I don't think the Deputy Public Prosecutor will think we're crazy when we forward your case to him."

Chong looks terrified, his face is twitching and he mumbles his words. "I swear, she was alive and sleeping when I left her in the car at the KTV. I *swear*."

"If she decided to leave with another person, I'm sure she would've called to inform you so that you wouldn't worry."

"She did not."

"What about you, did you call her to find out where she was?"

"She was drunk. All the time we were at the food court I could hear her phone ringing but she didn't answer. That was why I didn't call her."

"I find your answer hard to believe," Mislan says, shaking his head. "Why don't you tell us what really happened? Were you told by the judge to get rid of her?"

"No, Tuan asked me to *talk* to her to get an abortion. I talked to her, I offered her ten thousand but she refused. She said she wanted to have the baby. I swear," Chong pleads.

"Whose baby was she carrying?"

"I don't know. Tuan said Rita told him it was his baby but I don't know."

"Is it his baby?"

"I don't know."

"If it was not his baby, what was he afraid of? Why was he so determined to get rid of the baby?"

"I don't know if the baby was his, but I know he and Rita were having an affair."

"How do you know the judge?"

"Long time back D'Voice, the KTV I worked at, was raided and a few of my GROs tested positive for drugs. A police friend introduced me to Tuan. When I moved to the Champion KTV we met there again. When Rita come to work there, he saw her. He remembered she was one of the GROs I kawtim with him. He booked her and then they started to have an affair."

"That was why she was only fined five hundred for using illegal drugs," Johan says.

Chong nods.

"Apart from you and the judge, who else knew Rita was pregnant?"

"Nelly, because she asked my permission for Rita not to come to work every day, only when booked."

"Anyone else?"

"I don't know."

"Apart from the judge, who else were her regular clients at the KTV?"

"You have to check with Nelly, she will know."

"What do you think, Jo? Can we believe him or do we let him spend a couple of days in the lockup to think things over?"

Chong turns to face the detective sergeant, his expression beseeching to be spared the nights in the police lockup.

"Please, I swear I'm telling you the truth. I'm sorry I lied to you because I didn't want the judge to get into trouble. I regret it, but now I'm telling the truth."

"I think we should let him spend some quiet time by himself in our hostel. We'll talk to him again tomorrow. If he continues to lie, we should just pin the murder on him."

"No, no, I did *not* kill Rita. I swear I don't know anything about her death, *please*," Chong almost bursts into tears.

"I agree with Detective Sergeant Johan. One more thing, the next time I hear you treat my detectives arrogantly, I will personally escort you to the lockup. Do you understand me?"

"Yes, yes, I'm sorry. Please don't put me in the lockup. I swear I'm telling you the truth."

"We'll see about that tomorrow."

Back in the office, Mislan asks Johan if he still has the CCTV recording from the Champion KTV. Slotting in the DVD, he cues it to after his victim and the group left the KTV for supper. He keeps watching and at 12.01 am Chong is seen walking into the KTV. *That must be when he came back from the food court to his*

office, Mislan says to himself. Because the camera angle is from above the entrance facing outward, he sees a lot of people leaving but from the back, not their faces. He guesses they must be the KTV customers leaving at closing time: midnight. He continues watching. There is no sign of his victim entering the KTV. At 12.15 am, he sees many of the GROs leaving the KTV. At 12.25 am he sees Chong or someone wearing the same color shirt as him leaving.

He was telling the truth about stopping at the office from the food court. But it doesn't mean he did not stop somewhere to pass the victim on to his accomplice to be killed. From the food court to the KTV is what, one and half kilometers? He checks Waze for the time it takes from the food court to the KTV, it is eight minutes. *Shit, I should have asked him what time he left the food court to see if there was a sufficient window for him to do that. What time did Jo say they left the food court?*

Another possible scenario: His accomplice was waiting for him at the KTV carpark. What's the probability of that? I doubt it. He would not take the risk of being seen by the carpark attendant or the KTV customers or the GROs that were leaving.

If what Chong said is true, who would his victim go with? It had to be someone she knew, someone she trusted that would not take advantage of her, especially in her drunken state. Who could that someone be?

His office phone rings, it is the front desk telling him Superintendent Samsiah is back in her office. Pushing his thoughts aside, Mislan heads for her office.

"I heard you picked up the KTV manager," she says as Mislan takes a seat.

"Yes."

"What did you find out?"

"He admitted to lying about knowing the judge and introducing him to Gary. He also admitted to withholding information about joining the group at the food court and volunteering to send the vic home."

"But…?"

"He claimed, after the food court he stopped at the KTV to keep the day's collection and gather his things from the office. He claimed the vic was drunk and he left her in his car when he went into the KTV. When he came out, she was gone."

"And you believe him?"

"The CCTV captured him returning to the KTV at 12.01 am and leaving at 12.25 am. I can't dispute the CCTV," Mislan says.

"No you can't," she answers, smiling. "With the CCTV, Chong is exonerated from being a prime suspect."

"Not yet, there're still a few things I need to verify. How did it go with the judge?"

"As expected."

"Meaning?"

"A lot of interventions. But what's important, we got his DNA sample."

"Care to elaborate?"

"Let's just say the case is in the open and there'll be a lot of interested parties."

"Like?"

"The judicial community, those up there and the press."

"Hmmm."

"Do it right and there's nothing for you to worry."

"When will we know the result?"

"Two or three days' time. Get anything from the victim's phone record?"

"Jo is still reviewing it. He said too many triple X-rated chats."

Samsiah laughs. "Tell him not to dwell on them and get himself all excited. Focus on her friends, if she said something to them about someone that was angry with her, and threatening texts against her."

"I did, and he said he needs to read them all to know if there were any," Mislan says.

Back in the office, the inspector asks Johan if Andrew told him what time they left the food court with the victim.

"He said when he escorted Rita to Chong's car, he noticed the dashboard clock was at 11.52 pm. Why?"

"Trying to work out the timing. How's the vic's phone record?"

"So far nothing that would raise any suspicions. Just a lot of sales pitches."

"Who were her friends, that she always chatted with?"

"Murni, Nelly. She chatted with Nelly about her pregnancy and her thoughts on it."

"Like what?"

"She was having second thoughts about keeping the baby. She was saying what if the father didn't want the baby, what was she supposed to do, how was she going to manage financially and so on."

"Any photos?"

"Mostly of herself in sexy poses."

Mislan mulls, Chong left the food court at 11.52 pm and was seen entering the KTV at 12.01 am. That is nine minutes. Would he have the time to make a detour to offload the victim? Mislan supposes, the eight minutes according to Waze would be driving within speed limit. Then he had to walk from the carpark to the KTV entrance. No, he would not have the window to make a detour.

Any offloading of the victim to his accomplice would have to be done at the carpark. If so, there is a probability of the carpark attendant or customers leaving the KTV seeing something.

"Jo," he calls to his assistant.

"What?"

"Send the standby to pick up the carpark attendant for questioning."

"When?"

Mislan glances at the wall clock. "He should be working now, right?"

"Should be."

"Tell the standby to do it now. Can you chat with Murni and ask her if she saw or heard anything in the carpark on the night the vic was murdered?"

"I think it's better if we go there to talk to the attendant."

"Why?"

"He's a single operator, if we pick him up, he'll lose his carpark collection. When we're there, I can look Murni up and talk to her," Johan suggests.

"You'd like that, won't you?"

Johan beams.

"If you're done sex-citing yourself with the victim's chats, can we go now?"

Walking past the front desk, Mislan tells the standby detective to release Chong from the lockup.

"You putting him on bail?" Johan asks.

"No, release him unconditionally."

"Why?"

"The CCTV corroborated his story. Save the taxpayers some money."

27

In the car driving to the Champion KTV, Mislan tells Johan his thoughts on Chong's statement. He feels the claim made by Chong that he left the victim in the car while he went to keep the day's collection is plausible. There is also the CCTV recording of him returning to the KTV at 12.01 am.

"He's the manager, I'm sure he's the only one with the safe combination or key," Mislan says.

"And during this pandemic period, all entertainment and food and beverage outlets must close by midnight," Johan adds. "That makes sense, the bills would've been closed at 11.45 pm for the customers to settle them before closing."

"The question is, what happened to the vic while waiting for him in the car?"

"If she *was* in the car. You may be right, there was no time for a detour. But how long does it take to offload her from one car to another waiting car? Two minutes, three?"

The inspector remains silent.

"What if it all was preplanned? His accomplices wait for him by the roadside to the KTV. He drops her off and then goes ahead to the KTV. He knows there's a CCTV camera at the entrance that will capture him arriving back. Aside from his word, there's nothing to corroborate that the victim was in the car."

"There's also nothing to say she was *not* with him in the car. So why make up the story?"

"So he gets the benefit of the doubt. Unless, of course, we can prove otherwise."

"Did you check her mobile phone location?"

"Not yet, I'll do it after this."

The carpark attendant is an Indian man by the name of Ramesh. The space is rented from a developer by his uncle, and vehicles are charged on a per entry basis. During office hours, most of the vehicles belong to shop owners and their customers. In the evening, most are customers of the KTV and the GROs. While Johan goes to seek out Murni the gorgeous GRO, Mislan interviews the carpark attendant.

"How long have you been working here?" Mislan asks.

"Already four years."

"So you know most of the GROs?"

"Yes," Ramesh replies, shaking his head and smiling brightly. Indians shake their heads when it is a yes.

"You're the only one working here?"

"Morning, my nephew. Evening until close, only me."

"Do you know what car Mr. Chong the karaoke manager drives?"

"Mazda CX5, red color. He not arrived yet. He only coming around 5.30 or 6."

"How come you know the car model?"

"Every day I see cars in, out, parking. I also do security, rounding, checking if everything OK. So I know cars."

"Five or six nights back, did you see Mr. Chong enter the carpark around midnight?"

Ramesh tilts his head, his forehead crinkles as he searches his memory. "Yes, yes, that time customers already leaving."

"Why do you remember?"

"I stopped him. No cars can come in. I cannot see the car number plate because the car light is bright. When he stopped, he put window down. I see him and said OK can come in."

"I see. Was he alone?"

"One GRO with him."

"How do you know she was a GRO?"

"I always see her but I don't know name."

"Can you describe her?"

"Small, long hair, look little bit like Indian."

Mislan takes out his mobile phone and shows the victim's photo. "Is this her?"

"Yes, yes she the GRO."

"What time did Mr. Chong leave?"

"Sorry boss, I don't look cars leaving because they already pay parking. I only stop coming in cars to collect parking."

"That night did you see the GRO following Mr. Chong into the karaoke?"

"No boss, sorry. From here difficult to see."

"Did you see anyone stop at Mr. Chong's SUV?"

"No boss. I see many customers and GROs come carpark going home," Ramesh answers and then tilts his head as if he remembers something. "I got hear people laughing, I see three, four GROs standing. I think one GRO drunk and other GRO laughing maybe help I don't know."

"Where did this happen?"

Ramesh points to a spot in the carpark.

"Where was Mr. Chong's SUV parked?"

"Same place. I cannot see what happened. Mr. Chong car blocking."

"Then what happened?"

"After one minute maybe little longer, two GROs walked to cars."

"Can you remember who the GROs were?"

"I can recognize but I don't know names. Oh wait, mummy Nelly."

"You know mummy Nelly?"

"Yes, she good mummy. Always give me cigarettes, sometimes beers. She said customer leave in karaoke."

"That night, you are sure mummy Nelly was one of those laughing and helping someone drunk? And you're sure it was only the GROs and no customers?"

"Yes, very sure boss."

"OK, thank you."

Mislan makes a call to Johan. "Where are you?"

"With Murni."

"What's taking you so long?"

"Am I?" the detective sergeant answers, sounding surprised.

"Any longer and they'll charge you booking fee," Mislan mocks.

Driving back to the office, Mislan asks Johan what he found out from Murni. Johan tells him, nothing much from what she had told them during their meeting at Tapak Street Food.

"Then why were you talking so long with her?"

The detective sergeant gives the inspector a silly grin.

"Jo, something happened at the carpark on the night Chong claimed to have driven there."

"When he stopped at the KTV to go to the office? I did ask Murni, she said she heard some of the girls talking, that night Rita was at the carpark puking. Some of the girls attended to her but left after she said she was OK."

"Did she say who the GROs were?"

"No, she heard it from Lina."

"Did you speak to this Lina?"

"She's not working today but I got her phone number. I'll give her a call back at the office."

"Ramesh the carpark attendant said Nelly was there. Don't tell her that. Let's hear what she has to say first."

"OK."

"If she corroborates what Ramesh said, then Chong was telling us the truth and we need to find out where the vic went after he left her at the carpark."

"She either left with somebody or she wandered away through the footpath to the shops next to the carpark."

"Why would she do that? She was drunk and was in no condition to wander about."

"To meet with somebody that she called to help her."

"You said there was no outgoing call by her?"

"Yeah, I forgot," Johan admits.

"Maybe the vic felt Chong was taking too long and she asked for a ride from one of the girls."

"What if Chong went to the office and called his accomplice to come to the carpark and pick up the victim?" Johan asks.

"Not likely."

Johan glances at the inspector inquiringly.

"Ramesh would have stopped him or them. The carpark is closed after the KTV closes and vehicles are not allowed in. That was how he confirmed Chong and the vic returned to the carpark at midnight."

Johan nods.

Johan makes a call to Lina, the GRO who told Murni about the victim puking at the carpark. Lina sounds like she is having the flu. Her voice is coarse and muffled. She informs the detective sergeant that she is under home quarantine for Omicron infection.

"Are you OK to talk?" Johan asks.

"Yes."

Lina tells him she was walking to her car when she noticed the incident and approached them to find out what was happening.

"And what was happening?"

"Rita was bent over puking and mummy Nelly was massaging the back of her neck while the rest were just standing watching and making fun of her."

"Who were there?"

"Mummy Nelly, Christine, Puteri and Yati."

"Then what happened?"

"Then I left."

"And Rita, what happened to her?"

"I don't know. When I left they were still with her."

"You said the girls were making fun of Rita, what were they saying?"

"The usual jibes, like what a waste of good whiskey, a lady never pukes in public and so on."

"Did you know Rita was pregnant?"

"I heard the girls talk but I never asked her. It's none of my business."

"Thank you."

Johan updates the inspector on his conversation with Lina and the victim's phone locations detected by the transmission towers.

"The phone was last detected at Sri Hartamas cell transmission tower at midnight," Johan informs the inspector. "I assume it was when Chong returned to the KTV. Then it went off the air. It must have been powered off."

"After a phone is switched off, cell towers cannot detect the location?"

"No. Except in movies," Johan replies.

Mislan leans back in his chair and lets out a heavy sigh.

"This case seems to be going nowhere. We started with a clear picture of the means, motive and opportunity. Now we are without the motive and opportunity. And we don't even have a suspect anymore. Where do we go from here?"

Johan shares his frustration. He knows what an unsolved case can do to the mental wellbeing of an investigator. Not all investigators, but those who live their cases. He pulls up a chair and sits at the inspector's desk. Mislan looks at his assistant inquisitively.

"Let's go through what we have, see what we're missing," Johan says.

The wall clock shows 6.25 pm, about the time Superintendent Samsiah would make her rounds before calling it a day. They hear footsteps and turn to look at the office door. Sure enough, she appears. The officers stand to greet her and she waves for them to sit.

"Having a discussion?" she asks, approaching them.

"Not yet, I was just persuading Inspector Mislan to engage in one," Johan replies.

"The Posthumous Child?"

Johan nods.

"Let's hear it," she encourages the inspector. "I once attended a motivational course. The speaker said, talking to yourself aloud helps you see a clearer picture of what you want to achieve. I've never done it for fear people may think I'm crazy. But let's give it a try."

Reluctantly, Mislan narrates what he has thus far, laying out what is proven and also his deflated theories.

"If I understand you correctly, the carpark attendant does not allow vehicles coming in at midnight because the carpark is closing," Samsiah clarifies.

Mislan nods.

"If that's the case, the victim had to have left with someone coming out of the KTV," she deduces.

"That's what I thought too, but who? And what would be the motive for that someone to murder her?"

"Let's move on and see if it brings us there," she suggests. "The judge and Chong were not the last people to be with the victim alive. According to this Lina, after the judge and Chong there were four women who were with the victim alive. Speak to these women. One of them might know what happened to her."

"When we spoke to Nelly, she did not mention anything about the incident in the carpark," Mislan says.

"Because you probably did not ask her the question," she points out. "You only knew of the carpark incident today."

"I'm sure she would mention it, it's something crucial," Johan stresses.

"To you, us, but not to her. As a karaoke mummy she would've probably experienced such incidents daily. Whether it's her girls or the customers."

"Still, we were talking to her about a murder, not a drunken woman," Mislan argues.

"We were asking her about our victim," Johan reminds the inspector. "Trying to get to know more about our victim."

"Talk to her again, refresh her memory."

"We're going in circles," Mislan grunts.

"Musical chairs," she says, smiling. "And when the music stops the one standing is the one you interview and eliminate. Then when the music starts again they'll go round and round again until the last person sitting in the chair… he or she will be your prime suspect."

"The electric chair," Johan jests.

"Going back to this unknown person who may have, for whatever reason, given the victim a lift that night. The one who supposedly came out of the KTV. Only the four women, or one of them, might shed light on what happened to the victim," Samsiah suggests. "It could be one of her GRO friends or a regular customer she was friendly with. I advise you against jumping to conclusions that he or she had anything to do with the murder."

"Like we did with the judge," Johan interjects.

"Exactly. Conducting your investigation with tunnel vision. For all you know, the one giving her the lift could have been just a Good Samaritan helping a woman in distress."

28

Night is usually a busy time for them, when crime is open for business. Apart from the darkness brought by the night, there is an unexplained correlation between night and the commissioning of crimes. Murder, rape, robbery, housebreaking, mugging and many others. It is like nightfall flips a switch in the brains of criminals, perverts and wackos, telling them to begin. Something like the werewolf and the full moon.

Much as Mislan would like to revisit the Champion KTV to interview the three GROs and the mummy, he is not prepared to leave the fort for fear of call-outs.

"Jo, check with Lina if she has the three GROs' phone numbers," Mislan calls to his assistant.

Johan does as instructed and says, "She only has Puteri's number."

"Give it to me."

Mislan makes the call and after several rings it goes to voice message. He figures she must be in one of the karaoke rooms and did not hear the phone ringing. It can be really loud in there. He leaves a message for her to return the call.

He recalls the happy days when he and his ex-wife used to karaoke with some of her office friends. For that matter, when he was with Dr. Nursafia. She too enjoyed karaoke once in a while to wind down.

His office phone rings. "Mislan."

"Inspector Mislan, hi, I'm Puteri returning your call," the caller says. He can hear loud music in the background.

"Hi thanks, are you OK to talk?"

"What's it about? I've got a customer," she says, sounding harried.

"It's about the incident in the carpark about five to six nights ago."

"I'm sorry I can't hear you, what did you say?"

Mislan repeats loudly what he just said, attracting Johan's attention.

"Yes, what about it?" Puteri asks. The music has significantly reduced; she must have stepped out of the room into the hallway.

"I was told you were one of the persons that attended to Rita in the carpark."

"I was there, but it was mummy Nelly who attended to her."

"What happened after that?"

"Nothing. I mean after she vomited she said she was OK."

"Meaning?"

"She was standing, smiling and laughing about it."

"Did you see who she left with?"

"No – we, Yati and I, left."

"Christine and mummy Nelly?"

"They were still with Rita when we left."

"Have you got Christine's and Yati's numbers?"

"Only Yati's."

"Can you WhatsApp it to me?" Mislan says, giving Johan's mobile phone number.

"Sure."

"One more thing. Is Christine Chinese or Indian?"

"She is like mummy Nelly, Sarawakian."

"OK, thanks."

Johan's mobile phone beeps; it is a WhatsApp from Puteri with Yati's contact number. He looks at it, then at his lead investigator.

"New contact for your black book," Mislan says with a chuckle. "Give Yati a call and ask her about the incident in the carpark. Let's hear her story to see if it tallies with Puteri's."

Johan makes the call and identifies himself.

"Is it convenient to talk?" he asks.

"Yes."

"I'm putting you on speaker for my inspector to listen in, so I don't have to repeat what you said. Is it OK?"

"Whatever."

"A few nights back, one of the GROs was sick at the carpark. You were one of those that assisted her, right?"

"You mean poor Rita throwing up?"

"Yes."

"I was there with a few others."

"They were…?"

"Puteri, Christine and Nelly."

"Mummy Nelly?"

"Yes."

"Can you tell me what happened?"

"Nelly was helping Rita, the rest of us just watched."

"Then?

"Then when she was OK, we left."

"We meaning?"

"Puteri and I. Nelly and Christine were still taking care of Rita."

"Do you know who Rita went with?"

"No, we already left. What's this about? Oh my god, you think she was killed at the carpark and we had something to do with it?"

"Was she and did you?"

"NO, NO!"

"I'm joking," Johan says.

"It's NOT funny OK! You cops!"

The call is disconnected.

"Interesting," Mislan says.

"What is?"

"Both of them said Nelly and Christine were with the vic when they left. Puteri said Christine and Nelly are from Sarawak."

"What's interesting about that?"

"By itself nothing, but when you take into consideration that Nelly did not say anything about being with the vic on the night of her murder, it's a little suspicious to me."

"You're thinking the two of them murdered the victim?"

"Murdered I don't know… but had something to do with her death, probable."

"You're trying to work the judge and Chong back into the picture, aren't you?"

Mislan ignores that remark. "Why was she murdered? What could she have done to piss off the two Sarawakians to the point they wanted her dead?"

Johan keeps mum.

"I thought so."

Feeling triumphant, Mislan rewards himself with a cigarette. He knows Superintendent Samsiah has left and he has the office to himself.

"Jo, how much do you trust Murni?"

"As much as I trust any person I had two brief meetings with."

"Can you ask her about Christine and Nelly's relationship?"

"Like what? Are they a couple?"

"No. Like who brought Christine in. Are they from the same town or are they related in any way? You know, things like that."

"What are you getting at?"

"Just to know how strong their bond is. I'd also like to know Nelly's relationships with Chong and the judge."

"There you go again, back to those two."

Mislan grins at Johan.

"I'll have to ask her in person, not through the phone."

"There *you* go again, looking for an excuse to see her," Mislan mocks.

To the inspector's disappointment, there is only one call-out for the entire night. It is for road-rage where one of the drivers got shot. The person who fired the shot is a government employee who has a permit to carry the gun for self-protection. He claimed the other driver came at him with a hockey stick. The case is being handled by the district. Mislan expressed his dismay to his assistant, saying they could have gone to talk to Murni instead of sitting in the office. Johan, for a different reason, is also dismayed.

29

The next morning Mislan is gloomy; he feels he wasted valuable time last night in not chasing his lead. Even his favorite breakfast – nasi lemak which Johan went out to buy – does nothing to lift his spirits. Reeziana and the newbie Hartini notice his foul mood and stay clear of him.

"What's up with your boss?" Reeziana whispers to Johan.

"He is hung up with pinning the case on the judge and the KTV manager."

"What's stopping him from going after them?"

"Long story," Johan says, not wanting to go into detail. "Short version, his theory was blown to pieces when some of the GROs admitted to being with the victim on the night of her murder. They're the last to be with her alive."

"But…?"

"He's trying to spin it around back to the judge and the KTV manager."

"Why?" Hartini asks.

"Because they had a strong motive for wanting the victim dead."

"I see," Hartini says.

Mislan glares at the three of them whispering. The conversation immediately stops and both Reeziana and Hartini head to the pantry, leaving Johan smiling at the inspector.

The morning-prayer is brief with Mislan eager to get the day started. Leaving the meeting room, he signals for Johan to follow him.

"Where to?"

"Meet with Murni."

"I don't think she's up yet."

"Why don't you give her a call? We can meet for breakfast near wherever she lives."

Reluctantly, Johan makes the call. After several rings, a sleepy voice answers.

"Sorry, did I wake you up?" Johan apologizes.

"Yes, but it's OK. Why did you call?"

"My inspector is wondering if we can meet for breakfast somewhere near where you live."

"Umm, what time is it?"

"9.15."

"OK, why don't we meet at Johnny's at 10. Do you know where it is?"

"Which area? I can Waze it."

"Empire Damansara."

"OK, we'll see you at 10."

Johan drives out of the city, following the all-too-familiar roads he has driven through several times to the Champion KTV. Instead of turning to Sri Hartamas, he makes a left heading for Empire Damansara. Mislan Wazes the direction to Johnny's. Following the directions by the female voice, they reach their destination. Murni is already at the café sitting by herself at the open air section. She is dressed casually in shorts and a round neck T-shirt, hair ponytailed, no makeup except for a touch of light lipstick. She looks as beautiful as Mislan remembers from their first meeting.

"Hi," she greets as they approach her table.

"Sorry to inconvenience you and thank you for meeting us," Johan says, being the gentleman that he is.

"Have you ordered?" Mislan asks.

"No, I'm waiting for you guys."

Johan signals for the waiter. "What would you like?"

"The curry laksa here is good," she says, smiling.

"OK then, three curry laksa. Drink?" Johan asks Murni.

"Iced tea, please."

"Two iced tea and one iced coffee."

"Can we smoke here?" Mislan asks the waiter.

"No, but go ahead," the waiter answers, leaving them to place their orders.

"So, how do I pay you guys for the breakfast?" she asks when the waiter is gone.

Johan turns to the inspector.

"Murni, how well do you know Christine and Nelly?" Mislan begins.

"Christine, not well. She just joined about a month back. Mummy Nelly, quite a bit as she was already there when I joined."

"How close are Christine and Nelly?"

"They're from Sarawak and I heard mummy Nelly brought her in. I guess they're close. But how close, I don't know."

"What about Nelly and Chong?"

"I heard they used to work together before Champion, so they must have known each other a long time. Why are you asking me about Christine, mummy Nelly and Chong?"

"Just want to know more about them," Mislan answers vaguely.

"Wait a minute, you think they had something to do with Rita's death?" she says, shocked.

The waiter arrives with their orders and the conversation momentarily stops. As the waiter sets their orders, Johan notices Murni's disbelieving eyes never leaves the inspector's face.

"Let's eat while it's hot," Johan says, attempting to distract Murni's laser-beam glare.

Mislan notices it too and says, "I'm not saying they had anything to do with the case, but we need to cover all angles to be sure." With a chopstick, he picks up a prawn from his curry laksa bowl and holds it toward her. "Would you like my prawns? I'm allergic."

"Yes, please," she replies, smiling. "I love seafood."

Mislan transfers all his prawns to her bowl and starts eating. The curry laksa is really tasty, rich and lavish with toppings.

"This is really good," Johan says to Murni.

She beams with delight. When they finish enjoying the delicious curry laksa, Mislan offers her a cigarette which she declines. Digging into her shorts pocket, she holds up a soft pack of Marlboro Lights.

"I can never get used to Indonesian cigarettes," Murni says, lighting one of her own. "You know they burn your dresses if you're not careful."

Lighting one himself, Mislan continues, "What can you tell us about Nelly?"

"She's a divorcee, I think she lives in Ampang, exactly where I don't know. She drinks like a fish, whiskey, beer, anything with alcohol and she smokes the same cigarette as you – Sampoerna Menthol."

"How well does she know the judge?"

"Well, whenever he comes, mummy Nelly will always park herself in his room."

"Well enough to do favors for him?"

"You mean have sex with him? Maybe, but he has Rita, why would he want mummy?"

"What about Chong?"

"You mean like mummy and Chong having an affair?"

"Or more."

"More? I don't understand."

"Do something illegal for him?"

"Like what, sell drugs or something like that?"

"Maybe, or lie to cover for him?"

"We all would lie for the one we care for, right?" Murni answers with a sweet smile.

"True," Johan agrees.

"Nelly or Chong, do they have any other business?"

"I don't know. During the strict pandemic period I heard mummy sold food at one of the buildings in KL. It's funny, she said she wore the tudung so people would think she is Muslim and her food halal," Murni laughs.

"She's not Muslim?" Johan asks.

"Who, mummy Nelly? No, she is Christian or something but not Muslim."

"What about her and Rita?"

"Rita told me she thought about having an abortion during the early stage of her pregnancy, but mummy Nelly convinced her to keep the baby. She would drive her to medical checkups and took care of her when she was having morning sickness."

"Really?" Mislan is surprised.

"I personally don't know but that was what Rita told me."

"Did Rita say why mummy Nelly told her to keep the baby?"

"No."

"Did you know Rita was suffering from cancer?"

"No. Was she?"

"The pathologist found traces of chemotrophic medication."

"Oh my god. She never said anything to me. Was she dying?"

"We don't know."

"So sad."

"Murni, I advise you against telling anyone at the KTV about this meeting. I don't want them to think you are snitching on them," Mislan cautions her.

"Why? I didn't tell you anything that the other girls won't if you question them."

"You know that, we know that, but they don't. They may think that you're snitching."

"Tell me the truth, are they involved in Rita's death? The truth," Murni asks, looking intensely at the inspector's face.

"We don't know. We're still trying to figure out what and why it happened," Mislan answers truthfully.

"OK, I believe you."

"If you hear of anything you think we should know, please contact Jo."

"Why Jo? Why can't I contact you?"

"Because you don't have my number," Mislan chuckles.

Murni blows a raspberry to the inspector.

Mislan is quiet on the drive back to the police contingent HQ. He is at a loss. He has nothing to tie his most likely suspects – the judge or Chong – to the case. Apart from his victim working for Chong and having sexual relations with the judge, there is nothing. They were not even the last persons to be with her alive. The DNA result will be out and if it is proven the judge is the father of the unborn child, then maybe – and that is a big maybe – he will be allowed to bring him in for questioning.

In the meantime, all he has are three GROs putting Christine and Nelly with the victim at the carpark on the fatal night. *Were they the last two persons to be with the victim alive? Probably. Would they know where the victim went after puking in the carpark? Most likely.*

How does he navigate forward? Bring them in and do the hard interview? Or bring just Christine in to rat on the other? Leave mummy Nelly for last. She is a seasoned mummy, she has seen and been through enough not to be easily intimidated.

Why didn't she say anything about the incident in the carpark? Mislan mulls. *OK, we probably didn't ask her the right question during the first interview, like Superintendent Samsiah suggested. But the second time, when she was called to the office to identify the judge and victim in the CCTV recording, she knew we wanted to know where the victim went that night. Surely she could say something about the carpark incident. Yet she didn't. Why? Because she knew who the victim left with on that night – and for whatever reason she was protecting that someone.*

"Why so quiet?" Johan asks.

"Thinking about Murni," Mislan says, pulling his assistant's leg.

Johan laughs. "She is not your type."

"And what is my type?"

"The mature type."

"You mean old women."

"I said mature, not old."

"And in your opinion, Murni is not mature?"

"She is, but not your type of maturity," Johan jests.

"You want to know what I think? I think you're afraid of the competition that I pose," Mislan teases Johan. "You're afraid she may fancy a mature man."

"Let the best man win," Johan declares.

Mislan laughs heartily.

When they arrive at the office, they see ASP Ghani and his lapdog assistant in earnest low tone conversation with Reeziana and Hartini. Johan gestures discreetly to Mislan, asking what is going on. Ghani and his assistant never come to the investigators' office just for a chat. They have their own office away from the investigators. Mislan shrugs and heads for his desk. Noticing Mislan and Johan, their conversation stops. Ghani and his lapdog assistant leave.

There is bad blood between Ghani and Mislan. Although Ghani is one rank above him, they do not see eye to eye. On one of Mislan's cases, they crossed paths and he invited Ghani to his private smoking place. There Mislan got a little physical and said with no uncertain terms that should Ghani ever interfere again with his investigation, the consequence would be detrimental to both of them. The news of their private meeting leaked and reached Superintendent Samsiah's ears. They were reprimanded and given a last warning to behave or she would not hesitate to take necessary action. As agreed in Mislan's private smoking space, both of them said nothing about what happened. Not even to Superintendent Samsiah when questioned. Since then, they try to avoid each other whenever possible.

After Ghani and his assistant leave, Johan asks Reeziana what is going on.

"His CI was found dead by Rawang police," she says.

"How does he know?"

"Rawang police found his phone number and called."

"What does he want?"

"He wants me to call Selangor D9 and find out more."

"Why can't he call himself?"

"I don't know, why don't you go and ask him?"

"I'd rather not know the answer than to ask him," Johan snorts.

"Why are you guys back in the office?" Hartini asks.

"Just came back from talking to one of our sources, not a CI," Johan says.

"Yana, is Puan in?" Mislan asks from his desk.

"Let me check her leg-tracker," Reeziana replies, holding her mobile phone to him.

"Funny," Mislan snaps.

"What's wrong with him? Grumpy since this morning," she tells Johan.

X

Superintendent Samsiah gazes at her investigator's brooding face and knows the Posthumous Child case is challenging him. Mislan is many things, hardheaded and sometimes reckless, but he is never too proud or egotistical to seek opinions from others. A quality she likes in him. She knows this is one of the instances when he is seeking help.

"What's on your mind?" she probes. "I know it's not because Ghani is leaving us," she says, adding light humor to her inquiry.

Mislan flashes her a tiny smile. "Where's he going?"

"His first choice was General Operation, where I'm certain his paramilitary background will be an asset to them."

Mislan nods his agreement. He updates Superintendent Samsiah on his latest discovery.

"You've not interviewed the last two persons seen with the victim alive?" she asks, trying to read the inspector's face. "What's your reason?"

Mislan closes his eyes, searching his thoughts. "Puan, I'd like to bring them in, put them through the mill. I believe Christine is more likely to spill the beans – if there are beans to be spilled. Nelly is seasoned. She may not be easy to crack unless we can prove she had something to do with the case."

"I remember you saying because the carpark closes at midnight, the victim would have to leave with someone from the KTV."

Mislan nods.

"You're thinking the victim left with her or them?"

"Or with someone the killer arranged, and they were the ones making sure of it."

"A customer?"

"Perhaps."

"I don't think so. I know what you're thinking. Tell me if I'm wrong. The judge got Chong to get rid of the victim. Chong then arranged for the killer to be at the KTV. Nelly and Christine went to the carpark to ensure the victim was still there. To convince her it was alright for her to follow the man, although she doesn't know him. Nelly and Christine then walked the victim to the killer's car, probably saying Chong had asked him to send her home as he was delayed. The victim got into the car and they left. Too elaborate and too many people involved, the risk of being exposed is high."

"But it puts them all in the clear."

"Nelly and Christine would still be the last known persons to have seen her alive. Which means they would know who the killer is."

"They could say the same thing as the other GROs. The vic was OK and they left," Mislan argues.

"How do you know? You've not interviewed them."

Mislan nods.

"I'm torn between bringing Christine in and working on her first or bringing both of them in. Nelly was interviewed twice, including once at Waterfront. OK, we didn't ask the right questions because we didn't know about the carpark incident. But the second time when she came to identify the judge and the vic, she knew we were trying to trace the vic's movements. She should've said something then, but she didn't. She was so casual and calm when we spoke to her."

Superintendent Samsiah responds with a slow nod. "She was clearly hiding something. I suggest you bring both of them in but keep them separated. Keep Christine here and Nelly in Brickfields. Easier for you to work on her. When you're done with her, swap them: Nelly here and Christine in Brickfields."

"When I pick them up, I'm sure Chong and the judge will be nervous."

"Don't worry about them. I will handle their nervousness."

"Thanks.

"When are you picking them up?"

"Today. Tee is coming back tomorrow. That'll give me time to work on them before I'm on again."

"At the KTV?"

"Where else? I don't know where they live."

"Do it right."

"I always do."

Stepping into his office, Mislan tells Johan to go home, get some rest and come back at 4 in the evening.

"What's at 4?" Johan asks.

"We're picking up two chicks."

"Which chicks?"

"Yana, can you spare us the duty vehicle and a woman detective?"

"Sure. Take Kam, she's on today."

"Thanks."

30

The sky is dark with heavy rain expected when they leave the police contingent HQ for the Champion KTV. Johan is driving as Mislan does not have a police driving license issued by the Force to allow him to drive police vehicles. Mislan was told the training is for six months with no guarantee of you getting a license. Johan has a Police Force driving license from his days in the Mobile Patrol Vehicle (MPV) unit. When Johan drives out of the city, Detective Kamaliah, who is sitting in the back, asks where they are heading to.

"Karaoke," Johan says.

"You should've told me, then I can put on something sexy," she jests.

The sky opens up just as they turn the corner to the Champion KTV. In the pouring rain, Johan pulls up right in front of the entrance. The word 'POLIS' on the door of their car attracts the attention of arriving GROs. But with the rain pouring down, they have nowhere to go except into the KTV. Mislan suspects they must be saying to one another – *Shit, it's another pee-in-the-bottle night.* A few of the GROs hurriedly walk into the building, shielding their faces with hands or purses. Those must be the ones using drugs, Mislan presumes.

Mislan asks one of the staff at the entrance if Chong is in.

"Not yet, he usually comes in around 6," one of the greeters answers.

"Mummy Nelly and Christine?"

"In the locker room."

"Where's the locker room?"

"At the back, I'll show you."

The greeter leads the officers through the lobby along the dim hallway, with numerous karaoke rooms on each side, until they reach the back of the building. The locker room door is open and the sound of women chattering and laughing can be heard from the outside. The air is saturated with the odor of perfume, deodorant and body cream. Standing at the doorway, the staff calls for mummy Nelly and Christine.

"What?" a woman's voice calls back.

"Police want to see you."

Instantly the room falls silent.

A pencil-thin woman in her early twenties in a tight-fitting, very short blue halter dress appears. She smells like she just poured a bottle of perfume over herself.

"What do you want?" she asks Johan.

"Are you Christine?" Johan asks as mummy Nelly appears behind her.

"Yes," Nelly answers for her. "Why do you want to see us?"

"Please come with us," Johan says.

"To where?"

"To D9, IPK, KL."

Mislan notes the look of surprise on Christine's face, but Nelly's is unreadable.

"Why?" Nelly asks, doing all the talking.

"We'll explain when we are at IPK."

"I can't, I have a few bookings I need to attend to this evening."

Mislan notices a few of the GROs have gathered in the narrow hallway and doorway. Eager to listen, pushing and shoving, trying to get a ringside view of what is happening. One of them is Murni. She flashes him a tiny smile but he pretends he does not see it. For her own safety, he doesn't want the other GROs to see him smiling back.

"I'm sure another mummy can handle them for you," Johan replies. "Let's go," he says, signaling to Detective Kamaliah to escort the two women. When the detective beckons for them to follow, Christine steps forward to follow her but Nelly refuse to budge.

"You can come willingly or Detective Kamaliah will let you try on her stainless steel bracelets," Johan says firmly.

Nelly's mobile phone rings. She talks rapidly to the caller and then holds it up to Johan who in turn passes it to Mislan.

"Who's this?" Mislan asks.

"Chong. My staff said you are taking mummy Nelly and one of the girls."

"Yes, I am."

"Inspector, no need to take them. You can use my office or one of the rooms to talk to them."

"Thank you, but we have own interview rooms. You've been there, remember."

"What's this about? Mummy Nelly said you already talked to her a few days back."

"I did, and now I need to talk to her again."

"Can I come and bail her out?"

"Why do you need to? She's not being charged with anything."

"OK, OK, Inspector, I come to see you at your office."

"Please don't."

Mislan terminates the call and passes the phone back to Nelly.

"Let's go," he instructs his team.

Escorting the two women through the lounge, they notice the male staff in waiter uniforms are gathered at the bar. One of them calls out to them in a language which the officers don't understand. Mummy Nelly turns to answer but is nudged on by Kamaliah.

In the car, Mislan tells Nelly to sit in the front passenger seat, while he sits in the back with Christine sandwiched between him and Kamaliah. He instructs Nelly and Christine not to talk to each other.

He watches Christine's face all through the drive to the police contingent HQ. She notices his gaze and braves a smile, which is not reciprocated by the inspector. Once in a while he spots signs of anxiety in her eyes, but they are gone in a flash.

Mummy Nelly takes out a pack of cigarettes from her handbag and asks Johan if she can smoke.

"This is a police vehicle, smoking is prohibited," Johan answers, bringing a smile to Mislan.

His mobile phone rings, it is a number unfamiliar to him.

"Mislan."

"Inspector Mislan, this is Sallehnor."

"Yes sir," Mislan answers, surprised by the call. The judge is showing his hand.

"I was informed you and your team arrested two workers from the Champion KTV," Sallehnor says, his voice deep and calm.

"Yes sir."

"May I know the purpose of the arrest?"

"It's an ongoing investigation and I'm afraid I'm not at liberty to divulge any information on it."

"I thought I made myself clear to the OCCI and your superior Superintendent Samsiah, that I've nothing to do with the woman's death."

"Norita," Mislan says caustically. "Her name was Norita or Rita to her friends."

"Yes, I know. I also expressed my view that the people at the KTV are not involved. But you still..."

"I'm sorry, what did you base your views on? We've not concluded our investigation yet."

"I've known them for years, and I know they're not killers."

"Thank you for sharing your sentiment of them but as my superior always tells me, sentiments and feelings are not evidence."

The call goes dead.

Pulling into the police contingent HQ, Mislan's mobile phone rings. *It's starting*, he says, taking it out.

"Yes, Puan."

"Just got a call from OCCI."

"I got a call from the judge."

He hears Superintendent Samsiah chuckle. "What did he say?" she asks.

"That he knows the people at the KTV and they're not killers."

"OCCI called to ask about your arrest. He said a friend is inquiring."

"All of them are his friends except us," Mislan laughs.

"I don't have to remind you to do things by to the book. The heat is on."

"I will."

Mislan tells Detective Kamaliah to put Christine and Nelly in separate interview rooms, and get a standby to assist.

"Jo, get Kam to conduct a body search for drugs. Take their phones and personal belongings away for safekeeping." Heading to his office, he says, "And Jo, tell mummy not to make herself too comfortable, she's going to Brickfields tonight."

In the office, he asks Reeziana and Hartini to assist Kamaliah in conducting the body searches. It is Standard Operating Procedure for female detainees to only be body-searched by female personnel.

"Doing it by the book," Reeziana quips.

"Puan's instruction."

When Reeziana and Hartini leave, he heads to his private smoking area. Just as he lights up, Johan peeks through the door to tell him Superintendent Samsiah is looking for him. He puts out the cigarette and puts it back into the pack.

"Where is she?"

"Interview room 1."

"Who's in room 1?"

"Mummy Nelly. Inspector Reeziana is doing the body search. Inspector Hartini is searching Christine with Kam."

They hear footsteps, it is Superintendent Samsiah with Reeziana and Hartini.

"Puan," Mislan greets her. "Found anything on them?" he asks Reeziana and Hartini.

"Nothing," Reeziana answers. "What's your plan?"

"Like Puan suggests, send mummy Nelly to Brickfields and work on Christine."

"Why don't you get Hartini to sit in with you?" Samsiah suggests. "Jo and Kam can escort Nelly to Brickfields."

"Sure."

"Hartini, are you up to it?"

"Yes, Puan."

"Work out how the two of you want to get her to cooperate. Lan, remember they have a judge as their guardian angel."

"Why do you think he, I mean the judge, showed his hand?"

"Perhaps because he and Chong are not involved, so whichever way the wind blows he'll not be implicated."

"*Or* they're involved and desperate to kill the investigation before the evidence points to them," Reeziana counters.

Christine looks up from examining her fingernails when the two officers enter the interview room. Mislan introduces Hartini and himself, while placing his digital recorder on the table in front of her. She looks at the recorder and then back at him, raising her eyebrows.

Holding her identity card, Mislan reads out her name – Christine Lawi a/p Munggah. Age 22, with address listed in Sarikei, Sarawak.

It was earlier agreed that Hartini will start with the background interview and Mislan will observe and assess Christine's response. He nods to Hartini to begin.

"Christine, what is your relationship with Nelly?"

"She's my supervisor."

"Your personal relationship with her."

"We're from Sarawak."

"Apart from that?" Hartini asks with a warm smile.

Mislan notices that Christine is quite reluctant to elaborate on her answers. She just provides short direct ones. *Is she holding back because she is naïve – or afraid?* She seems tense and fidgety, examining her fingernails and avoiding eye contact.

Christine shrugs her bony shoulders.

"Is Nelly from Sarikei too?"

"I think so."

"Yes, she is. We checked her identity card too. In fact, her address is in the same postcode as yours."

Christine stares at Hartini, not saying anything.

"You came from the same area. Are you related to her?"

She does not answer, her facial expression and body language signifying nervousness. *What's she afraid of?* Mislan asks himself.

"Is she or isn't she related to you?" Mislan interjects firmly.

Christine turns to face him and her eyes answer his question.

"What is she, your aunt?" he makes a guess.

She replies with a tiny nod.

"Are you afraid of her?" he presses on.

"No," she answers timidly, but her eyes give her away.

Mislan sees fear in them. Suddenly her eyes dilate and the eyeballs roll up into her head. She leans back, her arms stiff and gripping the table edge. Her head tilts all the way back until she's looking at the ceiling. She groans like something is caught in her throat and her whole body starts shaking violently, like she is experiencing hysteria or a seizure. Hartini looks at Mislan, unsure of what is happening. Christine falls off her chair to the floor, wiggling and twisting wildly. Hartini jumps off her chair to check on her. Mislan opens the door, shouting for someone to call for the paramedics.

"Hartini, she seems to be choking, make sure her jaws are open," he says.

"I can't open her mouth," Hartini says as she pinches Christine's cheeks.

"Let me," he says, kneeling beside the wiggling Christine. Placing his thumb and index finger on Christine cheeks, he presses hard and with the heel of the palm of his other hand pushes down on her chin. He peeks into her mouth to see if there is any foreign object in it.

Reeziana appears at the door and Mislan asks her and Hartini to hold Christine down so she does not hurt herself.

"Yana, move the chair and table away so that she doesn't hurt herself," Mislan instructs.

"What happened?" she asks.

"I don't know, maybe a severe anxiety attack," Hartini answers.

"Tilt her head up so that her airway is clear," Mislan instructs. "Did anyone call for the paramedics?"

"Yes, Reeze did."

He hears Hartini reciting some Quran verses under her breath. Reeziana, who is kneeling next to her hears it too and turns to look at Mislan. After several minutes, Christine's wiggling weakens and slowly stops. Maybe the Quran verses Hartini recited works or maybe Christine is worn out – whatever it is, the officers let out a sigh of relief.

"Put her on her side so she can breathe easier," Mislan tells Reeziana and Hartini. "Stay with her."

The paramedics arrive, taking over from Reeziana and Hartini. They check Christine's eyes, pulse, heartbeat and for physical injury. She seems to have calmed down.

"What happened?" one of the paramedics asks.

"We were interviewing her and suddenly she started shaking and groaning," Hartini explains. "Is she going to be OK?"

"Her pulse and heart rate are still high, but she is breathing normally," he says, wheeling her to the elevator.

"Yana, she's a detainee, can you send Kam to be with her?" Mislan asks. "I'll see if Puan can get the district to arrange for the escort."

Johan arrives back from escorting mummy Nelly to Travers, Brickfields.

"What happened?" he asks.

"She had a seizure attack," Hartini says.

Johan gives her a funny look. "That's a first."

Mislan puts down the phone, saying, "Puan will arrange with Brickfields for their personnel to be with her. Yana, tell Kam to stay there until the Brickfields personnel arrives."

"What did Puan say?" Reeziana asks.

"Lodge a report of the incident," Mislan says. "I think Hartini should do it."

"Why her?"

"Yes, why me?" Hartini asks. "You're the lead and I'm only assisting."

"Because the ISCD will believe you more than me," he says with a tiny smile. ISCD stands for Integrity and Standard Compliance Department.

"But you did nothing wrong."

"You know it, I know it and maybe the ISCD will believe it but he," Mislan says, tilting his head upward, "won't. And I don't need any more run-ins with him."

Reeziana and Johan laugh. Hartini, not knowing the history between the inspector and the OCCI, looks baffled.

"I'll tell you one of these days," Reeziana tells Hartini.

"Or you'll find out yourself soon," Johan adds. "So, what really happened?"

"Nothing, we were asking her questions and suddenly she groaned, her body started shaking and getting wiggly, her eyes rolled up," Hartini answers. "She fell from the chair and..."

"What were you asking her about?"

"Her relationship with Nelly. Mislan asked if Nelly is her aunt and she nodded yes and then it started. No, Mislan asked if she was afraid of Nelly, then it started."

"Mummy Nelly must have some hold on her," Johan theorizes.

"Like what?" Mislan asks.

"Like black magic, supernatural stuff," Reeziana answers and laughs. "I told you to get a talisman to ward off the spell they cast on you. Did you?"

Mislan gives her a glare but Hartini and Johan seem to take it seriously.

"When Hartini recited the Quran verse, she started to calm down," Reeziana points out. "You still think I'm kidding?"

"Did she?" Johan asks.

Reeziana and Hartini nod.

"Holy shit!" Johan exclaims. "Puan is right about the what was it... anak kerak or the other one, the Thai thing."

"Kuman Thong, the Golden Boy," Reeziana answers.

"Yes, that thing. Believed to safeguard and protect its owner."

Mislan takes his leave when they start discussing supernatural beings and experiences they heard of.

"Hey, where're you going?" Reeziana calls after him.

"I'm not listening to this garbage," he answers and heads straight to his smoking hideout.

A few minutes later, Superintendent Samsiah appears on her normal rounds before calling it a day.

"Where's Mislan?" she asks them.

"Taking a break," Reeziana answers.

Johan goes to the emergency staircase to inform the inspector of Superintendent Samsiah's presence. Stumping his half-smoked cigarette and throwing it down the stairwell, he enters the office. Hartini is updating Superintendent Samsiah on what transpired in the interview room. Mislan joins them but says nothing.

"What was she afraid of?" Samsiah asks.

Hartini shrugs.

"Lan?"

"I don't know."

"Maybe she was afraid of her aunt Nelly," Johan suggests.

"But we've not questioned her about that night in the carpark," Hartini says.

"Maybe she knew what happened in the carpark, and it had to do with her and her aunt," Reeziana suggests. "In fear of being asked, she got all nervous and anxious. Like a kid getting his jab, the anticipation of it is what makes them resist and cry."

"Could be, she is after all just a kid," Samsiah says. "A village girl, with no experience of any run-ins with the police. Reality set in when the two of you started the interview."

The officers nod their agreement.

"Let's break for today and see how she is tomorrow. Brickfields will send their uniformed personnel to guard her. Lan, you and Jo should go home and get some rest."

"What about her remand?" Mislan asks.

"Our remand team will handle the suspect in hospital and Brickfields will arrange for Nelly."

"Thanks."

31

On his way home, Mislan stops at Kampung Pandan to buy dinner. Parking his car by the roadside, he walks to the stall where he usually gets his steamed rice with spicy fried chicken. It is closed. "Shit," he cusses under his breath. While walking back to his car, he hops into Kentucky Fried Chicken and gets himself a spicy snack plate to go.

After showering and eating his dinner, he sits at his bedroom workstation and lights a cigarette. His mind plays back the incident in the interview room. *What the hell happened?*

Christine was fine when they were in the car. She was smiling or braving a smile at him. Then when they reached the police contingent HQ, well he didn't pay much attention to her; Jo and Kam escorted them. When she was in the interview room, Kam and Hartini or Reeeziana did the body search. If they noticed anything suspicious or odd with her, he was sure they would have told him. She looked OK when he and Hartini started their interview. Yes, he noticed she was providing short crisp answers, not offering any elaboration to Hartini's questions. But that could just be her style. He did notice some level of nervousness but it was to be expected when you're being interviewed by the police.

Hartini was right, he first noticed signs of fear when she was asked about Nelly. Why was she afraid of Nelly? Could Reeziana be right, that she knew what Nelly did and feared the same would be done to her? What did Nelly do? Kill the victim?

And why would Nelly kill the victim? Murni said Nelly was the one who convinced Norita to keep the baby. She took care of her when she was going through morning sickness. Chong said Nelly was the one who asked for Norita to be excused from coming in daily and only when she was booked. After all that convincing and caring, why did she kill the victim?

Maybe it is not Nelly she's afraid of but the men Nelly handed the victim to. Maybe they warned her to keep her mouth shut, or she will be next. Maybe she was afraid for her aunt and herself.

What about the black magic suggestion and Hartini reciting verses from the Quran to chase or exorcise the spirit from her? Can he believe in such phenomena? As a criminal investigator – no.

His mobile phone rings, distracting him from his thoughts. It is his assistant.

"Yes Jo, anything?"

"I just left the hospital. The suspect's resting and the personnel from Brickfields has relieved Kam."

"Did you speak to the doctor?"

"The doctor was not around. I spoke to the duty nurse. She said the suspect had an anxiety attack but her pulse and heart rate are back to normal."

"When will she be discharged?"

"If there's no more attack, maybe tomorrow."

"Good. Did you speak to Christine?"

"No."

"OK, I'll see you tomorrow."

"After you left, we, Inspector Reeziana, Hartini and Reeze discussed about, you know..."

Mislan laughs, cutting Johan off mid-sentence.

"I know you don't believe in such things, but a lot of people do."

"And...?"

"Maybe you should consider that angle."

"Good night, Jo, we'll talk about it tomorrow."

Lying in bed, Johan's word plays on his mind. Yes, as a Malay he grew up with folklores and stories about black magic. It is an integral fabric of Malay society, urban and rural. Malays are Malays no matter where they live, even in a faraway foreign land. Like Superintendent Samsiah says, we all bring our beliefs and superstition wherever we go. He remembers seeing India's top-ranking male badminton double players on tour – Chirag Shetty and Satwiksairaj Rankireddy. Every time they entered or reentered the court, they would touch the sidelines with their rackets and kiss it.

Getting out of bed, he sits at the workstation and lights a cigarette, thinking. Christine and Nelly are not Muslim. Do they believe in something like Kuman Thong? Anak kerak is not well-known and is mainly confined to people from the East Coast. 'Deviant' teachings and practices in the country are closely monitored and acted upon by the Islamic agencies. Kuman Thong, however, exists in some Buddhist communities. Therefore, it is not under the purview of Islamic agencies.

He Googles Kuman Thong again. He rereads the literature to get a better understanding of how they are turned into the Golden Boy. None of the pages say anything about the fetus age, if it has to be early stage or full term. Glancing at his mobile phone, the time shows 9.18 pm.

Saying to himself that it is 8.18 pm in Thailand, he makes a call. After several rings, a woman answers.

"*Sawadee ka,* Inspector," Dr. Suthisa Ritchu, or Sophia to them, answers.

"*Sawadee krap,* Doctor," Mislan replies with the Thai greeting he picked up during his cross-border investigation. "Am I disturbing you?"

"No, no, I'm just relaxing watching television. Anything?"

"Doc, can you tell me about Kuman Thong?"

"About what?"

"Kuman Thong, the Golden Boy."

"Oh," she utters in surprise. "What do you like to know?"

"I've been reading about it on Google but there's something more that I need to understand which is not explained."

"May I ask, why are you interested in it?"

"I have a case where a fetus was stolen from a deceased mother. Superintendent Samsiah suggested I look at the possibility of black magic being the motive."

"She may be right. Other than for legal medical research, why else would you need a fetus? Back to the question, what do you wish to know?"

"For the purpose of making Kuman Thong, the fetus has to be at what stage of pregnancy?"

"The belief and practice of Kuman Thong as a divinity is strong here. In simple terms, there're two types of Kuman Thong:

the black magic and the white magic. The black magic is made from a fetus killed in the mother's womb. Usually, the mother is killed and the fetus stolen, but not necessarily so. The fetus can be obtained through abortion. It is used for evil purposes. The fetus can be at any term of pregnancy, as long as it is still in the womb." She pauses to catch her breath. "The white magic, these are made after the natural death of a baby, meaning stillborn or a miscarriage or an infant that died after birth. The spirits of these babies are transferred through prayer to a statue by a monk. Have I answered your questions, Inspector?"

"Yes. Is it legal in Thailand?"

"The white magic is. The black magic Kuman Thong is more widespread in Cambodia but not here. Here it's the white magic, even I have one in my house," Dr. Suthisa admits, laughing. "Oh, if you have a black magic Kuman Thong you have to feed it with food that a child likes: fruit, cake and sweet drinks. If you don't, the child spirit will be angry and harm you."

"How do you know if it's a black or white magic Kuman Thong?"

"Only the owner can tell you. However, if you locate a dried fetus wrapped in red cloth then it is black magic."

"What about white magic, I mean the fetus?"

"The fetus or baby is buried or cremated like for an ordinary death. It's only the spirit that is transferred to the statue."

"I read you can buy them in Thailand, is it true?"

"Sadly yes. As you know there are a lot of working women here. When they get pregnant they usually go for abortion, illegal abortion as it is not legal here unless of course due to medical reasons. Unfortunately, like in any other country there are unscrupulous people that take advantage of the situation to make money."

"Hmmm. Thank you Doc, you've been very helpful."

"Don't mention it. Give my regards to *P'*Samsiah and *Khun* Jo."

"I will."

"*Ratrisawat*," Doctor Suthisa says, meaning good night.

Not knowing what it means, Mislan answers, "Yes, *sawadee krap*."

32

Mislan arrives at the office happy to see that Inspector Tee is back on duty. Tee, Reeziana and Hartini are at the pantry having breakfast and chatting gaily. Earlier, Johan had called to tell him there will be no nasi lemak this morning as he is going straight to the hospital to check on their detainee, Christine. Putting his backpack at his desk, he joins them.

"Tee, welcome back. How was your New Year?"

"Hectic as usual, visit this uncle, this aunt, this cousin, that cousin, no ending."

Mislan laughs.

"It's only once a year," Hartini says. "Like my mother said, see them while they're alive, don't wait until they're dead to visit the grave."

"Yana and Tini were telling me about your detainee. Now I know why you asked me about kwai chai, the devil boy."

"He did? When?" Reeziana asks.

"A few days back. He called me but wouldn't say why."

"So, you do believe in it but pretend you don't," she says.

"I don't believe in it," Mislan says. "I just wanted to know more and see if it's a possible motive."

"And?"

"It's plausible."

"You're converted," Hartini points out. "Now a believer of the mystical supernatural beings."

"I said it's plausible. The killer or killers may have stolen the fetus for such a reason."

"But your victim was not murdered for the same reason," Reeziana states. "Are you saying the one who stole the fetus found your victim dead and decided 'What a waste of a good fetus for black magic' and stole it?"

Tee and Hartini laugh at Reeziana's suggestion.

"No. How do you dispose of a fetus, anyway?" Mislan asks. "I only know a bit about the Islamic teaching. What about the Chinese, Indian, and others?"

"What is the Islamic way of handling it?" Tee inquires.

"It depends on the stage of pregnancy, at this stage you need to do this and at this stage you need to do this and that. The gist of it, you still have to give it a proper burial. What about the Chinese?"

"As you know, a Chinese need not necessarily be Buddhist, they can be Taoist, Confucian, Christian or atheist. So the way they handle a dead fetus varies. In general, I think they offer prayers for the dead fetus so that it will not turn into a kwai chai and haunt you," Tee explains.

"The fetus, what happens to it?" Reeziana asks.

"I think, but you cannot take it as fact, most of them leave it to the hospital or clinic to handle it."

"You mean dispose of it?"

"Yes, the way they dispose of body parts."

"So, if an unscrupulous hospital staff takes and sells it, the mother would not know," Mislan points out.

"I suppose so."

"In other words, it's possible to get hold of a non-Malay fetus because most are left to the hospital or clinic to handle it, but not a Malay fetus. Interesting," Mislan says.

The front desk detective announces morning-prayer is starting in five minutes.

X

Superintendent Samsiah welcomes Tee back and hopes he had a good New Year. Hartini briefs on the call-outs during their shift. She gives a brief update on what transpired during the interview with Christine. As instructed earlier, she has lodged a police report on the incident.

"You? Not Mislan?" Samsiah asks.

"Mislan suggested that I make the report," Hartini answers.

"He is the lead and the senior. The report should be by him. Lan, what's your reason?"

"ISCD," Reeziana answers for him.

"I asked for a reason, not an excuse. You've done nothing wrong. I'll not tolerate similar behavior in the future. The lead or most senior officer shall take responsibility for what happened in his or her investigation. Do I make myself clear?"

All the officers nod.

"Ghani's transfer has been approved. He will be on leave before reporting to his new position at General Operation. I know he's not popular among you, but I'll be organizing a farewell dinner and I expect all of you and your assistants to attend, including detectives who wish to."

"In that case, why not have it at the office so that all can be there?" Hartini suggests.

"That's a good idea," Samsiah agrees. "Can I put you in charge of organizing it?"

"Glad to."

"Good. Let's have it this Friday at 7. I'll inform Ghani. Back to your case, how is the detainee?"

"Jo is there to make sure of her remand order. Last night he visited her and said she was resting. The nurse told him she had an anxiety attack. Her pulse and heart rate are back to normal and if all is stable, she'll be discharged today," Mislan updates.

"The magistrate will not be there this early," Reeziana states. "He or she will usually go after lunch after finishing with the in-court remands."

"Chances are the hospital will release her after lunch," Samsiah says.

"I don't mind going there to interview her," Mislan offers.

"I think you should wait for her to be released," Samsiah advises.

"It's better if I interview her there. Should she go into another one of her anxiety attacks, the doctor can immediately attend to her."

"Check with the doctor if you can interview her before you do."

Reeziana tags along with Mislan to the hospital. At the ward where Christine is detained, Mislan asks the duty nurse if he can speak to the doctor in charge. The nurse asks them to wait while she pages for him. They watch the detainee from the nurses' station. She looks fine and is chatting with the uniformed policewoman guarding her.

They see a doctor entering the ward and the nurse points them out to her. Dr. Siew introduces herself to the officers and asks what the visit is about.

"The patient, Christine," Mislan says, pointing to the detainee, "can we talk to her?"

"Yes, she is fine. We're waiting for her to be discharged."

"What was wrong with her?" Reeziana asks.

"She has a history of epilepsy and did not take her medication."

"Is she on it now?" Mislan asks.

"Yes she is but after her discharge we wouldn't know."

"What can trigger her epilepsy?"

"Not taking her medication is one of the triggers; stress, hunger, not enough sleep and many others. The trigger in every patient is different, hard to tell unless you dig deep into their history."

"In her case?"

"It was not taking her medication."

"Thanks."

Christine sees the officers coming and eye-gestures to the policewoman who is chatting with her and sitting on the edge of her bed. The policewoman literally jumps off the bed to stand.

"Christine, how are you feeling?" Mislan asks.

She replies with a smile.

"This is Inspector Reeziana," he introduces.

Again, Christine acknowledges with a smile.

"We're here to ask you some questions, are you up to it?" Mislan asks, taking out his digital recorder.

She looks at the policewoman as if asking her opinion. Mislan sees the policewoman nod. He notices the policewoman is wearing a nametag with **Lucy** and does not look Chinese. He guesses she must be from East Malaysia, Sabah or Sarawak. He asks Lucy to sit at the nurses' counter while they conduct the interview. Reeziana sits on the edge of the bed and Mislan pulls up a plastic chair.

"Christine, can you tell us what happened at the KTV carpark seven nights ago after closing time?" Mislan asks straight to the point.

"You mean the night the girl was vomiting?"

"Yes. Do you know who the girl was?" Reeziana asks.

"The one who died, right?"

Mislan shows her the photo of Norita from his mobile phone. "Is this the girl? Norita?"

"Yes."

"OK, tell us what happened."

"A few girls came to see, but then after a while they left."

"Who was attending to Rita?"

"Mummy."

"You mean Nelly?"

"Yes."

"Then?"

"Then the girl was OK and stood up."

"Then?"

"I left because my booking was waiting for me at the car."

"What about Nelly?"

"She stayed with the girl."

"Only Nelly was with Rita?"

"And William."

"William? Who is William? A customer?"

"Mummy's son."

"Your cousin?"

"Yes."

"Where did he come from? I mean, did he drive there to pick Nelly up?"

"No. From the KTV, he works as a waiter. They always go back together."

"So you saw Nelly, William and Rita leave together?"

"No, when I left with my booking they were still there."

"How do you know that?"

"My booking drove past them to go out of the carpark."

Mislan purses his lips, looking at Reeziana.

"Your booking, was it the whole night or a short game?" Reeziana asks.

"Short game."

"OK, so you went with your booking, then what happened?" When Reeziana asks the question, Mislan notices Christine blinking rapidly and then her eyes wander around the ward. She does not seem to be focusing on them anymore. "Shit," he curses under his breath. He has a feeling she's going to have another attack.

"Christine, what happened after you went with your booking?" Reeziana asks again.

Christine focuses back on them. Mislan sees fear in her eyes.

"Where do you stay?" Mislan asks, changing the subject.

"I don't know the hotel's name."

"We're not here about your booking. We're not from the Vice unit," Reeziana says.

Reeziana's reassurance calms her.

"I mean, where do you stay if you're not booked?" Mislan rephrases his earlier question.

"With mummy."

"At her house?"

"Yes, I don't have enough money to rent by myself."

"OK, so short game booking. How many hours is that, two, three?" Reeziana continues.

"Two hours."

"Then what happened?"

"My booking sent me home."

"To?"

"Mummy's house in Ampang."

"You mean Taman Kosas?"

Christine nods.

"Tell us what happened when you arrived at mummy Nelly's house."

Instead of answering, she stares at Mislan. Her lips quiver.

"It's OK, you can tell us, you're not in any trouble," Reeziana assures her.

"I opened the gate and William was carrying Rita out of the house. He told me she was drunk and he wanted to send her home."

"Where did William carry Rita to?" Mislan asks.

"The car I think, because he said he wanted to send her home."

"Did you see him putting Rita in the car?"

"No, because I was already entering the house."

"Where was mummy Nelly?"

"I heard her doing something in the kitchen."

"How did you know it was mummy Nelly? Did you see or talk to her?" Mislan asks.

"No, but who else could it be? Only three of us stay in the house. William was outside so it had to be mummy Nelly in the kitchen."

"OK, did you know what she was doing?"

"No, I went straight up to my room."

"What time was that?"

"Maybe 2.30 or 3 am."

"Did Nelly know or see you come back?"

"I don't know, but William knew."

"Did Nelly or William talk to you about that night?"

Christine shakes her head.

"Anything else you can tell us?"

Christine again shakes her head.

Mislan looks at Reeziana and she nods.

"You've been very helpful. Thank you, we'll let you get some rest now."

X

Leaving the hospital ward, Mislan makes a call to his assistant, asking his whereabouts. Johan says he just arrived at the office.

"Stay at the office and get the standby to be there too," Mislan instructs.

"What's up?"

"We've got a new lead. I'm on my way back to the office with Yana."

"What's she doing with you? She just finished her shift."

"Tagging along for the ride. Is Puan in?"

"Don't know. You want me to check?"

"It's alright. See you soon." He terminates the call.

Reeziana asks him what his next move is.

"Pick William up. Nelly's son."

"Didn't you know she has a son?"

"She did say it but it didn't occur to me to ask how old he was or where he was working."

"You think they killed your victim?"

Mislan glances at her.

"She didn't say anything about them killing her. She said she bumped into William carrying the vic out, William could be telling the truth, that the victim was drunk and he was sending her home," she suggests. "You said the doctor told you her blood alcohol level was high."

"At that hour? Why not just let her sleep it off at their house? The vic lived all the way across town in Kota Damansara. If they wanted to send her home, it would've been easier to go from the KTV, which is close by."

"Makes sense. But what was their motive for killing her?"

"I don't know. I hope to find out soon."

"You think it had anything to do with the judge or Chong?"

"Anything is possible. Until we get William in, no point in guessing."

Reaching the office, he tells Johan to check with Travers, Brickfields if Nelly is back from the court for her remand. He and Reeziana go to the office of Superintendent Samsiah, who is surprised to see Reeziana still there after her twenty-four hours shift.

"Why are you still here?" she asks.

"Don't feel like going back yet."

"Did you interview the suspect?" she asks Mislan.

Mislan briefs his boss on the interview and the new lead.

"So she saw Nelly's son carrying the victim out of the house, but did not see them killing her," says Samsiah.

Mislan opens his mouth to say something but Samsiah raises her hand to stop him.

"Let's examine her statement before we make any move. Remember there's a judge involved. She did not know if the victim was dead or alive when she saw Nelly's son carrying her. She did not see Nelly but heard someone in the kitchen. Am I right?"

Mislan and Reeziana nod.

"Your deduction that they killed her is based on…?"

"One, the son was working at the KTV so he did not come from outside to the carpark as we theorized. Two, Christine said they were the last two persons with the vic. Her short game booking drove past them. Three, she said Nelly and son always went back together. Four, she bumped into the son carrying the vic supposedly to the car between 2.30 to 3 am. Five, she said she heard someone doing something in the kitchen when she went upstairs. Six, the vic was staying across town, if they were to send her home it would be nearer from the KTV."

"And their motive would be…?"

"I don't know, perhaps as we theorized: doing a favor for the judge or Chong," Mislan says desperately.

"Let me play the devil's advocate. If they killed the vic, why do it at their house? Why not do it along the way and then dump her?" Samsiah probes.

"The fetus. They couldn't be cutting the vic up by the roadside. They needed to do it somewhere private, where they felt safe and without being seen. What better place than at their house?"

"Yana?" Samsiah asks.

"I'm with Mislan."

"What's you next move?"

"I need a search warrant for their house and car."

"Anything else?"

"When Nelly comes back from remand, I want her here."

"And the son?"

"Here too. I want to pit the mother against the son, see who will break first."

"You want Tee to assist?"

Mislan turns to Reeziana. "Are you up to it? You know the whole story and the witness statement. Tee just came back from holiday and he's not familiar with the case."

"Give me a couple hours of shut-eye and I'll be ready."

"It's settled then."

33

Chew Beng Song from Federal Forensic and his team are already waiting in front of Nelly's house when Mislan and his team arrive with the search warrant. The house is an intermediate double-story terrace with a small front yard. The police presence attracts the neighborhood residents and within minutes the road in front of the house is crowded with them. Most of them are holding up their mobile phones videoing the police.

Mislan and his team walk up to the front door, knock and announce their presence. After several knocks, the door is opened by a very sleepy man in his early twenties.

"William?" Mislan asks.

The man rubbing his sleepy eyes nods.

"We have a warrant to search your house and car. Please stand aside," Mislan instructs and signals for the forensic team to come forward. "Jo, place William under arrest."

Syed gets William to turn around, and cuffs him.

"Chew, can you start with the kitchen?" Mislan asks. "The witness said she heard someone doing something back there when she arrived."

"Will do," Chew says and leads his team to the kitchen.

"Jo, Syed, take William to the kitchen to witness the forensic search."

Unlike in the US where the house owner or occupant need not be present during the search, here it is a must – unless, of course, it is an abandoned premise or the owner is not traceable.

Mislan hears one of Chew's technicians call out, "We got blood, lots of blood." He walks to the kitchen and sees a technician shining the blue light on the floor of the bathroom next to it. The whole floor, especially around the water discharge trap, lights up under the blue light. The technician takes several swabs of the blood around the trap and passes them to Chew.

"We got hairs too," the technician says.

Mislan sees him picking up several strands of long black hair with plastic tweezers and putting them in an evidence bag. One of the technicians is examining the kitchen knives. He swabs a knife handle and drops a few drops of Luminol on the cotton swab.

"I've got blood on this knife," he says, showing the light blueish cotton swab.

"It could be chicken or fish blood. How do you know it's human blood?" Mislan asks Chew.

"Human blood contains hemoglobin that makes the blood illuminate when it comes in contact with Luminol. Most animal blood does not contain hemoglobin. Anyway, when we get back to the lab we'll be running more tests and DNA sampling. For now, we take it as human blood."

"Good. Let's finish here and go up to the bedrooms."

Walking out to the living room, Mislan observes William's face for reaction on the discovery of blood in the bathroom and on the knife. William probably isn't so much sleepy as hungover, so he doesn't seem to understand what is going on. Most of the time he is leaning against the wall with his eyes shut.

Mislan walks out of the house. The crowd has grown and he thinks a few of them are from the press. He lights a cigarette and sits on a stool by the door.

He hears a familiar voice call his name. Looking around, he spots Audi smiling and waving. When they make eye contact, she walks up to the gate. A detective stops her and she says something to him, pointing to Mislan sitting on the stool. The detective turns to look at him and lets her through.

"You can't come in here," Mislan says, "it's a crime scene."

"I'm just talking to you outside here," she says, poking her head to peek through the open door. "What did you find?"

"Nothing," he lies.

"If nothing, how come it's a crime scene?"

Mislan smiles at her.

"The neighbors told me this house belongs to a karaoke mummy. Is she a mummy at the same KTV as your victim?"

Mislan nods.

"Tell me what you found."

"You can't broadcast it, not until the lab confirms it."

"Of course."

"Blood."

"You found blood, where?"

"In the bathroom."

"It could be menstruation blood. You know the house owner is a woman."

"It could be." Mislan smiles at her silly suggestion, knowing she is fishing for information.

"But it's not," Audi says. "Your victim was killed by strangulation, so you think the baby was removed from the womb here."

"I don't know, we're still investigating."

"That's the reason you're looking for blood. That makes sense. What could be her motive?"

Mislan shrugs.

He hears Johan calling for him.

"I've got to go. Please go back out to the road."

"Call me after you're done," Audi says, walking out.

The forensic team is done with the kitchen and is going upstairs to the bedrooms. Mislan follows them, with Syed tugging William in tow. At the landing, Mislan tells Chew to speed things up; some of his technicians can do the suspect's car. Chew agrees and instructs two technicians to do the car.

"Don't remove anything unless the suspect is called to witness it," Chew says.

Chew's team starts with the master bedroom.

"Whose room is this?" Mislan asks William.

"Mummy's."

"OK, sit there." Mislan points to the bed.

A technician examines the bathroom, while Johan and another technician search the cupboard and drawers. In one of the drawers, the technician finds a mobile phone hidden between panties and bras. After snapping a few photos, he bags it and shows it to Chew.

"Can you switch it on?" Mislan asks.

Chew presses the on button but nothing happens. "I think the battery was taken out."

"Whose phone is this?" Mislan asks William.

He shakes his head.

The same technician finds a woman's black clutch bag in the bottom drawer. It contains a coin purse, lipstick, condoms and some pills. He bags the items and hands them to Chew.

"Chew, you can test the lipstick for DNA?" Mislan asks.

"Should be able to."

"And dust the clutch bag and all the items for prints."

"We'll do that too, back at the lab."

Johan, who is searching the cupboard, calls Mislan over. "You may want to have a look at these."

Johan pushes the hanging dresses to one side. Behind the dresses is hidden a small red cloth the size of a handkerchief with black characters, in a script he doesn't understand, on it. There is a ball of light brown gunny string next on it.

"What is it?" Johan asks Mislan.

"I've seen it before in my research on Kuman Thong. I think it's something you wrap the fetus with."

"Serious?!"

"Check it out," Mislan tells him.

"No way, I'm not touching that thing."

"Chew," Mislan calls him over, "take a look at this."

"What is that?" Chew asks.

"I think it's some sort of prayer cloth."

Chew asks a technician to take photos of the red cloth and the roll of string. He nonchalantly picks them up and places them in an evidence bag.

"There are two pieces of cloth," he says.

"Are you not going to check them for DNA?" Johan asks.

"Any reason to check for DNA?" Shifting the hanging dresses to another side, Chew checks if there is anything else to be found.

"Inspector Mislan thinks the cloth is used to wrap fetuses."

Mislan shows Chew a photo of Kuman Thong from his mobile phone.

"The cloths look like they have not been used," Chew points out.

"Give it a try, who knows?"

They hear one of the technicians examining the car calling for William to be brought down. Johan and Syed escort him down to the driveway.

"What did you find?" Johan asks.

"Hair on the passenger seat and in the boot. Same color as those found in the kitchen bathroom," the technician answers. "We also found a pair of black high heels in the boot which I don't think belongs to the women staying in the house, it looks too small compared to those in the house. Just to be sure, we'll bag them too."

"Anything else?"

"Prints on the door and a folded scarf with crumples on both ends. Like it was used to tie something. We'll check it for foreign matter back at the lab."

"Good work."

34

By the time his team arrives back at police contingent HQ, it is 2.45 pm. According to the front desk, his detainee Nelly is already in holding. Entering his office, he sees Reeziana at her desk.

"What time did you arrive?" Mislan asks.

"About fifteen minutes ago."

"Had your lunch?"

She nods. "How was the search?"

"Forensic found blood and hair in the back bathroom, possibly the knife used to cut her up, and two pieces of red cloth with black characters written on them and a ball of gunny string. A woman's black clutch bag, containing lipstick and condoms. We also found a mobile phone but it had no battery, so Chew has to work on it at the lab. Oh, I think we have the murder weapon, a scarf."

"Woah, so much damming evidence."

"Yes, but we still have to wait for the DNA results on the blood to put the nail in her coffin."

"The son said anything?"

"Didn't question him yet. Best if we do it here, get video statements from him and her."

"You want me to interview him or her?"

"Let's both do her and let Tee do him."

"Check with Puan, maybe she can sit in with Tee."

Johan comes in with packed lunch for himself and Mislan.

"Jo, has William been given lunch?"

"I told Syed to get for him."

While Mislan and Johan are having their late lunch, Superintendent Samsiah walks into the office. She signals for Reeziana and Tee to join her at the pantry.

"I heard you had a successful hunt," she says.

"More than successful," Reeziana answers for them.

"Good job." She pauses, looking at Mislan. "I don't know how this will play in your investigation. The judge's DNA matched the parental DNA taken from your victim."

Mislan, Reeziana, Tee and Johan gawk at her, stunned. Then all eyes turn to Mislan.

He looks lost. Initially his prime suspect was the judge, because he had the means, opportunity and motive. Halfway through his investigation, his theory went south. When his investigation started moving on a fast track, he discarded his first theory. Now, this DNA links his struck-off prime suspect back to the case.

"The judge paid Nelly to do it?" Johan surmises.

"I'm not too sure he did," Mislan says.

"Why is that?" Samsiah asks.

"We found two pieces of red cloth with prayer writing on them… fetus wrappers in her bedroom. This may sound silly, but I'm thinking she did it on her own or with her son. I think she's selling them like the case I read of the British Taiwanese man."

"How would she market it?"

"She's a karaoke mummy, I'm sure she has many contacts, especially businessmen. Times are bad and they believe divine spirits can help them prosper again. In fact, come to think of it, I saw small boy figurines in the KTV and also at Gary's office."

"I saw one too at Andrew's office," Johan points out.

"I think we should leave the judge out of this for the time being. Let's interview them and hear what they've got to say," Samsiah suggests. "You're doing it simultaneously?"

"I'm thinking Yana and I will do Nelly and Tee can do the son."

"I'll sit in with you, and Yana can do it with Tee. As you said, she knows the case," Samsiah suggests. "What time are you starting?"

"In thirty minutes."

"I'll get D6 to set up the videos." The D6 is the Technical Aid department.

"Thanks."

One of the detectives informs him the videos are set up and the detainees are ready; Nelly in room 1 and William in room 2.

Mislan makes a call to Superintendent Samsiah, saying they are ready. Mislan walks with Reeziana and Tee to the interview room and sees Superintendent Samsiah standing in the hallway.

"Room 1," he informs her.

Nelly is wearing the baggy orange lockup outfit. Her hair is rumpled, with dark bags under her eyes with no makeup to hide them. She looks haggard from spending the night in the police lockup, like she had not slept the whole time. Probably, also because she was deprived of her nicotine fix. Murni did say she is a heavy smoker, his brand of cigarettes.

Sitting facing her, Mislan tries to read her expression, but her eyes are just red, watery and blank. No emotion or reaction. He indicates to the D6 technician they are ready to start. The technician gives the thumbs up and leaves the room.

Mislan states, for the purpose of the interview, the date, time, case number and those present.

Reading from the detainee's identity card, he says, "Nelly Kalong Tukiet, can you tell us your present house address?"

"23, Jalan Mawar, Taman Kosas, Ampang, Selangor."

"Who's staying at the address with you?"

"My son and my niece."

"Their names?"

"William and Christine."

"And the address in your identity card, who's staying there?"

"My mother and brothers."

"Where are you currently working?"

"Champion KTV, in Sri Hartamas."

"Your position there?"

"Mummy."

"By mummy you mean supervisor?"

She nods.

"Please answer verbally for the video," he says.

"Yes."

"What do the GROs, staff and customers of the Champion KTV call you?"

"Mummy, or mummy Nelly."

"Do you know of a GRO by the name of Norita Mokhtar, also known as Rita by the GROs and customers of the Champion KTV?"

"Yes."

"Rita, was she under your supervision?"

"Yes."

"Three nights before Chinese New Year, can you tell me what happened at the carpark around midnight?"

She looks at Mislan without answering his question. Mislan thinks he sees a miniscule grin. But he definitely sees a flicker in her eyes.

"Let me remind you that you're to answer the question by Inspector Mislan," Samsiah says.

"I repeat, three nights before Chinese New Year, can you tell me what happened in the carpark next to Champion KTV around midnight?"

"You know what happened," Nelly answers mockingly.

"I'd like to hear your version of it," Mislan says.

No answer from Nelly.

"Did you see Rita at the carpark?"

No answer.

"Since you're not willing to answer my question, let me tell you my version of what happened in the carpark on the night in question. If I'm wrong, you can correct me. How does that sound to you?"

She pouts and shrugs, as if saying – whatever.

"Several witnesses put you in the carpark around midnight, assisting Norita when she was sick and vomiting."

"What's wrong with that?"

"Nothing. Then what happened?"

No answer. As there is no response, Mislan continues.

"When Norita said she was OK, the witnesses left, leaving you and your niece Christine with her. Then your son William came from the KTV to join you. Christine had a booking, so she left, leaving you and William with Norita. Am I right so far?"

"If you say so."

"Why don't you finish the story for me?" Mislan offers with a smile.

No response, just a tired blank expression on her face. Mislan knows she is a tough cookie. He remembers how calm and collected she was when they first interviewed her. She will not offer or admit to anything unless he can present strong evidence against her through eyewitnesses or forensic evidence. He has no eyewitness except for what happened before the fact in question. Forensic evidence will not be available to him until tomorrow or the day after. Superintendent Samsiah recognizes and feels her lead investigator's frustration. She whispers to Mislan to terminate the interview.

Mislan states for the record the date and time the interview is temporarily suspended, and turns off the video. He calls for a standby detective to guard the suspect and they step outside. Mislan tells Superintendent Samsiah he needs to go to the washroom. She knows he is going for his nicotine fix.

While having a smoke, he makes a call to Chew.

"Chew, I know you won't get the DNA result until tomorrow but I just need to know if the blood found in the washroom and knife is that of a human," he asks.

"Yes, we did the test and it is positive for human blood, type O."

"What about the clutch bag and its contents? Have you checked them for prints?"

"We did and got some partials, insufficient to hold up in court as a positive match. Sorry."

"Don't worry about court, who did the prints match with?"

"We did manual comparison of the partials and I can safely say it's your victim but…"

"Thanks, that's all I need to know for now."

Superintendent Samsiah is brewing a pot of tea when Mislan returns from the washroom. She asks if he wants a cup, which he declines.

"I know you're a coffee person but you should give tea a try. It's calming and good for your health," she says, walking back to her seat with her cup of tea.

Mislan smiles at her suggestion.

"Lan, your frustration is showing and I'm sure the suspect can see it too. What are you after? Her admission?" she asks.

Mislan sighs heavily.

"You know with the latest amendment to Section 113 of the CPC, admissions cannot be used in court."

Mislan nods.

"Even if she admits it, you still have to prove your case through evidence."

"I just want to hear it from her mouth. I want to hear her admitting to killing the vic and cutting the baby out," he says.

"You don't know what happened, I mean who killed your victim. It could be her or her son. That's a missing element in your case."

Mislan nods.

"*If* your victim was killed at her house or in the car…" she says. "The statement by Christine was she bumped into William carrying the victim between 2.30 to 3 am coming out of the house. We may presume the victim was already dead at that time."

Mislan nods.

"This is my suggestion. Come up with a story that points to the son as the killer. Whether it was done in the car or in their house, it does not matter."

Mislan gazes at her, his forehead winkling.

"She's a mother. As a mother, I'm sure she would not throw her son under the bus."

"You think she will take the blame?"

"I don't know, but I'm sure she will offer her version of the story to protect her son. That's what a mother does."

"A normal sane mother," Mislan sneers.

"You said yourself, you don't think the murder was premeditated. She may not deny that her son killed the victim, but she comes out with a story that it was an accident. Her son wanted to have sex with the victim but when she refused, he became angry and chocked her. He didn't mean to kill her but it went too far. So, it's culpable homicide not amounting to murder, prison term not more than ten years."

Mislan raises his eyebrows at the plausibility of the suggestion to create reasonable doubt.

"Anyway, I called Chew, he confirmed the blood is human, type 'O'. He managed to lift partial prints form the clutch bag and items found in it, but it's insufficient for a positive match. He did a visual comparison and said the minutiae matched with the vic's print."

"Use that to loosen your suspect's tongue."

Inspector Mislan and Superintendent Samsiah reenter the interview room. Nelly is napping, with her head on the desk facing away from the door. Mislan slams his palms on the table, rudely startling the suspect awake. She stares menacingly at Mislan, accompanied by saying something in the Iban language. The manner it was said tells him it is not complimentary.

Mislan instructs her to sit properly and switches on the video, stating the date, time, and those present.

"I'll continue from where we left off, my version of what happened," Mislan begins.

Mummy Nelly responds with body language saying – *whatever*.

"You told Rita that Chong was delayed and that he had asked you to send her home. She believed and trusted you. You and your son put her in the front passenger seat while you drove with your son in the backseat. On the way, your son used the scarf he found on the backseat, put it around Rita's neck and strangled her to death."

Nelly stares with narrowed eyes at him, jaws clenched tight, biting her lower lip. From her expression, he believes he has gotten it right.

"This is where I've not figured it out yet: why didn't you stop him? Perhaps you didn't realize what was happening. It was dark and you were driving, concentrating on the road. And perhaps even a little tipsy yourself."

Mislan pauses to read Nelly's reaction. She just holds her stare.

"But you know what? I'm inclined to believe you and your son were in cahoots. Mother asked the son to kill, that was why you did not stop him from strangling Rita to death. Never mind, let's continue, you can correct me later," Mislan says.

He sees a flicker of rage in her eyes as she frowns.

"Then when you reached home, you decided to cut the fetus out to throw us off track. You knew the judge had an affair with Rita and that she was pregnant. By cutting her baby out, you hoped the police would suspect the judge as the murderer or was involved with it. Well, you almost succeeded."

The suspect is not willing to say anything. He looks to Superintendent Samsiah for support.

"Nelly, this is your chance to tell your version of the story," Samsiah says. "We've strong forensic evidence that Rita was strangled to death by your son using a scarf found in your car. We also have blood and hair evidence that Rita was dissected in the washroom next to your kitchen. We've evidence of blood on the knife being used. We found her mobile phone in your room. If you don't say anything, we'll charge you and your son for the murder of Norita."

"My son has nothing to do with it," Nelly mumbles.

"Then tell us how your son is not involved. We have witness testimony that your son was carrying Rita's body out from your house."

"He's a good son. He was only following my instructions."

"You instructed him to strangle Rita?"

"No."

"Then, you're saying *you* strangled Rita?"

Nelly remains silent. To Mislan's relief, her stare shifts to Superintendent Samsiah. Her mouth twitches like she is chanting something. *Probably calling on her Kuman Thong to do its evil deeds for her*, Mislan says to himself. As if she read his thoughts, she turns to stare at him. "Shit," he cusses. Her unblinking eyes are red with rage. *She's turning into the devil itself! Can she?*

Superintendent Samsiah's mobile phone rings, distracting his thoughts. She holds up the phone, saying she needs to take the call, and steps out, leaving Mislan with the red-eyed suspect.

Mislan flashes Nelly a smile, hoping to pacify her. It has the opposite effect. Her eyes seem to become redder, if that is possible. Suddenly, she utters something in a language he does not understand.

"Are you casting a spell on me?" Mislan asks.

She replies with a nasty grin and narrowing of her eyes.

"I can tell you, that shit don't work on me," Mislan says, chuckling to hide his trepidation.

Superintendent Samsiah reenters the interview room, saying to Mislan the OCCI wants to see her now. Relieved, Mislan terminates the interview and calls for a standby detective to guard the suspect.

35

Bringing her notepad, Superintendent Samsiah decides to take the stairs two floors up to the Officer in Charge of Criminal Investigation (OCCI), Assistant Commissioner of Police Baharuddin Mohd. Sidek, whose office is nicknamed the Ego Chamber by officers. His personal assistant greets Samsiah and ushers her in. Standing erect at the door, she greets the OCCI, who returns her greeting with uncharacteristic warmth.

"Samsiah, come in, come in," he says with a wide smile, pointing to the visitor's chair.

Instantly she is on guard. Taking a seat, she wonders what the hell she is in for.

"How have you been keeping? Busy as usual I'm sure," he says, shaking his head. "I don't know what this city is turning into, with the crime rate increasing by the day."

"I'm fine, thank you, sir. Is there something that you want, because I'm in the middle of interviewing a suspect," she says, hoping it will cut the meeting short.

"I won't take too much of your time. Judge Sallehnor came to know that his DNA matched that of the parental DNA of the stolen baby. And he…"

"How did he come to know this information?" Samsiah interjects, looking Baharuddin straight in the eye. "Only D9 and D10 know it."

"It doesn't matter how he knew," Baharuddin says defensively. "He called to ask me if we can keep it out of the public's knowledge ... the media."

"It looks like it can't – because even when only D9 and D10 know it, he somehow was informed," she mocks.

"Yes, yes, but can your department not reveal it to the public?"

"It depends on the testimonies and evidence. If it leads to him, it will have to come out. If not now, later during the court case. Apart from us in D9, there are many other people that are privy to the information."

"D10?"

"One of many. The hospital, the DNA data technicians and others."

Baharuddin sighs heavily.

"Is that all, sir?" Samsiah asks, standing.

"Yes, yes thank you."

Walking down the staircase back to her office, she feels sorry for the OCCI. A man who makes promises to please others, to get into their good books … promises he has no way of keeping.

Reeziana and Tee are concluding their interview with William when they hear loud eerie screams and wailing coming from the adjacent interview room. They look at each other, puzzled.

"What the hell is Mislan doing to the suspect?" Reeziana asks no one in particular. "Tee, get a standby to escort William to the lockup," she instructs, standing to go investigate what is happening.

She sees the detective guarding Nelly standing outside the interview room, his face ashen with fear.

"What's going on?" she asks.

"I didn't do anything," the detective declares, obviously scared. "She was looking at me, smiling, and I smiled back. Suddenly, she started screaming and wailing, staring at me like she wanted to eat me alive."

Reeziana peeks into the room. Nelly glares at her, her eyes red, but she thinks the suspect is smiling – or is she snarling, baring her teeth like an angry dog? She hears footsteps coming towards them. It is Mislan, Johan, Syed and several other detectives.

"Syed, you're the ustaz. Go in and see what's happening," Reeziana says. "I think she's possessed or something."

From the doorway, Syed loudly recites the Azan. Nelly glares and growls at them. Pushing Syed aside, Mislan enters the room He sits in front of her, looks directly at her and firmly says, "Cut the crap, your fucking shenanigans don't work on me."

Nelly turns to face him, growling, leaning forward with both hands on the table, like she is about to crawl onto the table to get to him.

"Behave yourself or I'll put you in a looney jacket and throw away the bloody key."

Nelly stops growling, pushes herself off the table and sits down. She smiles. Mislan takes out his pack of cigarettes, the same brand she smokes.

"You want one?" he asks.

Nelly nods.

"Syed, release the cuff on her left hand," Mislan instructs.

He takes a stick and hands it to her. With a shaking hand, she takes the cigarette and puts it to her lips. Mislan leans across the table and lights it for her.

"That feels good, doesn't it?" he says as she takes deep drags. "Syed, you stay here with the standby. Do you want a drink?" he asks Nelly.

She nods, mumbling, "Thanks."

"Get her a drink. When she finishes, cuff both her hands."

Walking back to the office, Reeziana asks how he knew Nelly was putting on an act.

"Christine, her niece, suffers from epilepsy, she must have seen her in one of her attacks. Or she must have heard of her niece's relapse and being sent to the hospital. Much better accommodation, bedding and food than the lockup. Same trick as our politicians serving prison sentences – now and then, they claim illness and get admitted to the hospital. Single room, soft bedding, friend and family visiting them with food and drinks. What a joke. They should be placed in the common ward, handcuffed to the bed. No visitors. What's the point of sending them to prison if they're treated like VVIP?" Mislan sneers. "They're common criminals."

"What if you were wrong?" Reeziana asks, ignoring his tirade.

"Then Syed's azan and recital of the Quran could deal with it," Mislan laughs.

Superintendent Samsiah joins them in the office. She tells them of the OCCI's request.

"Why do we have to keep his name out?" Reeziana asks, annoyed. "Ooo, I know, to protect the boy's club."

"If the investigation leads to him, there's no reason for us to keep his name out of it. Otherwise, I don't want it to be us that leaks his name. It's a Syariah matter, nothing to do with us,"

Samsiah says. "We're not here to judge people. Do I make myself clear?"

The officers nod.

"I heard something happened with the suspect Nelly, another supernatural incident?" she asks.

"She tried to pull a trick like she was possessed, but Mislan saw through her and put a stop to it," Reeziana answers.

"She was having nicotine withdrawal. Nothing that a stick of holy cigarette can't exorcise," Mislan says with swagger.

Reeziana laughs.

"What did you two manage to get out of the son?" Samsiah asks.

"Like Mislan discovered, after all the GROs were gone, only he and his mother were left with the victim. Nelly told him to bring the car around. When he did, she put the victim in the front passenger seat while she sat in the back. The mother told him to drive home. When they hit Jalan Ampang, he heard the victim groan; turning to look, he saw his mother pulling on a scarf which was wrapped around the victim's neck. He saw the victim's legs shaking and kicking under the dashboard. He focused on the road. He was scared other road users might see what was happening. When they reached the traffic light near Great Eastern Mall, the victim was quiet and his mother was leaning back and breathing hard. The scarf around the victim's neck was gone. When they reached home, the mother asked him to carry the victim to the kitchen. He laid the victim on the kitchen floor and went up to his room because he was scared and feeling sick from seeing what had just happened to the victim." Reeziana pauses to catch her breath.

"What did he think happened to the victim?" Samsiah asks.

"Died," Tee answers.

"My account of what happened was not far off. I was wrong on who strangled the victim," Mislan says.

"Then?" Samsiah asks.

"About two hours later, when he was about to fall asleep, he heard his mother call," Tee picks up where Reeziana left off. "When he went down to the kitchen, he saw the victim on the kitchen floor. His mother told him to carry the victim and put her in the car boot. His mother was in the washroom, pouring water on the floor. He noticed the water was red and smelt horrible. He carried the victim and when coming out of the house, bumped into Christine coming home." Tee pauses. "Coming back into the house, his mother asked him to follow her out. They got in the car and she drove. She stopped at a playground and asked him to carry the victim out of the boot. She told him to place her at the bottom of a slide and go wait in the car."

"Didn't he ask her why she killed the victim?" Mislan asks.

"No, he was too afraid," Reeziana replies.

"You saw your mother killing a woman and you're too afraid to ask?!" Mislan says unbelievingly.

"You saw what he was like when you searched the house. Did he say or ask anything?" Reeziana asks. "No, right? You can see that this is a man-boy, not really fully wired upstairs. He can pass for fully wired but he is not."

"He drives."

"Without a driving license, only because his mother told him to."

"He fears his mother," Samsiah says. "Maybe caused by his traumatic upbringing."

"Puan could be right. His father left them when he was ten and he was raised by the mother. She was probably a GRO then, always not around to care for him, so she must have raised him with an iron fist to keep him in line."

"Shit."

"Check with the mother," Samsiah instructs, "if he is indeed of diminished mental capacity. If he is, we need to send him for psychological evaluation."

"Ask Christine, she may know," Reeziana suggests. "She's more cooperative."

"Did you ask him about the red cloth with the prayer characters?" Mislan asks.

"We did," Tee answers. "He said it's his mother's business. She buys amulets, talismans and figurines from Thailand and sells them to her KTV customers or their friends."

"But she's Christian," Mislan says.

"Her ex-husband, William's father's, was Chinese," Tee answers.

"Maybe that was how she learned about the mumbo-jumbo."

"Let's call it a day. We continue tomorrow with the mother," Samsiah says.

"Yana, can I get a copy of William's interview?" Mislan asks.

"I'll get D6 to make a copy."

"Tell D6 to set up for tomorrow at 10."

"OK."

"Who will follow up on Christine?" Samsiah asks.

"I will," Tee volunteers.

36

Sitting at his workstation, Mislan watches the video of William's interview. He studies William's demeanor. The suspect looks timid, scared and is avoiding eye contact with Reeziana and Tee. His head is bowed low, with the forehead almost touching the table in front of him. His voice is sometimes inaudible and the officers have to ask him to repeat what he says. He displays the mannerism of, to quote Reeziana, a man-boy.

Listening to him, Mislan has the feeling he answers all questions truthfully, not understanding who or what his answers may implicate. Mislan does not believe William has the mental capability to come out with the story unless it was the truth. He did what he did because he was told by his mother. Anyway, what motive could he have to murder the victim? Mislan doesn't believe Chong or the judge would conspire with him. They would certainly know of William's mental state. Would they even consider him to be a part of their plan to get rid of the victim? Highly unlikely. The other thing which convinces Mislan that William is incapable of doing it is his non-aggressive behavior. He is far too gentle.

It brings his thoughts back to mummy Nelly. With the forensic evidence, once he gets them, he can positively pin the murder on her. But the evidence would have to be corroborated by William and other testimonies. The problem is, he does not feel it is fair to put William on the stand, make him face his mother. To put his mental condition through severe scrutiny by the defense to discredit his testimony. It would be demeaning for William, through no fault of his.

Mislan wonders: *Would Nelly, knowing her son's mental state, dump the blame on him? Knowing that if his condition is medically certified, he will not be held liable for his actions.* The mother, however, could still be charged for abetting – which would be the same as if she had murdered the victim herself.

But what was her motive? What did she do with the fetus?

William was asked about the fetus but he didn't know anything about it. The house was searched from top to bottom, they couldn't find it. *So, where the hell is it?*

Mislan decides only Nelly can tell them. How does he make her talk? What can he offer her to loosen her tongue? Offering a reduced charge is not in his power.

Frustrated, he decides to sleep on it.

The next morning, Mislan is in the office early. Tee, Reeziana and Hartini are at the pantry having breakfast. Making a mug of coffee, he joins them.

"How was last night?" he asks Tee.

"Nothing interesting. Did you go through the interview?"

Mislan nods.

"How?"

"Yana's right, he's like she said, a man-boy."

"Did you notice how he avoided eye contact?" Reeziana asks. "I don't think because he was lying but because he was afraid of us, of authority."

"I noticed, especially you. I don't think he once looked at you."

"Probably Yana reminded him of his mother," Tee mocks.

"And you, his runaway father," Reeziana laughs. "Do you believe what he says?" she asks Mislan.

"People like him always tells the truth, they don't know how to make up stories. What they see or do, they'll tell you. The only thing that stops them from telling is when they're scared shit of someone. Even then, they'll not lie but just keep quiet."

"How do you know so much about them?" Hartini asks.

"TV," Mislan deadpans.

Johan walks in with a plastic bag containing a pack of nasi lemak, holding it up to Mislan.

"Your stimulant has arrived," Tee jokes.

Opening the nasi lemak pack, he asks, "No sambal sotong?"

"Finished, I got you the paru goreng."

"Thanks. Jo, I need you to get hold of Nelly's mobile phone and go through it."

"Anything in particular?"

"Anything about the fetus."

"Can you do that?" Hartini asks.

"What?"

"Go through the suspect's phone?"

"Why not?"

"I'm sure there's a law against us doing it."

"There's a law against us doing everything," Mislan snaps. "But that shouldn't stop us from doing our work: investigating a murder."

Reeziana and Tee look at Hartini, grinning.

"Now you know why Puan put you under Yana and not him," Tee says, smiling.

"Jo, ask Nelly for the passcode. If she gives it to you, that means she consents to us going through the phone."

"If she doesn't?"

"Get D10 IT to unlock it."

The morning-prayer is brief and after Tee updates the team on his call-outs, Superintendent Samsiah inquires on Mislan's plans for today.

"I'll have another go at Nelly, see if she's in a talkative mood today after another night in the lockup."

"You want Yana to sit in with you?" she asks.

"If she is up to it."

"Yana?"

Reeziana nods.

"What about the son, William?"

"I believe he has told us all he knows," Mislan says. "Can we get D11 psychologists to evaluate him?"

"I'll check with them. Something on your mind?"

"I'd really like to avoid him being dragged to court. To me, it's just not fair for him to be a subject of debate by the prosecution and defense to establish if his testimony can be used as evidence. The mental anguish he'll have to endure and the experience testifying against his mother would be traumatic and could permanently damage him emotionally."

"I understand, and we do have all the evidence to pin the murder on her without his testimony," Samsiah agrees.

"We have abundant forensic evidence recovered from the house that we can nail her with. My concern is that by going to court, William will have to be dragged in too. I'm hoping we can make a deal with her. She pleads guilty and we'll not charge William as an accomplice."

"We cannot make such deals. It's up to the AG."

"Can we at least propose it to the AG?"

"I'll have a chat with D5 and see what they say."

"In the meantime, it would help if we could get D11 psychologists to come up with their assessment of him."

Nelly looks more haggard, if that is possible, than she did yesterday. The bags under her eyes are darker, and her blonde hair looks stiff and coarse, probably from not being shampooed for more than two days. He knows shampoo and soap are provided in the female lockup but he guesses they are not her brand. He is sure he even notices fresh wrinkles on her face.

"Morning," he greets, "had your breakfast?"

Nelly looks at him coldly, then shifts to Reeziana.

"Sleep well last night?" Reeziana asks with a smile, taking her seat.

The D6 technician asks if they are ready. Mislan nods; he switches on the video recorder and leaves the room. Mislan goes through the same preliminary motions.

"Let's continue where we left off yesterday. As I remember, it's your turn to tell us your version of what happened in the KTV carpark on the night in question," Mislan begins.

Nelly remains silent.

"Your son, William," Reeziana says and instantly the officers notice her eyes widen with interest, "is he suffering from any illness?"

"What do you mean? Did you torture him? I know the police beat suspects to get them to confess," she snarls. "He's slow but he's not a retard."

"No, he was not tortured and no he's not retarded. As you say, he's just a little slow but a very honest man," Reeziana replies. "Has he been diagnosed or seen any doctor?"

"Maybe 14 or 15 years back but there was nothing they could do for him... *special child* they said," Nelly sneers. "What's special about being slow?"

"Which hospital?"

"GH."

"Is he on medication or anything?"

"No, as I said they told me he's normal, just slow. No medication, no further therapy."

"Your ex-husband..."

"Don't you dare speak of him to me. That useless piece of cow dung, he left the day William was diagnosed. I hope he's dead and his corpse eaten by mad dogs," she interjects before Reeziana can finish her sentence.

Oh shit, Mislan says to himself, *this is one woman you don't want to be angry with you.*

"Here's the deal, William told us on video everything about the night in the carpark with Rita. What we need is to hear your version of it."

Nelly once again goes into her silent mode.

"If you don't, we'll have no alternative but to charge both of you for the murder of Rita."

Nelly's eyes widen again, staring first at Reeziana then Mislan and back again to Reeziana. The officers note that every time her son's name is mentioned, she reacts or steps out of her silent mode. Mislan's mobile phone rings, it is Johan. He shows the phone to Reeziana and steps out.

"Yes, Jo."

"There are a lot of coded chats between Nelly and Gary Lai and the words 'thing' and 'it' used regularly."

"Example?"

"*You sure or not you can get it? When can you get it? I've the thing already, when do you want it. Are you sure it is real.* There are many more chats about the 'thing' and 'it'."

"Where are you?"

"Office."

"I'm with Yana interviewing the mummy. Give me a few minutes to complete the interview."

When Mislan and Reeziana enter the office, they see Johan standing next to Hartini, who is examining Nelly's mobile phone and making notes.

"What have you got?" Mislan asks.

"I'm copying down the WhatsApp chats with the word 'thing' and 'it' in it," Hartini says without taking her eyes off the phone.

Mislan goes to the pantry to make a mug of much-needed coffee and lights a cigarette.

"Done," Hartini announces.

"Let's see it," Mislan calls from the pantry.

Hartini places the A4 paper in front of him, and all eyes focus on the notes she made.

"The first was from Gary, asking if she can get 'it'," Reeziana points out. "That was like a month back."

"She replied; *I can try, how much are you willing to pay?*" Hartini says. "Then she says: *We talk when I go to there.*"

"I think that was the time the plan was hatched in her head," Mislan theorizes.

"I think so too," Hartini replies. "Then she sends this to Gary: *I've the thing already, when do you want it.* That was like five days back?"

"Two days after the vic was murdered," Mislan says. "Then he asked her: *are you sure it's real.*"

"You're thinking the 'thing' or 'it' mentioned by them is the fetus?" Reeziana probes.

"It had to be something illegal, otherwise why use the word *thing* or *it* instead of what it actually is," Mislan says.

"What is more illegal than a murdered baby?" Johan stresses.

"There's a boy figurine in Gary's office, and in Chong's," Mislan says.

"In Andrew's office too, same," Johan points out.

"What boy figurine?" Hartini asks.

Mislan Googles Kuman Thong and shows her the picture. "Similar to this. I can't remember what it's called, Luk something. Luk Thep, that's it, the figurine."

"So now what?" Reeziana asks.

"I need search warrants for all three offices."

"For what?"

"The vic's fetus. I have to speak with Puan."

37

Inspector Mislan, Inspector Reeziana and Inspector Hartini, each armed with a search warrant, lead teams to search the three premises simultaneously. As Forensic (D10) does not have sufficient manpower to accompany all three teams, they will only be called if any of them find a fetus or any trace evidence that require their presence.

Mislan assigns himself to Gary's office, Reeziana to Chong's at the Champion KTV and Hartini to Andrew's in Jalan Ipoh. They are instructed to bring back any figurine of a boy similar to what Mislan had WhatsApped them. Gary, Chong and Andrew are not to be arrested but brought in for questioning to assist in the investigation.

He gets into his car to go to Gary's office, but the engine won't start and Johan laughs.

"Nelly must have known we're going to Gary's office and sent her little devil boy to mess with your car," Johan says.

Mislan gives him a stare. "Don't you start with that hocus-pocus."

He tries again and the engine still refuses to start. He pops the hood and asks Johan to have a look at it. His assistant knows more about engines than he does. Johan does something and calls for him to give it another try. He turns the ignition key and the engine comes to life.

"What was wrong with it?" he asks as Johan gets back into the car.

"One of the battery heads was loose. The little devil boy must have loosened it."

"Yeah, right."

Johan guides Mislan through the back lanes shortcut to get to where they parked when they first visited Gary's office. Parking the car, Mislan surveys the surrounding areas looking for any suspicious character watching them, worried about his jalopy being stolen.

Entering the liquor display shop, the officers are told by the staff that Gary is not in the office. Mislan asks the staff to call Gary to the office and if he refuses, they will conduct the search with one of the staff present. He steps out to the pavement to have a smoke. Halfway through his cigarette, he sees Gary walking hurriedly towards him.

"Inspector, my staff said you have a search warrant, what search warrant?" Gary asks, puffing from the walk.

"Where did you come from?" Mislan asks.

"Around the corner, I was having a late breakfast with friends. What are you looking for?"

Mislan flicks his cigarette into the drain, saying, "Let's go inside."

"What are you looking for? I've nothing to hide," Gary protests. Taking out his mobile phone, he makes a call. Mislan has stationed one of his men in the display showroom and another at the office door, with instructions to stop any staff from removing anything. Once inside, Johan serves him with the search warrant and ushers Gary who is still talking on the phone to the office.

Gary terminates the call and makes another. The officers hear him explaining that the police are at his office with a search warrant.

Then he says, "Yes, Inspector, you're sure, OK, OK." Terminating the call, he plonks heavily on his office chair. Mislan asks him to move to the sofa.

"What are you looking for?" Gary asks again, his voice desperate.

"It's in the warrant, read it," Mislan says.

"If you tell me, I can assist. You don't have to search all the cabinets and drawers."

"Are you afraid we may find something more than what we are looking for?"

Gary grins like Tom Selleck as the NYPD commissioner in *Blue Bloods*.

Mislan sees Johan standing in front of the boy figurine; his mouth is twitching and he looks around without touching it. *Probably reciting Quranic verses to protect himself from the devil boy*, Mislan thinks to himself with a tiny smile.

"It's easier to see if you move the thing," he tells Johan and receives an are-you-crazy look.

"Someone's still got to carry it to the car," Mislan says with a chuckle as he searches the liquor cabinets. "Jo, check the desk drawers."

Mislan notices that all the liquor is displayed without boxes but on the top shelf at one end there is a liquor box. The Hennessy XO Cognac box is larger than standard liquors boxes, and the photo on the box shows that the bottle is bell-shaped. Mislan reaches for the box, stopping just before touching it and turns to look at Gary. It shows on his face. The fear is unmistakable. Fear of him taking the box or fear of what the box's contents will do to him, Mislan is unsure.

"Inspector," Gary calls, standing up. "Please don't take that," he says nervously.

"Why not?" Mislan asks as Johan looks on.

"It's a prayer thing for business."

"What prayer thing?" Mislan plays dumb.

"Buddhist prayer thing, Malay people don't understand."

"You mean Kuman Thong, kwai chai?"

Gary looks at the inspector, shocked.

Mislan turns to his assistant. "Jo, cuff him." Turning back to Gary, he says, "You're under arrest for suspicion of abetting in the murder of Norita Mokhtar."

Gary's face turns ashen and he almost faints. He drops back onto the sofa, trembling. Johan puts the cuffs on him. Mislan makes a call to D10 to come to their location.

Waiting for D10 to arrive, Gary asks if he can pray for forgiveness in front of the boy figurine. Johan looks at Mislan questioningly. Mislan nods. Gary is assisted from the sofa to the figurine. He kneels in front of the figurine, hands cuffed behind his back and head bowed low, and mumbles something in Chinese. Then his head bobs up and down three times before he struggles to his feet. Johan gives him a hand and guides him back to the sofa. His face is wet with tears.

Mislan gets a call from Kevin of D10, informing him that since Chew did the house in Taman Kosas, it is better for him to also do Gary's office. He has already informed Chew and they are on their way.

Waiting for the Crime Forensic team to arrive from Cheras will take at least half an hour, and Mislan steps out of the shop for a smoke. At the front door, he bumps into a Chinese man and an elderly Chinese woman in office attire.

"Are you Inspector Mislan?" the man asks.

"Who would like to know?"

"I'm Tan from Tan and Tan. This is Shirely from Shirely and Co. We're here on behalf of Mr. Gary Liu."

"Lawyers? I don't see any need for him to see lawyers now. He has not been charged with anything yet. We're executing a search warrant and your presence at this stage is not required."

"Can we at least talk to him?" Shirely asks.

"Once we finish, but not at the moment. By the way, how did you know of our presence?"

"That's privileged information," Shirely answers lawyer-like.

"From what I understand of the law, privileged information is only applicable for conversations between counsel and client. Not for another party that contacted you to come here. As the lead investigator, it's my belief that if Gary is allowed to talk to you now, it will jeopardize my search for further physical evidence related to a case I'm investigating."

The two lawyers look at each other. Mislan walks between them, saying, "Now if you'll excuse me, I need my nicotine fix." The lawyers follow Mislan out and leave him to his unhealthy habit.

Mislan calls Reeziana, asking if her team found anything. She tells him except for the boy figurine, she found nothing which resembles the photo of Kuman Thong wrapped in red cloth.

"Check the liquor cabinet," Mislan suggests. "I found mine in a Hennessy XO box in the liquor display cabinet."

"Checked, nothing."

"What about Hartini?"

"Just asked her, nothing."

"OK, take just the boy figurine with you. Maybe it is inside it."

"Are you breaking it open?"

"No, we'll get it X-rayed."

"OK."

The white Crime Forensic van pulls up in front just as Mislan is about to reenter the display shop. He sees Chew stepping out of the vehicle and decides to wait for them.

"That was quick," he greets Chew.

"We were finishing up at Bandar Tun Razak when Kevin called. What do you have here?"

"I think we found the fetus but I've not checked it yet. When I was about to take a box down, the suspect's face turned white and he begged me not to touch it."

"What makes you think it is the fetus?"

"Some Thais or Buddhists believe in this thing called Kuman Thong, which is made from a dead fetus. I think the Chinese call it kwai chai, the devil boy."

"Let's see what it is."

Mislan leads the forensic team to Gary's office and points out the Hennessy XO box. A technician takes several photos of it before Chew casually takes the box down from the shelf. He opens the lid and peeks inside. The technician again takes several photos of the inside of the box. Mislan turns to look at Gary, who by now has turned ghostly white. He closes his eyes, refusing to witness what is happening while mumbling prayers or something.

"What's inside?" Mislan asks.

Chew puts the box on Gary's desk and pulls out something wrapped in red cloth with black prayer characters inked on it. The lower part of the wrapping is tied with a light brown gunny string and the top opens like a flower bouquet wrapper. The office falls eerily silent. Mislan feels the hairs on the back of his neck stand and is sure the others feel the same. All eyes are fixed on the hellish bouquet. A tiny head that seems oblong at the top back, with big hollow eye sockets, flattened nose and lips stares at them. The hands are crossed across the chest, pointing upward to the chin. The skin appears dry and wrinkled. *How could a person do such a thing to an innocent unborn child?* he wonders.

Placing the bouquet on the desk next to the Hennessy XO box, Chew asks his technician to snap several photos. Mislan takes a couple with his mobile phone. Then Chew carefully places the items into evidence bags.

"Is that all?" Chew asks Mislan.

"We need to take this too," Mislan says, pointing to the boy figurine.

"Just one?"

"Yes. Can you take it back to the lab and X-ray it to see what is inside?"

"We don't have an X-ray machine that can penetrate porcelain. You'll have to use the airport machine."

"I think our bomb squad has them. Why don't you ask them?" Johan says. "I've seen it used at one of the bomb-hoax calls."

"Good, I'm putting you in charge of getting all the figurines to our bomb squad unit," Mislan says, smiling at his detective sergeant.

"Syed is the ustaz, he can handle them," Johan answers.

"Chew, you can get DNA from the thing, right?" Mislan asks.

"It looks dry. I don't know if it has been treated with chemicals or whatnot. I'll check at the lab."

"If my Google search was right, the ritual is to roast it over an open fire at the graveyard by a monk while chanting and calling for the spirit. Why don't you Google it to understand better?"

"What is it again?"

"Kuman Thong," Mislan says, spelling it.

38

When Mislan and his team arrive back at the office, they see two groups of men in office attire milling at the front desk talking. When Johan and Syed escort Gary to the interview room, two of the men call to him. Syed nudges Gary on, not allowing him to stop to talk to the two men. One of the men calls out, "I'm his lawyer, I've the right to speak to him." Johan and Syed ignore his calls and urge Gary on to the interview room.

Reeziana and Hartini are already back from their search. He sees two figurines by the side of his desk.

"Why did you put them here?" he asks.

"You're the lead, where else do we put them?" Reeziana replies.

"Put them at Jo's desk. He's in charge of taking them to the bomb squad."

"You're going to blow them up?" Hartini asks, surprised.

"No, they have an X-ray machine to see if there's anything inside them."

"Like what?"

"A fetus. Where are Chong and Andrew?"

"We found nothing incriminating in their offices. I checked with Puan and she said there is no need to bring them in for now. We put them on notice to come in should we need them to assist in our investigation," Reeziana answers.

"You got the search list?"

"Here," Hartini says, handing him the search list for both the offices.

"I'm going to see Puan, want to join me?"

Both of them nod.

When the officers reach Superintendent Samsiah's office, they see a man in a black suit sitting in front of her desk. Samsiah sees her three officers outside her office's open door and beckons them in.

"Anything urgent?" she asks.

"Yes," Mislan answers.

"I'm sorry Mr. Lim, I need to speak with my officers."

The man is reluctant to leave but the three officers walk in, prompting him to take his leave. Mislan closes the door after him and takes a seat. As there are only two visitor chairs, Hartini leans against the cabinet.

"Sorry to disturb you and your guest," Mislan says.

"Don't be, I'm glad you came."

"Who was that?"

"Sallehnor's lawyer, asking us not to make public his involvement with the victim."

"There're a few of them out front, I think they are Gary's team."

"I'll handle them. Yana and Tini did not find anything except the figurines. But I heard you did," Samsiah addresses Mislan.

"Yes," he answers, showing her the photo of the hellish bouquet he snapped with his phone.

Samsiah cringes on seeing the photos and passes the phone to Reeziana and Hartini.

"It looks exactly like the photo you showed us from Google," Hartini says. "But somehow it's more eerie seeing it on your phone."

"Because it's for real," Mislan says.

"Where did you find it?" Samsiah inquires.

"Hidden in a Hennessy XO box in the liquor display cabinet."

"What did he say?"

"Have not questioned him yet. But as I reached for it, you should have seen his face. White, like he saw a ghost. Then he asked if he could pray in front of the boy figurine. He was bowing and crying. I've never seen anything like that before, he was scared shitless, like the thing would harm him."

"If you believe that it can, it probably could. If not physically… mentally," Samsiah says.

"But if you don't, like *you* don't," Hartini says to Mislan, "then it can't harm you."

"Mislan doesn't believe in anything," Reeziana jests.

"Chew will try and get DNA from the fetus but looking at its condition, he is not sure he can. They'd roast the fetus, so I doubt if we can get DNA. Even if we do, it would probably be damaged by the roasting," Mislan says, frustrated.

"Hope for the best," Samsiah says. "Interview Gary and find out where he got it from. That'll be another link in your chain of evidence."

"Can we charge him for having a dead fetus in his possession?" Hartini asks.

"Check the Birth and Death Registration Act, perhaps there's something we can use against him," Samsiah suggests. "After you gather all the evidence, I suggest you reinterview Nelly."

"Oh before I forget, Puan, can you call our bomb squad and ask if they could assist us in X-raying the figurines?" Mislan asks.

"What do you hope to find?"

"Dried fetus."

Samsiah smiles. "Aren't the figurines factory-made?"

"I don't know. Yana, Hartini, did you inspect them for an opening, you know like a porcelain piggy bank?"

Reeziana laughs. "I'm a believer, no way I'm inspecting them. Get Syed to do it, he is the ustaz here."

Gary Liu is startled when the door opens, and he stares at Mislan and Reeziana as if they are alien beings. *He probably thinks we are ghosts or some reincarnated creatures coming to get him*, Mislan figures. Telling the standby detective to leave, he switches on the video and takes his seat. He goes through the usual preliminary motions.

"Gary, hey Gary," Mislan calls, snapping his fingers to get him to focus back to the world of the living.

Gary turns to look at Mislan. His eyes start blinking and Mislan knows he is back among them.

"Gary, can you tell me, what is this we discovered in your office?" Mislan asks, showing him the photo of the red cloth with the dry fetus bouquet from his mobile phone.

Gary turns away, refusing to look at it, mumbling something in Chinese.

"Is this Kuman Thong?"

Gary nods without looking at Mislan.

"Where did you get it from?" Mislan asks, putting his mobile phone with the photo facing Gary.

Gary slowly turns to face Mislan, avoiding looking at the phone.

"Inspector Mislan asked you where you got it from," Reeziana says. "If you don't answer him, we're going to charge you for abetment in the murder of Norita Mokhtar. Do you understand me?"

"I don't know anything about the murder," Gary says, his voice shaky. "I bought it from mummy Nelly. She deals with prayers items. She said she got it from a woman working in a tour agent shop in Penang."

"You mean this Kuman Thong?"

Gary nods in earnest.

"How did you know she deals in prayer paraphernalia?"

"Chong told me. He bought the statues from her."

"You said Nelly got them from Penang? Who in Penang?" Reeziana asks.

"She said a woman who runs a travel agency at Komtar. She sells van tickets to Hatyai, Thailand. If anybody wants them, she gets the van driver to bring them in from Thailand."

"Do you know the travel agency's name?"

"No, I never asked."

"The border is closed. How did Nelly get the Kuman Thong?"

"I don't know. She said she could get it."

"How much did you pay her for it?"

"She said it's difficult to get because of the pandemic and no cross-border movement and asked for 50 but I paid her 45 thousand."

"How did you pay her?"

"She wanted it in cash."

"When and where did the transaction take place?"

"Two days after CNY, at my shop in the office."

"Do you know Kuman Thong is made from human fetus?" Reeziana asks.

Gary nods.

"The one she sold to you, did you know where she got the fetus from?"

"Nelly told me she bought it from an abortion clinic in Thailand. I swear I don't know where she got it from."

"Who else bought Kuman Thong from her?"

"I don't know. I know Chong, Andrew and Wong bought the Luk Thep statue from her but that was a long time back. I bought one too, the one you took from my office."

"If you already have the Luk Thep, the boy figurine, why do you want a Kuman Thong?" Reeziana asks.

"Since the pandemic two years back, my business stopped. All the pubs, hotels and entertainment outlets are closed. I cannot pay my bank loans and creditors. My friend told me about Kuman Thong and asked me to get one to help my business."

"Inside the Luk Thep, is there a fetus?" Mislan asks.

"No. The temple will put the spirit into the statue. My friend said, it's not strong like Kuman Thong."

"Which temple?"

"Nelly said the woman from the travel agency got them from Thailand."

"How do you know it's true?" Reeziana asks.

"Prayer things, people don't lie. The spirit will haunt you and make bad things happen to you and your family."

"Cannot lie but it's OK to kill and make a profit," Mislan mocks.

"I swear on my ancestors' graves, I didn't know about the killing. I only heard about it through the news."

"If the fetus DNA matches the fetus from Norita, you'll be charged with abetting murder," Mislan says.

Gary's face ashens. "I didn't know, she told me she got it from an abortion clinic. Please, I'm telling you the truth," he pleads, crying.

39

Mislan gets a call from Johan; the X-rays show nothing in the hollow figurines. Mislan tells him to bring back the figurines and contact the owners to collect them.

"Where do you want me to put them?" Johan asks.

"Put them at the front desk."

"It's past lunch time, do you want me to get them something to eat?" Johan jokes. "You said if they're hungry they'll cause trouble."

"Ask them for 4D numbers. If they give you, then feed them," Mislan deadpans.

Terminating the call, he calls Chew.

"Chew, did you manage to get DNA from the fetus?"

"The DNA was compromised due to the roasting, sorry."

"So we have no forensic proof it's our vic's fetus."

"I'm afraid not. Inspector, since you're on the phone, the DNA from the blood found in the suspect's washroom and the knife from the kitchen is a positive match to your victim. Also the DNA from the hair in the washroom and car, as well as the high heels and scarf. You've enough forensic evidence to put the victim at the suspect's house, car and boot of the car."

"Thanks, that's good news."

Mislan updates Superintendent Samsiah on the interview with Gary, the result of the X-ray by the bomb squad and the forensic evidence found by the crime lab. Samsiah tells him that William is being evaluated by a D11 psychologist, who will give a professional assessment.

"That's good, I hope we don't have to involve him," Mislan says.

"I agree. Yana told me, when the two of you interviewed Nelly, she was only responsive when her son was mentioned."

Mislan nods.

"I suggest, put it to her that you're trying not to involve her son. She has to own up to the murder and that her son's involvement was on her instructions. The psychologist evaluation will show that the son's diminished mental capacity made him unable to refuse or defy her instructions."

"And Gary?"

"Since the lab cannot obtain DNA from the roasted fetus, use him as a witness. I've checked the Birth and Death Registration Act, there's nothing to say a person cannot keep a fetus at his house or office. Anyway, the offences are related to not registering a birth or death, and the fine is only a few hundred ringgit."

"I'll give Nelly another go. What about the travel agency that Gary claimed supplied Nelly with the Kuman Thong?"

"If you can get the travel agent's name, I'll forward the information to Penang for their action."

Nelly looks as haggard as she did in the morning interview session. However, Mislan notices a sense of calmness about her. Her eyes, although red from lack of sleep and nicotine withdrawal, have no anger in them. When Reeziana asks if she has had lunch, she actually nods with a miniscule smile. Mislan supposes, she must have accepted the fact that the game is over for her. The only thing left is to salvage whatever she can from the situation.

Before starting the interview, Mislan offers her a cigarette which she gladly accepts. When she finishes her cigarette, Mislan switches on the video, states the case number, date, time and those present.

"Let's start with the night Norita Mokhtar or Rita was sick and vomited in the carpark at Champion KTV," Mislan begins.

"What you said about me assisting Rita on that night is true," Nelly says calmly. "When all the other girls left, I was there with Christine. Then my son came and Christine left. I told my son to bring the car around. When he left to bring the car, I told Rita that Chong had asked me to send her home. I helped her into the front seat and I got in the back. Rita was sleeping, drunk, I put on her safety belt and she leaned back." Nelly pauses, as if thinking how to go on. "You see, she never wanted the baby. I persuaded her to keep it, helped her to go to the clinic for checkups. She had ovarian cancer and was taking medication for it. She was afraid the baby would be deformed. She also told me that Tuan did not admit to being the father and had asked her to terminate her pregnancy. Rita was worried, if she had the baby who was going to take care of her and the baby? Especially if the baby was deformed."

"The Tuan you mean is the judge, Sallehnor?" Mislan asks.

"Yes, but he is Tuan to us."

"Was it his baby?" Reeziana asks.

"I don't know. About two months back, Rita was really depressed and started talking about suicide. She stayed away from her friends, even Murni. I was afraid she would start taking drugs again and go ahead with it … suicide."

"Let's get back to the night in question," Mislan says.

"She wasn't supposed to drink, and certainly not so much until drunk. She was pregnant. I know what can happen to the baby if you drink too much. Look at William."

"Then why did she drink?" Reeziana asks.

"The Tuan and Chong made her drink, yam seng, yam seng when he booked her."

"She didn't have to."

"Yes, but she wanted to please the Tuan."

"Go on."

"That night she was saying the Tuan wanted to break up with her. She started talking about committing suicide. Maybe jump from a building or cut her wrists or swallow sleeping pills. She said this time she would do it for real to get back at the Tuan. I tried to calm her but she was determined. Inside the car, she was still mumbling about suicide. After all that I'd done for her, helped her, cared for her, she wanted to commit suicide. I lost my head. I saw my scarf on the seat. I took the scarf and wrapped it around her neck and pulled from the back until she was…" Nelly leaves her sentence hanging.

"Dead," Reeziana says it for her.

Nelly looks at her and nods.

Mislan recalls the pathologist saying there were two spots of light abrasion about 12 centimeters apart on the victim's back. It had to be from the headrest buttons when her neck was pulled back against them when she was strangled from the back.

Mislan sees remorse and sadness in her eyes. "Then what happened?" he asks.

"You know what happened. You searched my house and found all the evidence," Nelly says, not in anger but as a matter of fact.

"We want to hear it from you," he says.

"Reaching home, I asked my son to carry her to the kitchen. I undressed her, pulled her into the bathroom and cut out the baby. When she stopped bleeding, I taped the stomach, put her clothes back on and asked my son to put her in the boot. I cleaned the bathroom and knife. Happy?" she says, looking at Mislan.

"Our forensic found traces of detergent on the masking tape. Did you use detergent on the victim before you cut her stomach?"

Nelly shakes her head.

"Did you use gloves?"

"Kitchen gloves."

"You mean dishwashing gloves?"

Nelly nods.

Mislan stops the recording and hands her the pack of cigarettes. Nelly gratefully takes one and he lights it.

"You're not such a bad person," Nelly says to him.

Mislan laughs, "Smokers' courtesy."

Nelly laughs for the first time since her arrest. When she finishes her cigarette, Mislan restarts the video.

"Where did you take Rita's body?" Mislan continues.

"Rita always had big dreams. She said one day she'll marry a rich man and they'll live in Bangsar. Breakfast at La Bodega and shop at Bangsar Village or Bangsar Shopping Centre where all the mat salleh go. The least I could do for her was to make her last resting place Bangsar. But I couldn't place her in front of a bungalow or Bangsar Village. So I placed her at the playground facing the bungalows, where I knew her soul would be happy."

"That was thoughtful of you," Reeziana says.

"The baby or fetus, what did you do with it?" Mislan asks.

"Gary had a long time back asked if I can get a Kuman Thong for him. But with the pandemic, the border is closed. So my contact cannot bring it in. After I, you know…to Rita, I remembered Gary once asked for it, I mean Kuman Thong. He was willing to pay a lot of money for it. I needed money for my house mortgage, car installment and the loan I took to open my failed food business during the pandemic. So, I did what I did and sold it to him."

The officers notice that Nelly could not bring herself to say she killed the victim or the baby.

"Where did you go to do the prayer and chanting?" Mislan asks.

"Oh, you know about that too," Nelly says, surprised. "I don't know where to do it here. So I slow-roasted it on my stove in the kitchen and then wrapped it in prayer cloth like the one I saw in Thailand."

"Where did you get the red prayer cloth?"

"Petaling Street. There're a lot of shops selling prayer items."

"How did you know which red cloth and prayer characters to buy?"

"I just bought red cloth with prayer writing. I don't know and I'm sure Gary doesn't know what was written on the cloth. It's in Sanskrit."

"So, it's not a real Kuman Thong," Reeziana asks, fascinated by Nelly's ingenuity.

Nelly shakes her head. "I'm a Christian, what do I know about all their magic and superstitions? He wants a Kuman Thong, I sell him a Kuman Thong."

Mislan smirks. "What about the Luk Thep?"

"I got them from my contact in Penang. For all you know, she may have gotten them in Penang and not Thailand. Who's to know if the statues were blessed or not? There's nothing to indicate it. People who believe in superstitions, they are easily suckered," Nelly says, not hiding a smile.

"Your contact in Penang, what's the name of the travel agency?"

"I don't know the shop's name, it's outside Komtar, the same row as McDonald's. The woman's name is Lilian. She's in my phone list."

"Anything else you'd like to tell us?"

"My son, he's not involved in this. He's a good boy. His only crime is to be the child of a hopeless father who left him with a bad mummy. I'll admit to all that I've done but please spare him."

"William is being evaluated by our psychologist. I'm sure they'll make the right assessment of his condition. We've no intention of prosecuting him but it's not up to us. The case will be forwarded to the Attorney General for his consideration. However, I can tell you my superior Superintendent Samsiah, who was present during your first interview, and Reeziana here, who interviewed your son, and I will put forward our recommendation to support him being excluded in this matter."

"Thank you," Nelly says. "I did already say you are not a bad person, didn't I?"

Mislan sees she's at peace with herself and it shows on her face. Mislan switches off the video and gives her a last cigarette before calling for the standby detective to take her away.

"She is in a better place," Nelly says softly.

"Who, Rita?" Mislan asks.

Nelly nods.

Mislan and Reeziana brief Superintendent Samsiah on the conclusion of their interview. Reeziana does the talking while Samsiah and Mislan listen in silence. When she finishes, Samsiah asks if Mislan wants to add anything.

"I'm not saying what Nelly did was OK, but I can feel her frustration."

Samsiah nods.

"She cared for the vic, helped her whenever needed and when the vic kept on talking about killing herself, I think Nelly lost it."

"But it still did not give her the right to take the victim's life."

"What if the vic *did* end her life?"

"Then, it is on her and not Nelly."

Mislan nods. "I feel sorry for William. Who is going to care for him?"

"We'll try and locate his relatives in Sarawak. See if they're willing to take him in."

"Sorry for not listening to your suggestion," Mislan says.

"About?"

"People and their stupid superstitions and crazy beliefs."

Samsiah smiles. "Don't be, you're a crime investigator. You based your investigation on facts and scientific evidence because that's what the law requires to prove innocence or guilt."

Samsiah stands up, picks her bag.

"It's late. Go home and get some rest. Good work, both of you."

X

That night while Mislan is at his workstation, his mobile phone rings. It is Audi, the investigative journalist.

"Yes?"

"Have you checked Twitter? Oh sorry, I forgot you don't use social media."

"What's there?"

"Viral posting of 'Judge's Illegitimate Unborn Baby Used for Black Magic'."

"Serious?!"

"Yup. You can see what's trending on Google, or ask Jo, he has a Twitter account … hashtag #judgedevilchild."

"What did it say? Did it name the judge?"

"No. It says a Malay judge's mistress was found murdered and the fetus ripped from her womb. It was later discovered the fetus was used for black magic, a Kuman Thong, bla, bla, bla. Read it yourself. It's true then, the judge was having an affair with your victim?"

"This is not from me OK."

"Nothing ever comes from you," Audi chuckles.

"Yes, the DNA confirmed he was the father."

"What's his name?"

"You're the investigative journalist, dig it up yourself."

Audi laughs heartily.

N
O O
V